By Kakeru Kobashiri

Art by Takashi Iwasaki

Original Design of Select Characters by Yoshinori Shizuma



1

# The Dawn of the Witch

## The Remedial Student and the Witch of the Staff

At last Saybil fell backward, and found himself flat on the ground, looking up at the witch straddling him.

Los held his face with both hands and slowly, very slowly, pulled her lips away.

**Hort**

The most talented student at the Academy of Magic. Despite her stellar grades, she volunteered to participate in the special field training program.

"You can count me out of this supervised shit."

"You're pretty cool, Saybil."

**Kudo**

A lizard beastfallen and student at the Academy of Magic. Though his speech and conduct leave much to be desired, his grades are top-notch.

Loux Krystas

The Dawn Witch, on a quest to read the Grimoire of Zero, the book which heralded the advent of magic. She has agreed to chaperone Saybil and the others in the special field training program.

"Special...field training program?"

Saybil

A young man with no memories of his life before enrolling at the Royal Academy of Magic of the Kingdom of Wenias, he's been put in the special field training program because of his terrible grades.

"Why dost thou wish to become a mage?"

# CONTENTS



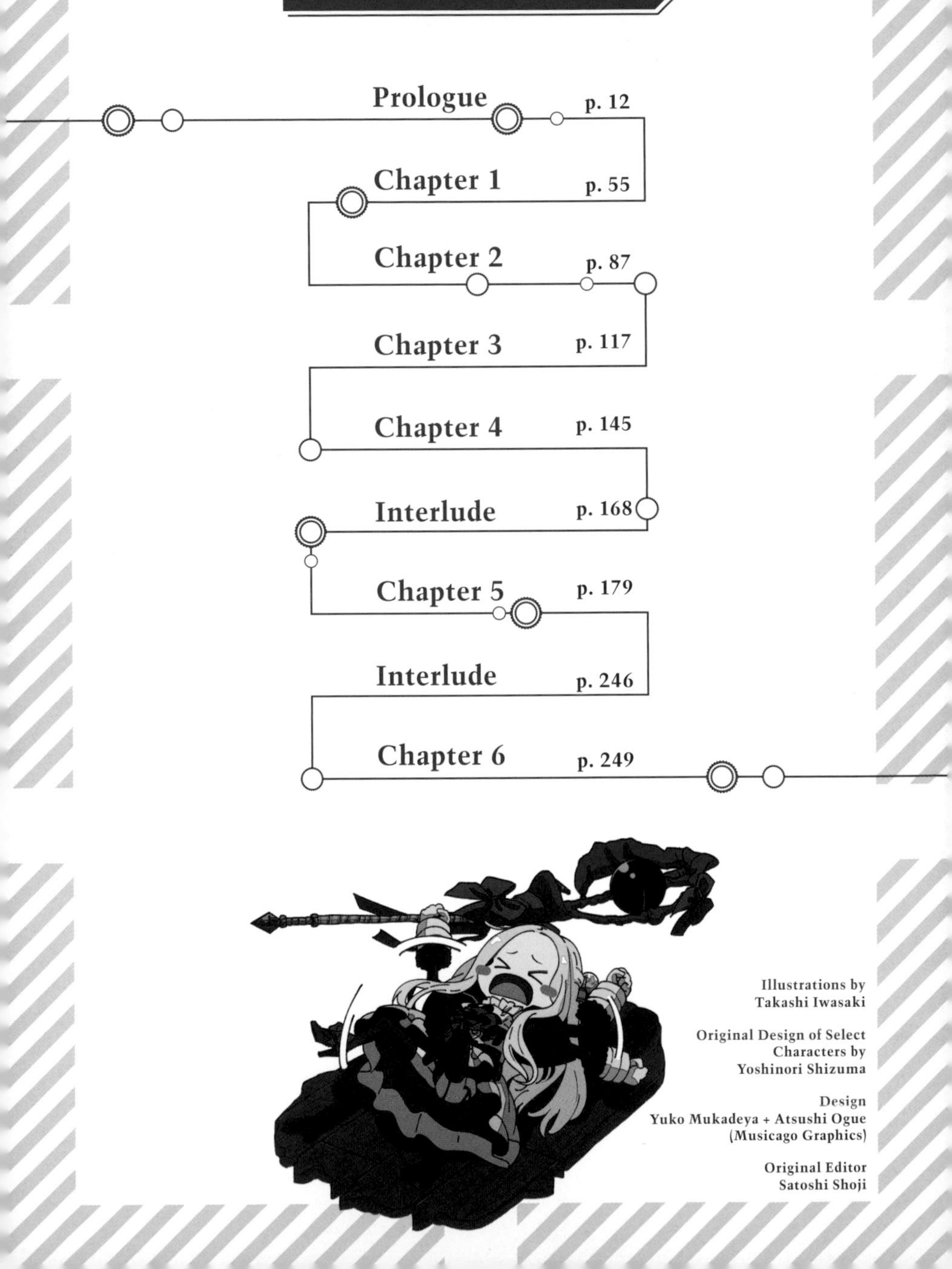

Illustrations by
Takashi Iwasaki

Original Design of Select
Characters by
Yoshinori Shizuma

Design
Yuko Mukadeya + Atsushi Ogue
(Musicago Graphics)

Original Editor
Satoshi Shoji

# The Dawn of the Witch

1

## The Remedial Student and the Witch of the Staff

By Kakeru Kobashiri
Art by Takashi Iwasaki
Original Design of Select Characters by Yoshinori Shizuma

Translated by
Alexandra McCullough-Garcia

KODANSHA

**The Dawn of the Witch 1**
**The Remedial Student and the Witch of the Staff**

**A VERTICAL Book**

Translator: Alexandra McCullough-Garcia
Editor: Daniel Joseph
Production: Tomoe Tsutsumi
Grace Lu
Proofreading: Micah Q. Allen



Publication for this English edition arranged through Kodansha, Ltd., Tokyo.
English language version produced by Kodansha USA Publishing, LLC, 2022.

Originally published in Japan as *Mahoutsukai Reimeiki: Rettousei to tsue no majo* by Kodansha, Tokyo, 2018.

ISBN 978-1-64729-185-3

Printed in the United States of America

First Edition

Kodansha USA Publishing, LLC
451 Park Avenue South, 7th Floor
New York, NY 10016
www.kodansha.us

# The Dawn of the Witch

## The Remedial Student and the Witch of the Staff

The boy awoke suddenly. He knew his name: Saybil. It was the only memory he retained. Everything else had disappeared.

"Congratulations. You are now a student at the Academy of Magic."

"...Wha?"

A document lay on the table in front of him. Though he couldn't read the writing, the bloody imprint on the paper and the prickle in his thumb told him he had signed some sort of contract.

"Now then, let me show you to your room. Come, you don't have anything to worry about," the woman told him. Gorgeous and golden-eyed, her abundant blonde hair stretched down the length of her back to her waist.

*Wait, something's off. She's not the one.*

"...Where did she go?" Saybil asked.

The woman's eyes widened in surprise. "...You remember?"

"Umm... I think she brought me here..." He trailed off and shook his head. His fingertips had just grazed the elusive recollection—

*—Hmm. You have my eyes, young man.*

That gentle voice.

That sweet scent.

The warmth of her body.

*—Come. I shall take you to a world which befits you.*

It had been raining. The woman had opened her long cloak, welcoming the grimy Saybil into its folds.

*That woman—*

*Who was she?*

Long silver locks. Enigmatic bluish-purple eyes.

She was beautiful.

Saybil trembled before the fleeting recollection of her fearsome beauty, his sole memory.

# Prologue

# 1

*This can't be good.*

As soon as Saybil read the note pinned to the bulletin board outside his classroom, he broke out in a cold sweat.

+++
*Student Summons*
*Saybil*
*Mouse House, Year Three*
*Proceed to the headmaster's office directly after class*
+++

The spring of Saybil's third year at the Academy had come, and he was on the cusp of advancing to his fourth. Getting slapped with a summons to the headmaster's office during this delicate period could only mean bad news. A ring of students began to form around the note and its subject. They cast glances Saybil's way from a safe distance, whispering among themselves.

—Wait, who's Saybil again? He really a third-year?

—You know, that forgettable guy who sticks to the back row. He's so deadpan, makes you wonder if the muscles in his face are just flat-out dead.

—What do you think he did to earn a summons from the headmaster?

—He's got literally the worst grades in our year. Maybe they're gonna kick him out?

They weren't mincing words. But Saybil was getting minced. To be fair, he *was* pretty forgettable, and he did have the worst grades in his year. He couldn't deny the part about his facial expressions, either. Even in that moment, he looked sleepy at best, with a permanent air of unaffected apathy.

—The headmaster's, like, crazy scary, don't you think? And the direct descendent of some super famous witch, I hear.

—Well, I heard the headmaster got all these beastfallen and locked them up in an underground prison, then exsanguinated them.

—Beastfallen?

—You know, those part-human, part-beast monsters. Haven't you seen the ones we've got here?

The whispered gossip showed no signs of abating. Every word drove another anxious knife into Saybil's heart.

The headmaster was a busy person. The students only rarely caught a glimpse of their principal, with whom almost none of them had ever spoken. Saybil, for one, had never even seen the elusive head of the Academy. Apparently it was customary for the headmaster to briefly greet new students at the yearly matriculation ceremony, but Saybil hadn't enrolled until a little after the start of term. The receptionist had been sitting there in front of him when he came to, and the next day she had been the one to introduce him to his classmates as a "transfer student."

*Not sure if showing up a week after school starts really counts as transferring, but...*

In any event, Saybil had never met the headmaster. And he never would have guessed the principal of his own school would be the subject of such exclusively negative gossip.

*There's got to be at least one positive rumor going around, right?*

He pricked up his ears to catch his classmates' conversations.

—D'you think the headmaster really poisoned the last king? You know, the one who backed the anti-witch faction?

—I mean, that's what the professor said, right? That the headmaster took on a whole country alone—at sixteen, no less!

*Nope. This is only making things worse.*

Saybil prepared himself to accept his fate. As he pursed his lips and turned on his heel, the ring of students surrounding him and the bulletin board parted down the middle to give him a wide berth.

*Gahhh...* "This can't be good."

That said.

Saybil couldn't very well ignore a direct summons, so he begrudgingly trudged down the hallway leading to the headmaster's office.

The Royal Academy of Magic of the Kingdom of Wenias had only been established four years prior. As the course of study took five years to complete, no one had yet graduated. If the headmaster did expel Saybil, he'd earn the dubious honor of being the first student in the Academy's short history to fail out of the school. And expulsion would, of course, mean he could forget about ever becoming a mage. Not only that, all of his knowledge of magic would be sealed away—he wouldn't even retain the memory of getting kicked out! Of this, at least, he was certain, since the woman who'd helped him enroll that first day had told him as much.

The prospect terrified Saybil to his core. He could hardly remember anything from before he'd awoken there, so sealing away his memories of the Academy would leave him completely and utterly empty.

*I can't let myself get kicked out. Anything but that.*

Saybil wished he could entreat the headmaster to let him stay with a teary performance, but alas, his frozen facial muscles would not play along. He tried to practice contorting his stubborn face into a sad frown in a mirror in the hallway, but he only wound up looking like a corpse just after rigor mortis had set in. Not that he really expected his muscles to suddenly spring into action after three years of total inertia.

*It's not like I don't feel anything, though—*

For whatever reason, Saybil had resisted all powerful emotions, instinctively suppressing any feelings that threatened to express themselves externally or have any physical effect.

The young mage-in-training stepped out of the dark corridor and found himself before a pair of stout, perfectly smooth ebony doors: the entrance to the headmaster's office. Devoid of any adornment or even handles to open them from the outside, the doors could have easily been mistaken for a section of wall. Like silent sentinels, their cold, intimidating presence warned away any who approached. Saybil was overwhelmed by their imposing power—

"These blasted doors! Why have they no handle? I was told this was the way to the headmaster's office, but was it a lie? Have I been duped yet again?"

—or at least he would have been, if not for the presence of an earlier arrival: a young girl—most likely around Saybil's age, if not younger—was pacing furiously back and forth before the doors, muttering to herself and shaking her fist at them, which shattered the office's gravitas like a bull in a potions shop.

"Oi! Come out here at once, Albus!" she raged, calling the headmaster by name. "Cower in there if it please thee, but thou shall not escape me today of all days!"

*Pretty bold to call out the headmaster without so much as an honorific, even for an angsty teen.*

It wasn't his problem, but Saybil still felt a chill of fear race down his back all the same.

"I know very well thou art in there! Oiii!" the girl railed, then began mumbling to herself. "Can she perhaps not hear me? In which case I would be making a complete fool of myself, would I not? That won't do... No, not at all... If it came to it, 'twould be much preferable to be ignored..."

"Excuse me."

At Saybil's voice, the girl froze. Looking terribly displeased, she turned around and blinked eyes so big they seemed in danger of popping out of her head entirely. Her long, honey-blonde locks—so long as to trail down to her heels—looked as if they might melt at first touch, and leave a sweet taste on the tongue. Vivid purple ribbons were woven through her braided hair, tied off with exquisite spheres of glass. Pale scarlet flowers bloomed softly within the translucent orbs, marred by neither scratch nor bubble. Even a master artisan would struggle to craft such perfect baubles. And even Saybil, with his amnesic, piecemeal understanding of the world,

could guess that to enclose the flowers so delicately within would require skill of the highest order.

Nevertheless, these beautiful glass spheres adorned not only the girl's hair but glittered all about her clothing and accoutrement. And yet they did not look gaudy on her; if anything, they suited her as perfectly as a favorite ribbon a girl her age might wear every day. A rosy blush bloomed on her puffed cheeks, and her eyes, open wide in surprise like a startled feline's, were of a mysterious shade no words could describe. In one hand she held a staff that towered disproportionately over her, which in turn boasted another orb, this one black and big as a clenched fist.

"What is it, lad? What business might a sagacious young man such as thyself have with me?"

As a student in such imminent danger of failure, this address left Saybil at a loss. Not to mention the fact that he hadn't actually come to see this young girl at all. As his silence dragged on, she frowned with ever greater displeasure.

"Come now, hast thou naught to say? Rather taciturn and altogether dull of thee, wouldst not agree? Thou couldst at the very least display some small joy at being complimented upon our first meeting by a girl so beautiful as I."

"Wow, if you don't say so yourself..." Saybil blurted without thinking, but the girl winked flirtatiously, not in the least bit offended.

"'Tis naught but the truth, as thou canst see for thyself. The vice of humility serves but to waste time. I need not wait for others to assure me with coos of 'No, thou truly art adorable!' as I am more than fully capable of evaluating mine own worth," she asserted. "And, as thou canst also see, I am terribly occupied at the moment. Begone, shoo!"

Saybil almost obeyed reflexively as the girl waved him away, but then he remembered that he himself had business on the other side of the door. Silently he pointed at it, whereupon the girl's expression instantly brightened.

"Thou hast business here? Beyond this confounded door?"

"Yes, ma'am. The headmaster summoned me," Saybil replied, a certain politeness unintentionally slipping into his address. The girl was his age—or maybe even younger—but perhaps her antiquated way of speaking had influenced his choice of words.

"Not with me?"

"Not with you."

"Wonderful! I withdraw my previous sentiment!" She clapped happily, then ran around behind Saybil and pressed herself against his back. The young apprentice was on the taller side, and she was exceedingly short, her head just barely reaching the level of his chest. Nevertheless, she pushed him forward with a surprising amount of strength for one so tiny, urging him on with a cry of "Come, quickly now." Saybil did what he could to resist, but his thin frame gave way to her insistent shoves, and he was nudged closer and closer to the headmaster's door.

"Thou hast business within, correct? And must pass through these doors? Every river requires a bridge, and I welcome thee as mine! My good will and support are thine to enjoy. Now, be a good lad and open this bedeviling door that has so stubbornly denied me thus far."

*Ughh, what do I do? This feels like a bad idea.*

As Saybil hesitated, the enigmatic girl's wide eyes narrowed into a glower. "Here now, child. I am not known for my patient disposition. If dost value thine own safety, I advise thee to heed my request while I maintain such even keel."

"And what will happen if I don't?"

"I shall whack thee with my staff," she informed him in earnest. The large, heavy-looking staff in her hand seemed perfectly suited to double as a blunt instrument.

"Looks like it would hurt," Saybil noted, equally earnest.

"That it would. Enough to draw blood, at times."

*Well, that clears that up. She's not playing around. I've got a feeling a full-force blow from that thing could crack my head open like a nut.*

"But unless I'm mistaken, the fact that the headmaster hasn't opened the door means you haven't been invited, right?"

"...Hnh."

"So if I sneak you in, the headmaster'll be angry with me. And honestly, that sounds scarier than a beating from your staff..."

Saybil's academic future already hung by a thread. He desperately wanted to avoid anything that would further tarnish his standing with the head of the school. Given the choice between losing a little blood and losing his place at the Academy, Saybil would unquestionably choose the former.

"Hnnngh...! A sound argument. And I have a great love of sound arguments. Very well, rejoice in my pardon! How about this, then!"

Adjusting her grip on the staff, the girl swung it around in a great circle. In that one swift motion, the black sphere imbedded in the weapon transformed into a razor-sharp blade, which pressed against Saybil's throat before he could so much as cry out.

He held his breath. Not out of fear, though: more than anything, the staff's glorious transformation and the girl's dexterous movements had astonished him, like a child enthralled with a magic trick.

The corners of the girl's soft, full lips rose into a mischievous smile. "How now? Surely this is more perilous than a beating, no? Wishing to save thine own life is more than sufficient cause to plead for entrance. Now, weep! Beg for thy life! Not even Albus could deny me entry once thou—"

"Oh." Saybil raised his head to see a figure looming behind the halberd-wielding girl. That's when he realized the door to the headmaster's office had opened. A tall half-beast, half-human monster—a wolf beastfallen—had silently appeared from within and now stood directly behind the girl, his clenched fist raised in the air.

"Oh," the girl repeated after Saybil. Realizing the danger, she managed to twist around and face it, but the staff—currently in the form of a halberd—she held menacingly against Saybil's throat impeded her ability to dodge. In that split second of delay, the lupine beastfallen ruthlessly brought his fist down upon her skull.

"Loux Krystas! What the hell do you think you're doing?! Get your hands off that student!"

"Ouch!" the girl yelped, crouching down and cradling her head in her hands. Her staff clattered to the floor, and the blade that had formed at the end melted away and was absorbed back into the black orb.

Curious as to how it worked, Saybil reached out to pick it up—

"STOP! Do you have a death wish?!"

—but the beastfallen grabbed his wrist and kicked the staff away.

"My staff!" The girl leapt after it, then rose to her feet, rubbing the sore spot on her head. Tears welling in her eyes, she angrily thrust her precious staff toward the beastfallen.

"Holdem, thou vile fiend! How darest a third-rate manservant such as thyself strike a blow 'pon my cranium, repository of all wisdom! And, unsatisfied by the grievous nature of thy crime, thou hast defiled my hallowed treasure, my little Ludens, with thy revolting foot! 'Tis a transgression worthy of a thousand deaths!"

"Too long—didn't get. Try again, but simpler this time."

"How darest thou hit me, thou third-rate fiend!"

"Stuck with the 'third-rate' bit, huh..." Saybil once again blurted out, then clamped his hands over his mouth. The beastfallen called Holdem stared icily at him, while the girl—"Loux Krystas"—guffawed.

"...Since you're standing out here, I take it you must be Saybil?" the wolf inquired.

"Yes. I was summoned by the headmaster..."

"We expected you sooner. I was actually on my way to get you... when *she* got in my way. Apologies for the trouble this intruder must have caused you."

"Oh no, it was..." *no trouble,* Saybil was about to say, but stopped short when he remembered how close he'd come to getting killed. "Um... Is she an acquaintance of yours?"

"I suppose so, technically," Holdem scowled. "If you can call a pest who incessantly shows up at your door an 'acquaintance,' that is. I'll let you decide."

"Quite the insolent analogy from a third-rate manservant. What harm canst thou claim I have caused?"

"Your very presence is a pestilence," Holdem growled. "Come on, Saybil. Forget her and head on inside. The headmaster's waiting."

"I will join you."

"The hell you will! Go back to whatever hole you crawled out of!" the beastfallen barked, mercilessly pushing Loux Krystas back as she tried to follow Saybil into the office. At that, the girl's porcelain cheeks flushed red and she began to flail her arms, wailing,

"Nay! Nay!" in protest. The tears in her eyes added the finishing touch to the pathetic picture.

*What could this girl possibly have done to make Holdem hate her so much? Sure, she's pretty weird, but she came all the way here—would it kill them to hear her out?*

Holdem caught Saybil's curious gaze and let out a sigh. "Don't let her appearance fool you, kid."

"Huh?"

"She's not as young as she looks. The old bag's over three hundred years old."

"......Huh?"

In the wake of Saybil's exceedingly muted show of surprise, Loux Krystas aggressively swept Holdem's hands off her, snorted a petulant *Hmph!,* and struck the floor with the butt of her staff.

"Age matters naught when one is this adorable. Or, do you lot truly hold age so dear? Or is it simply appearance as determined by age that you love so?"

"Who gives a damn about appearances?!"

"Thou didst bring it up!"

"Oh, shut up! The only reason I said anything was that your innocent little girl act was hurting this *actual* innocent boy here!" snarled the beastfallen, roughly flicking Loux Krystas's forehead with his claw.

"Desist, Third-Rate!" she shouted, swinging her staff at him.

With such a commotion going on outside the door, it was only a matter of time before the office's occupant came out to take stock of the situation.

"Quite the racket you're making, Holdem." The voice was calm, androgynous, powerful. "What in the world could be so difficult about going to fetch a single student?"

From within the office appeared a beautiful woman with long, blonde hair that stretched down to her waist. While her facial features were as androgynous as her voice, slightly lower down Saybil found an eloquent argument for her gender, and quickly averted his eyes from the ample bosom that bulged beneath her robe.

"Oh."

I know this person.

"You're the receptionist who helped me with my enrollment."

For a moment, time stopped. The blonde woman, Holdem, and Loux Krystas all turned toward Saybil with expressions so similar, it almost seemed like they'd rehearsed them in advance.

*Was that such a weird thing to say? Wait. Something's clearly off here.*

"...Why would a receptionist be in the headmaster's office?" Saybil wondered aloud.

"Because I *am* the headmaster."

*Aaahhh, there goes that.*

Saybil inwardly accepted his now all-but-certain expulsion. This whole time, he'd been under the mistaken impression that the headmaster of the Academy of Magic was just a receptionist.

*Well, I guess this means I* did *meet the headmaster when I first got here.*

An awkward silence hung thick in the air. Saybil felt like he should probably say something, but the fear that he'd only dig himself further into this embarrassing hole left him tongue-tied. Headmaster Albus waited patiently for Saybil to speak, a placid smile on her face.

Until—

"Ahahaha! Marvelous! Magnificent! A receptionist, he says? What a perfect occupation for a youngster such as thyself, Albus!" Loux Krystas's mirth reverberated from the high ceiling like a carillon of tiny bells.

Eyes flashing wide in surprise, the headmaster turned toward the little girl—then shrieked, "Gah! Loux Krystas?!"

"What, hast thou only now taken note of my presence? Rather careless, wouldst not agree? One must be wary of intruders at all times."

"Pretty rich, coming from the intruder herself...!" Albus retorted. "What are you doing here anyway?! How did you manage to sneak in?!"

"My disarming cuteness?"

"Are our security measures really that pathetic?! Holdem! Security is your purview, isn't it? What the hell have you been doing?!"

"D-Don't blame me!" Holdem spluttered. "We're dealing with a three-hundred-year-old ancient witch here. No ordinary security protocols are going to keep her out! And anti-sorcery defenses are *your* purview, aren't they?!"

"Aha! Is my manservant really trying to shift the blame for his own failings onto his master?!"

The fight was on. The intimidating headmaster who struck fear into the hearts of thousands, and her bodyguard, the beastfallen upon whose lupine shoulders the very nation's defenses rested, started screaming at each other like petulant children.

Headmaster Albus was the first to notice that Saybil was standing there with his mouth hanging open. She snatched his hand and began dragging him toward her office.

"A-A-Anyway, let's go on in! This is no sight for the students!

It'll ruin my air of dignity!"

"Hfff..."

"And what of me? Am I to enter as well?"

"All right! Fine! I don't care anymore, just get inside!"

"Huzzah! Oi, Third-Rate, fetch some tea. As a servant thou mayest be third-rate, but thy tea is unquestionably first-class." Loux Krystas flounced into the room like she owned the place, her buoyant verve a perfect contrast to Albus's aura of despair.

In the face of the headmaster's explicit permission, even Holdem had to abandon his dogged battle to deny Loux Krystas entry to the inner chamber. He listlessly shut the office doors once the others were all inside, ears and tail drooping in defeat.

## 2

Saybil took a seat on the sofa provided for guests, directly across from Headmaster Albus. Beside him, Loux Krystas pestered Holdem with endless plaints: "Why hast thou deprived me alone of tea?" and, "How fiendish!" and, "Some for me, too," and, "Please, I beg of thee!"

"So," Headmaster Albus began, exercising impressive mental fortitude to ignore the ruckus. "Do you know why I've called you here?"

"Because...I'm failing?" Saybil ventured.

The headmaster smiled wryly. "Indeed. Your grades are the worst ever recorded in our Academy's short history. As things stand, there's simply no way I can allow you to advance to the next year of study."

"Right... Of course..." Saybil's shoulders sagged. He'd seen it coming, but even so, hearing it from the headmaster's own lips was like a punch in the gut. "Headmaster...I promise I'll try my best. I mean, I *am* trying now, of course, but I'll try even harder! I'll even start over from year one if I have to. Just please, don't expel—"

"Which is why I wanted to discuss a special field training program with you."

"...Huh?" Saybil blinked, feeling like the rug had just been pulled out from under him. "Special...field training program?"

"Oh hoh, what a lovely ring that 'special' has to it. I have a great fondness for special treatment. Uncommonly talented individuals should receive all the special treatment there is to be had—especially ones as exceptional as myself."

"Loux Krystas. I'm trying to have a conversation with Saybil right now. This is work," the headmaster chided. "If you can't sit quietly, I'm going to have to throw you out."

"Thou art welcome to try. However, shouldst thou resort to force, I, the illustrious Loux Krystas, am thoroughly prepared to respond in kind with the full measure of my might. And yet thou mayest find more elegant means of silencing me. I have a great love of thoughtful consideration. And I imagine thy clever mind should at the very least suffice to discern the simplest solution here."

Veins bulging faintly on her forehead, Headmaster Albus wordlessly offered her own plate of sweets to the guest at her side. The witch's eyes glittered with delight as she stuffed her mouth full of the delicious confections. In the ensuing silence, the headmaster hurriedly returned to the matter at hand.

"So, back to the special field training course—tell me, Saybil. Are you aware of how people treat witches and mages outside the Kingdom of Wenias?"

"Yes. The neighboring countries are welcoming enough, but anti-witch sentiment grows stronger the further south you go...and in some cases it can even lead to witch hunts. That's what it said in my textbooks, anyway."

That's right—his textbooks. Aside from what he'd gleaned from such written materials, Saybil knew practically nothing about the world outside the school. The inner workings of the Magical Academy itself and the recent magical history he'd learned in class were about the only things he could confidently claim to *know* about this world:

Five hundred years of conflict between the Church and the witches, with peace achieved only a few years prior.

The shift from cumbersome sorcery to simpler magic.

Witches like Albus, who wielded those more ancient arts, and mages like himself who had studied the newer evolution of the practice.

"Exactly. You clearly know your stuff. In Wenias, witches and mages like us can walk tall and proud, but it's still not safe to openly proclaim ourselves in the southern reaches of the Great Continent. Though Loux Krystas may be able to give us a more accurate picture of the current situation," the headmaster remarked, turning to the visiting witch. "Weren't you traveling in the South up until recently?"

But Loux Krystas did not even glance in her direction. "Who can say? Thou art busy talking with this Saybil lad, art thou not? I dare not interject, lest I be thrown out. I must say, however, that these dainties are quite scrumptious."

"...Holdem," Headmaster Albus called quietly to her manservant. His hand quickly found the sword hanging from his waist.

"Want me to toss her out? Just say the word."

"Pour some tea for Loux Krystas. And bring some more sweets while you're at it."

*She took the high road. The highest, most mature road there could be.*

No sooner had Holdem set to preparing the tea and pastries as he'd been ordered, than Loux Krystas leaned forward and began divulging the information Albus had requested.

"From what I've observed in my travels these last few years, the South is—well, rife with murderous intent. Fundamentalists of the church in every corner of the land have been clamoring for witch hunts."

"But," Saybil broke in, "didn't the Church…didn't the Bishops of the Seven Great Cathedrals accept peace with the witches?"

"Maybe so, but their holy texts have demonized witches for over five centuries and only changed course a handful of years ago. 'Twould be inconceivable for a simple declaration of peace to persuade life-long adherents to relinquish such beliefs overnight," Loux Krystas explained.

"Huh…" *Is that how things go?* Saybil wondered. After all, he knew very little about the world.

"The Church is no longer monolithic. In the wake of the Disasters of the North, it has split into incessantly bickering factions: those who support peace with the witches, and those who would seek to suppress us. If anything, the division has led the suppressionist faction to intensify its witch hunts. Come, I shall illustrate the situation such that even this uninitiated youth can understand."

Loux Krystas lightly shook her staff. In response, a black liquid oozed out of the orb embedded in it and spread out to cover the low table between Saybil and Headmaster Albus. As Saybil watched, the sludge bulged and stretched into a three-dimensional map of the Great Continent, a landmass shaped like an overfed crescent moon. The witch pointed to the center of the map.

"This is the Kingdom of Wenias where we now sit, in the heart of the Great Continent." As she said this, a small replica of the Academy of Magic bubbled to the surface. Saybil lost himself in the map, entranced by what looked to him like a clay creation come to life.

The witch's finger slid to the northern region of the map. "To the north of here lies a barren wasteland called the Remnants of Disaster. Though the area around the capital came away relatively unscathed, the further north one travels, the more pervasive the devastation becomes, until hardly any natural life can be found. To quote a certain text, however, monsters like 'the nightmares of a deranged artist' run rampant there."

As if on cue, tiny figurines of centipedes with human hands and feet, deer with savage blades for antlers, and other deformed monstrosities crawled out of the murk.

*How does that thing work? Man, I really want to touch it—but Holdem asked if I had a death wish last time I tried, so maybe I'd better not.*

Many of the implements wielded by witches—particularly those witches of ages past—were as dangerous as they were useful, which was why almost every class in the Academy's curriculum strictly warned students never to carelessly touch any such objects.

"Saybil, do you know about the Remnants of Disaster?" Headmaster Albus asked, to make sure the student was keeping up with the discussion.

"Oh, yes, of course," Saybil spluttered in a mild panic, but then checked himself. He slowed down and chose his words carefully so as to not give an incorrect answer. "Six years ago a single witch summoned an unbelievable number of demons and destroyed the northern part of the Great Continent, right? The witch was eventually killed, but the monsters created by all those demons still roam the area...so now we call those monsters, and, well, all the ills that survived the witch's demise, the 'Remnants of Disaster.'"

"Oh hoh? What's this? 'Twould seem that despite thy befuddled air, thou hast rested not on the laurels of thy talent, but toiled away diligently at thy studies. Well done, child. I have a great love of industrious pursuit." As she said this, Loux Krystas reached out a hand and gave Saybil's head a few appreciative pats, then turned once again to the map on the table.

A little girl had patted him on the head. Loux Krystas was in reality ancient beyond human reckoning, so perhaps it was fair to say that it was more like receiving the affection of a nice old lady, but since she looked like a little girl, it still made him feel weird.

"Now then." With a flick of her finger, Loux Krystas drew what looked like a border across the map just south of the Kingdom of Wenias. "Down to roughly this point, the people enjoy the benefit of having in their midst mages who keep the threat of the northern beasts at bay. Many of them consequently view witches kindly. In sum—"

"The further south you go, the less people benefit from the presence of witches, and the more their opposition intensifies...?"

"Verily. Humans are exceedingly simple creatures. They accept whatever serves their needs, yet focus on naught but the danger associated with what does not. Granted," she added, "it *was* a witch who brought this calamity upon the world, and pockets of anti-witch sentiment *do* also fester within the Kingdom of Wenias. What's more, one imagines those unfortunate souls who hail from the ravaged North harbor complicated feelings on the subject."

"Complicated feelings?"

"And why not?" Loux Krystas cocked her head quizzically. "'Twas a witch who laid waste to half the continent, yet witches also were those who vanquished her and saved the people from her reign of terror. 'Witches' earned the hatred of humans, but also their gratitude. As a result, people have come to realize that what falls under the overwhelmingly broad term of 'witch' cannot be so simply defined. This prevents them from fully subscribing to either the conciliation or suppressionist movement. There are good witches in the world. But there are also evil witches, 'tis as simple as that." A wry grin that seemed out of keeping with the witch's youthful appearance crossed her lips. "Nevertheless, in sorting out who is evil and who is righteous, 'tis a much neater and less taxing affair to tar all 'witches' with the same brush. Should the anti-witch faction succeed in readying a decisive blow against magic, war is a very real possibility. They are no doubt even now endeavoring to engineer the downfall of magic, much as the Church did five centuries ago. As history shows time and again, it is conflict above all else that spurs the advancement of technology."

With another flick of her finger, Loux Krystas set the map wriggling again. Countless human figures rose to its surface, and war erupted across the land. Mages unleashed spells from the North, while great cannons spurted flame in the South.

A tired sigh escaped Headmaster Albus as she gently tilted her head back. "Thank you, Loux Krystas. What a great relief to confirm my suspicion that there isn't a single ray of positive light to be found in this bleak picture." She turned to Saybil. "What do you think? A lot worse than you'd imagined, I'll bet?"

"Y-Yes, ma'am."

"But not hopeless. No matter how deep the roots of this conflict run, people are surprisingly simple. And, just as Loux Krystas pointed out, they'll accept magic in their lives as long as they decide they can benefit from it. So if we can just get more people in the South thinking that magic is convenient, that not *all* witches are bad—" Here the headmaster grinned. "It might take time, but don't you think their antagonism would soften of its own accord?"

Saybil blinked. If witch persecution intensified the further south you went because the people there no longer benefited from magic, it made sense to assume that their opposition would wane if they started seeing those benefits too.

"Fear is rooted in ignorance. So all we need to do is make magic familiar, expose people to it so they can't help but grow accustomed to it. We just need to make magic a part of everyday life."

"But how?"

"With this special field training program."

Suddenly, they had circled back to the beginning. Headmaster Albus ploughed ahead, leaving no room for the dazed Saybil's attention to wander.

"To tell the truth, Saybil, I enlisted the help of several witches to establish a nice, visible outpost in the South before we even opened the Academy."

"You mean like…a fortune-teller's shop? One of my textbooks said that five hundred years ago, back before the Church and the witches went to war, you could find them in towns sometimes."

"Something a little grander than that. What I created was a 'village with witches,' a community where witches are an accepted part of everyday life and can go about their business freely. A village where witches are treated as ordinary people."

*I had no idea. None of the teachers ever said a thing about*

*Headmaster Albus founding a village like that.*

"I'd like you, as a participant in this special program, to spend some time in that village."

"Huh?"

"And, over the course of a few years, I want to see you accomplish something as a mage—it can be anything you choose."

Saybil stared at Albus for a few moments. "...So, am I being... expelled...?"

"Not exactly. But I don't see you improving if you remain here at the Academy. That's why I want to send you to a new environment, so you can mature as a mage."

"But, what am I supposed to accomplish...?"

"The sky's the limit. For example, you could use your magic to get the village's agriculture on the right track, or become a healer and reduce the mortality rate. The only stipulation is that you have to serve the village in some way, and compile the results in a report."

"A report, huh..."

*Come to think of it, I'm pretty sure they taught us how to write reports in class:*

*1. Establish your goals.*

*2. Present your proposed methods and conditions.*

*3. Explain your results.*

*4. Discuss areas for improvement.*

*Write that all out, then hand it in to the instructor.*

"Mage" was an occupation that hadn't existed for very long. More study was still needed to see what kind of effect mages would have on the world, what they would actually do—at least, so Saybil's professors had said. That was why every Wenisian mage had to write reports on their activities and submit them to the Society of Mages.

*Maybe this training program is a part of that whole process?*

"But, don't they hunt witches in the South...? Won't the Church faithful attack the village...?"

"No need to worry on that front. I've enlisted the help of a witch with the power to destroy the entire world if she felt like it." Headmaster Albus grinned playfully. Saybil caught his breath. She talked about the end of the world with a smile on her face, but he could tell she wasn't joking.

Just then, Holdem brought Loux Krystas her tea. The pleasant fragrance of the leaves wafted through the room, and Saybil went to take a sip from his now slightly cooled cup as well. It was refreshing, with a gentle sweetness to it, a flavor that relaxed body and mind. The young mage could hardly believe it had been prepared by the hands of this fearsome beastfallen.

"So...what happens after I submit my report?"

"If we approve the work you've done in the village, you'll be able to graduate as a bonafide mage. That said, graduating from the Academy is just the first step. It'll probably take you a much longer time to fully master the art of magic..."

"Aha! So if I'm not mistaken, this is what thy proposal amounts to," Loux Krystas interjected through a mouthful of sweets, as she reached for her tea.

*I wouldn't have guessed anyone could speak that clearly with their mouth stuffed so full*, thought Saybil, his admiration going perhaps somewhat astray.

"Students who achieve grades satisfactory for graduation are enlisted directly into maintaining the kingdom's peace or some such task, while those who cannot achieve passing marks are whisked away to a remote corner of the land to continue their studies whilst laying the groundwork for the expansion of thine influence—correct?"

"Well, yes, in a word, but...you don't have to put it quite so bluntly..."

"Brilliant! I have a great love of efficiency. Very well! I hereby agree to lead thy students on the treacherous journey to the village!"

## 3

Everyone but Loux Krystas had the same thought: *Huh? Why?*

No one said a word, but their faces all instantly froze in the same confused expression.

"...Thanks, but that's taken care of. I've already hired a mage to lead the group—"

"Ah, yes. I sent her away."

"Come again?" Headmaster Albus said, no smile on her face now.

Loux Krystas jiggered her staff, and the black substance once again oozed down from the gem embedded in it, this time molding itself into the likeness of a witch Saybil didn't recognize.

"Is this not the witch in question? As it happens, I chanced upon a familiar face headed for the Academy. Scampering after her, I asked what business brought her hither, and she rather resentfully recounted her task of chaperoning some students from the school. When I offered to take on the troublesome duty in her stead, she gleefully handed over the responsibility and scurried away to resume her own research. Here, the letter of commission," Loux Krystas said, thrusting a lambskin scroll toward the flabbergasted headmaster, whose jaw hit the floor when she saw the airtight legal document before her. "I had half a mind to rip the agreement to shreds should the task have sounded wearisome upon learning the details, but it sounds surprisingly entertaining! Rejoice, for I accept the post!"

"You...Youuuuuu idiot!" the headmaster erupted, her patience at long last depleted. "This! This is why I can't stand witches! You ancient ones are the worst! Unfailingly selfish, hedonistic... You always put yourselves first, and you have absolutely no notion of cooperation! I wouldn't trust you as far as I could throw you—much less rely on you for anything like this!"

"'Tis only natural, is it not? The more skilled the witch, the less she comes to concern herself with the affairs of others. Lest thee forget, the witch in question *did* make certain another would faithfully carry out her responsibility. Rather conscientious, I should say, so far as it goes."

"Obviously!! She was the one I chose to take care of our students after painstaking scrutiny! Do you have any idea how difficult it is to find a witch without any current ties to the school who's appropriately sociable, not too aggressive, and won't abandon the students at the first sign of danger?! Of course not, and yet you, you—!"

"I tell thee, I accept the post. I meet all thy stipulations. Where dost thou find fault?"

"Your very existence is a danger to us all! I'll never understand where you get the audacity!"

Ruffling her hair with both hands in enraged frustration, Albus reared back and practically toppled over. Her trusty manservant Holdem wrapped an arm around her shoulders and repeated a soft "Whoa, whoa there," like someone calming a frenzied horse.

*Wait, hang on.*

"Her existence is...a danger?" Saybil peered at the diminutive witch. "You're talking about Loux Krystas?"

"'Los' will do. 'Tis what all my closest acquaintances call me. I, in turn, shall call thee Sayb."

Saybil wasn't aware they'd become close, but he also perceived that it might not be the wisest course of action to make things awkward by saying so.

"Is it really all that surprising?" Holdem interjected. "She almost killed you a few minutes ago, remember?"

Los puffed out her cheeks in annoyance.

"It was an act! An act!" she insisted. "Anyone with eyes could see 'twas naught but an empty threat. I'm well aware that I would not escape unscathed should I lay a hand on one of Albus's students."

"Wait. You tried to kill one of my students? While my back was turned?"

"I merely threatened him with my staff."

"You're not chaperoning anyone."

"No faaaair! I wish to do iiiit!" Los wailed, flailing her arms and legs in protest at Albus's blunt rejection. Forget being three hundred years old; the tantrum made her seem even *more* childish than her youthful form would suggest.

"She doesn't seem that dangerous to me..." Saybil muttered to himself.

"*She* isn't," the headmaster conceded. "Loux Krystas herself isn't the danger, per se. It's that staff of hers." Albus ran her eyes over the towering staff Los held clutched to her chest.

*Guess it really must be a special staff.*

"What exactly is it? It seems... I don't know how to put it, but, like...awesomely...awesome. That is, what I saw *was* really awesome..." Even Saybil could appreciate that the staff's awesome power defied description (evidently).

"Right? Dost see it? One cannot help but notice how truly awe-inspiring is my little Ludens!"

"I mean, it turned into a halberd, and then a map... There's no way you could spin that as ordinary."

In the brief time he'd known Los, Saybil had seen enough to know the staff was indeed irrefutably awesome. Headmaster Albus, for her part, stared at the witch's treasured possession with horror in her eyes.

"It's a demon in the shape of a staff."

"A demon?" Saybil repeated, puzzled.

"...Nothing much surprises you, does it...?"

"No, I'm totally freaking out right now. This is just the best my facial muscles can do..." Saybil pried his eyes open wide with his fingers in an effort to demonstrate just how shocked he actually was.

"Now it just looks like you're mocking me. Stop."

"Sorry."

"Don't be. That's on me. I knew from the start you don't emote much," Albus admitted.

"You did?"

"I *am* the headmaster, you know."

*Whoa. Pretty badass headmaster.*

Saybil's respect for the head of the Academy deepened—not that you could tell by looking at him. Albus continued her explanation.

"The Staff of Ludens is actually quite famous in the witching world."

"Quite," Los agreed. "It all began four hundred years ago—"

*"Four hundred years?"*

"It's a long story, so let's cut to the chase," Albus said, mercilessly truncating the witch's tale.

"Blasphemy!" Los squawked, but the headmaster spared her not even a glance.

"The Staff of Ludens runs amok if any witch but Loux Krystas wields it."

"Runs amok? How could a staff…run amok?"

"By draining whoever touches it of all their magic, or possessing them… Anyway, the point is, it's cursed. Which is why I wish she'd lock it away somewhere safe instead of strolling around with it like it's some kind of harmless pet."

"Prejudice against demons does not become thee, Albus! And it foments anti-witch discrimination as well, I'll have thee know! Consider the anguish this groundless abuse must cause my little Ludens! Dost feel no pity?"

Los cradled the staff lovingly in her arms, nuzzling it with her cheek. The mysterious black ooze stretched down from the staff's orb and embraced her in return. Evidently, it did in fact have feelings.

"There are more than enough grounds to criticize that thing, Loux Krystas. Don't tell me you haven't heard its notorious nickname? People call it 'The Witch Eater.'"

"I have not been eaten."

"Because you formed a pact with it, remember?! But do you have any idea how many witches' lives it devoured before that…?!"

"How many witches' lives *did* it devour?" Saybil asked, his curiosity piqued.

Headmaster Albus raised a finger, then stood up abruptly and walked over to a bookcase. She pulled out a tome, flipped through its pages, and turned back to Saybil. *"While the total number of victims remains unconfirmed, a great many witches lost their lives to the staff."*

"I see." *The typical vague phrasing you find in reference books.*

"In any event, that's why there is absolutely no chance I'd ever let Loux Krystas chaperone my precious students anywhere."

"Quite the coddler, I see. So long as none of thy pupils take Ludens in hand, they run no risk of losing their mana. If it worries thee so, why not procure a bit of consecrated cloth from the Church and have it fashioned into gloves for the students? While thou art at it, order some breastplates, that they might not be stabbed in the heart with a knife or some such."

"That's not the issue here, you kn—"

"That is *precisely* the issue here," Los insisted. "My little Ludens is indeed dangerous. However, a simple knife may just as easily rob a person of their life. Magic itself is outrageously perilous. Yet to teach what is treacherous and to prepare thy charges with the tools to protect themselves—is that not the meat of education?"

Headmaster Albus said nothing, but she glanced over at Holdem, who shrugged. Whatever means of silent communication connected them was beyond Saybil. But—

"...And what would you have in return?" Albus finally asked. Her next words carried the promise of a negotiation. "I can accept you as the group's chaperone, but only under the stipulation that we sign a proper contract. For your part, you will lead my students safely to the designated village. Now what do you want in return?"

Los grinned mischievously. "Dost thou not know, Albus? I wish to read the *Grimoire of Zero*."

The *Grimoire of Zero*—the tome that ushered in the age of magic. In ancient times, the miracles witches conjured were all referred to as sorcery, a form of spellcraft which required decades of study to master, and days—sometimes years, depending on the rite—to invoke. These witches of old summoned dangerous demons, and through them, worked wonders. That was sorcery.

Magic, in comparison, called not on such demons themselves but on their power. Not only could the necessary skills be acquired within five short years, the incantations took only seconds, or at most a few minutes, to recite. Magic was, in every sense, an incomparably simpler practice than sorcery.

The *Grimoire of Zero* was the first treatise laying out the fundamental theories of magic: what it was, and how to utilize it. Rumor had it the tome was kept secure somewhere in the Academy—but.

"How many times do I have to repeat myself, Loux Krystas? I can't let you read it. It's forbidden."

"Why?! What cause dost thou have to seal away the book? 'Tis but a handbook of magic, not an incitement to mass murder!"

"Absolutely. The *Grimoire of Zero* is inherently good. Even so, it's a dangerous book for anyone just getting started with magic to read. It's *too* instructive, it discloses far more than is safe to know," Headmaster Albus argued. "That tome takes its author, the Mud-Black Witch, as its standard. While she was unquestionably a witch of rare genius, however, she had a deeply impoverished grasp of the world when she penned the *Grimoire*. She knew nothing of the contradictory impulses that motivate so many humans to resort to force in the pursuit of pleasure or revenge, even when to do so is detrimental to their own interests."

Tension crackled through the air like an electric current. Flames flickered in Headmaster Albus's golden eyes—flames of war, of witch hunts, of all the conflagrations she had witnessed throughout her life.

"I am no untutored fledgling, Albus. Nor will I scurry off to commit some pointless plunder once I have read the great *Gri-*

*moire,"* Los scoffed. "Books are, in essence, finely honed blades of knowledge. Whether that blade is employed to cut through adversity or to cut down an object of contempt is entirely up to the one who wields it."

Albus raised an eyebrow at the dramatic turn of phrase, but Los paid her no heed. "Look at me, Albus. Revisit what memories thou dost possess of me. I am the Dawn Witch, she who seeks incessantly for all that is novel, who revels in all life's pleasures. Yet I do not love the suffering of others. Were I wicked, I would simply take my darling Ludens in hand and have my way with the world, with no need to read a single page of the *Grimoire of Zero.* I understand thy dread of the *Grimoire.* None has been more deeply wounded by that blade than thee. Which is why thou didst take it up thyself and wield it."

"...You have an awful way of putting things, Loux Krystas."

Saybil had learned in history class of the influential role Headmaster Albus had taken in the civil war between the witches and the Kingdom of Wenias. Spurred on by the death of her grandmother, Sorena, an august witch of old who lived for over five centuries and was killed in a witch hunt, Albus took what magic she had learned and joined the war, pitting herself against the forces of an entire kingdom. She was said to have been only sixteen years old at the time. Nevertheless, she exposed the schemes of the mastermind behind the war and defeated him.

Thirteen—that was the moniker of the notorious and wicked sorcerer who stole the *Grimoire of Zero* from the Mud-Black Witch, bringing magic to the Kingdom of Wenias and kindling the flames of war. To this day, some refused to denounce his actions. While he did start the conflict, they argued, that same war was exactly what led to the peace the kingdom now enjoyed.

The Academy of Magic, however, refused to accept such claims. Thirteen had not set out in search of peace; he had aimed to put witches in a position to subjugate the population. The Academy held that one could not excuse his crimes simply because they ultimately led to the advent of peace.

In fact, the one who finally slew the sorcerer Thirteen was none other than Headmaster Albus herself. Though he had manipulated her for a time, she eventually saw through his lies and marshaled the mages who stopped his evil in its tracks. Headmaster Albus was no ancient witch; she had not yet outlived any human lifespan—and even now she continued to devote her life to creating a world where humans and mages could coexist in peace.

"I do not say it to blame thee. That war was bound to happen. And the experience thou didst gain in the midst of that tumult is what has brought thee to act as shepherd to the practice of magic. I hold no rancor for errors once made. They are precisely what qualify thee to be a leader."

Silence.

Headmaster Albus drew in a deep breath and let it out slowly.

"I...no, *many* witches abused magic—even the revered witches of old," she admitted. "That's why I put a seal on all magic within the Kingdom of Wenias: so that we could start fresh. And why only those with my permission can cast spells within the kingdom. That's the basis of the current magical licensing system. You're right. I made terrible mistakes. That's why I'll never allow myself to make one again."

Then she doubled down: "You'll get no special treatment from me, Loux Krystas. I cannot grant you access to the *Grimoire of Zero.* As long as you remain unaffiliated with our Academy, that is."

"Huh?" Saybil blurted out. "So, if she's part of the Academy... she can see it?"

"So now we come to it!" exclaimed Los, thrusting her staff in Saybil's face. "Blasted Albus tells me that, should I graduate from the Academy and receive permission to conduct research furthering the field of magic, the *Grimoire* would be mine to read! And yet as soon as I tell her to enroll me, she denies me outright! 'I cannot expose my students to that risk,' she says!"

"You leave me no choice!" Albus shot back. "You refuse to sign a contract with me. Every student admitted to the Academy is required to sign the same contract, swearing eternally to use magic only for the greater good and never for evil ends."

The seal on magic had no effect outside the borders of the Kingdom of Wenias, so in order to prevent mages from running amok in other lands, everyone who enrolled at the Academy first had to sign a formal contract with Headmaster Albus herself:

*I vow not to use magic without the express permission of the Society.*

*I vow not to teach magic without the express permission of the Society.*

*I vow not to devise new magic without the express permission of the Society.*

*I agree to forfeit for all eternity the use of demonic power should I violate any of the above terms.*

Every single person who studied magic in the Kingdom of Wenias and became an official mage of the realm had to sign this contract, without exception.

Los snorted, looking deeply disgusted. "I have no love for restrictions. Nor will I suffer to be prohibited in any way, by anyone. I would never use magic to evil ends, contract or no. And as for that last bit! About forfeiting the power of demons for all time! Should I be so prohibited, I would no longer be able to draw on little Ludens's power! Wouldst thou be a murderer?!"

"That wouldn't happen as long as you didn't break the terms of the contract!"

"But what if I should slip and violate them unintentionally?!"

"That's exactly what I'm trying to avoid! One little slip could cost lives! It's why we have the contract in the first place! In any event, I cannot grant you access to the *Grimoire of Zero*."

"Miserly monkey!"

"So now you're *talking* like a child, too...? I haven't finished, Loux Krystas. Hear me out." The headmaster raised her finger, and Los fell silent. "I can't let you see the *Grimoire*, but... Yes. I *could* facilitate a meeting with its author."

For a second, Los didn't even breathe. Then she bent back as far as she could go before flinging herself forward toward the headmaster.

"With—the Mud-Black Witch?! Dost mean to tell me thou knowest where she is, she who vanished so thoroughly after the Disasters of the North?!"

"All part of the job."

"M-My lady, that's—" Holdem tried to interject, but Albus raised her hand, cutting his protest short.

"So what'll it be? It's a pretty good deal, if you ask me," the headmaster said, all the while jotting down the contract on a lambskin scroll, which she then signed in blood. This she proffered to Los, along with a map to the village. Quick as a snake, Los snatched the contract from Albus and added her own name. Saybil couldn't believe how easily she'd caved.

"I'm warning you now, though, I can't guarantee the Mud-Black Witch will talk to you about magic. She doesn't take orders from anyone. She does carefully consider requests, however. I can get you two in the same place, but there's a chance you won't even realize who she is."

"Nonsense. What sort of witch dost thou take me for?" Los held the signed contract to the flame of a candle. "I am Loux Krystas, the Dawn Witch, she who pursues the one shining truth in a sea of myriad falsehoods. No matter how the Mud-Black Witch may disguise herself, she shall not deceive me."

Flames licked the scroll bearing both witches' signatures—the final step in a sorcerers' blood contract. Whosoever violated such a contract would lose their soul to the demons who stood witness to the pact. Saybil had only ever heard about blood contracts in class, but he knew they were far too dangerous to be signed casually. Only true witches would tie their fates to these soul-risking pacts as if it were as natural as breathing. That willingness was probably one of the fundamental differences between them and mages like Saybil.

Finally, the fire devoured the last of the scroll.

"Albus, Mooncaller Witch, thus our pact has been sealed. Now, 'tis time to make ready for our long journey!" Los proclaimed. "Sayb, I shall await thee three days hence at the South Tunnel!"

And with those scant parting words, Los flew out of the headmaster's office like a gust of wind. Dazed and befuddled in her wake, Saybil looked to Albus. "...The South Tunnel?"

"Mountains surround the Kingdom of Wenias on all sides, so the only way to leave is through a tunnel. There's one leading out in every cardinal direction," she explained.

The additional information put Saybil's mind at ease. He had a rough grasp of the kingdom's geography, but couldn't immediately pinpoint any locations by name.

"I'll have Holdem help you prepare for the journey. He'll take you to the South Tunnel by carriage."

"Th-Thank you very much. And…thank you for finding a way for me to graduate, even though my grades are so awful. I can't tell you how happy it makes me," he said, giving the headmaster his best attempt at a smile. Whether the sentiment reached her, however, he had no way of knowing.

"Whether or not you graduate is going to be up to you. I imagine you'll face more hardships than you would have studying here at the Academy—and more temptations, too. But I'll be praying you don't stray from the path."

"…Can I ask you something?"

"Hmm?"

"The day I first came here…I asked you, 'Where did she go?'"

"Ahh… That's right, you did."

"My memories from that day are pretty hazy, and I can't remember how you answered."

"I didn't." Albus smiled. "I didn't answer your question. Nor do I intend to."

"But…she brought me here—"

"Saybil." Suddenly, the headmaster sandwiched Saybil's cheeks between her hands. She pulled him close, and he gazed into her golden eyes. "Any memories you truly need will return to you. Otherwise, they're best left forgotten. This little head of yours—" and here Headmaster Albus lightly knocked her forehead against his, "—has so much else it needs to absorb. Don't chase the past. You don't want to lose your future."

"What…do you…?"

A pat on the chest, and the headmaster's warmth moved away from Saybil's body. That's when he realized a lambskin scroll had been slipped into his hand.

"Holdem, help Saybil with whatever he needs for the trip."

"You got it."

Ushered away by the lupine beastfallen, Saybil left the headmaster's office more than a little confused. He unrolled the scroll in his hand, read its contents, and took a deep breath.

*Apprentice Mage Saybil*

*You are hereby dispatched to the Witch's Village as a Special Field Training Student.*

*Restrictions (Permissions)*

*Forbidden from conjuring magic harmful to people.*

*Exception: In a matter of life and death, this restriction shall be considered lifted.*

# Chapter One

# 1

The Kingdom of Wenias was nestled in a valley encircled on every side by a range of mountains. In order to leave the kingdom, one had to either hike over their peaks or pass beneath them through one of the four tunnels in the east, west, north, and south. The road from the North Tunnel led to the barren wasteland known as the Remnants of Disaster, while the path from the South Tunnel stretched on toward the village where Saybil and the other field program students were headed.

Or so Saybil had heard.

He came by all these piecemeal details second-hand. As far as Saybil could recall, he had never set foot outside the Academy, much less passed the kingdom's borders. He was beyond sheltered.

Holdem had helped Saybil gather everything he needed for the trip, and even given him a ride to the South Tunnel by carriage. As soon as he was on his own, though, the mage-in-training immediately found himself at a loss.

"She said the South Tunnel, but...which end did she mean?"

The tunnel that carved its way through the mountains was so long and wide that a peek inside provided no glimmer of the light at the other end. Shops and throngs of travelers lined the passage's interior, while just outside the mouth of the tunnel stood a prosperous and bustling post town. Street vendors called out to potential customers, lost children wailed at the top of their lungs, and buskers played their flutes. And yet, Los had not specified where amid this crowded scene Saybil was to find her. Should he meet her at the entrance? The exit? Not even that was clear.

*I might not ever find her.*

The worry wasted no time worming its way into his mind. And Saybil, who had no recollection of taking any sort of journey before, had no hope of making it to the village without Los. He didn't have so much as a map to tell him where it lay. And so—

"Oh, thou hast come, Sayb! Here! Over here!"

—Saybil was surprised at just how relieved he felt at the sight of the witch hopping up and down, her head bobbing in and out of the crowd, having caught sight of him more or less as soon as he arrived. That said, he also couldn't deny the impulse to walk right by as if he didn't know the deranged girl waving a dangerous magical staff as if it were a signal flag.

"Why the sour scowl! Why dost look so put off?!"

"Nothing, it's just... I don't really like to draw attention to myself..." Saybil hedged.

"And nor do I! Yet wouldst thou have preferred I cower in embarrassment and leave thee stranded there forever with that look of utter despair on thy face?"

Saybil couldn't argue with that. Still, he had to wonder whether they couldn't have avoided drawing such attention to themselves in the first place if the witch had just specified where they were to meet beforehand.

"What now? Why the troubled look? Rejoice in my pardon—if dost have words for me, out with them!"

"Oh, uh... No, I don't..."

"Goodness, what a reserved sort thou art! A lad as young as thee should throw caution to the wind and forget about social niceties! 'Twould be more enjoyable for me, at any rate."

"It's just... You were talking about my face..." Saybil pointed at it. "Did my expression change?"

"Heavens, no. 'Tis as if thou wert wearing a mask."

"But, you said I looked put off..."

Los cackled. "A witch sees more than mere surface expressions, my lad. We follow the flittering of thine eyes, the fall and rise of thy breath, the beating of thine heart, the flow of thy gestures, the air that hangs about thee—every possible aspect of thy being is part of the 'face' I see. The muscles of thy countenance may have gone on strike, but the emotions are still plain to see. Though it would appear thou dost suppress these somewhat."

"I'm not...suppressing my..."

*At least, I'm not trying to.*

Saybil laid a hand on his chest. Heartbeats.

*Huh. My heart might actually be beating a little faster than usual.*

"These are thine effects, I presume? Let's see what we have here." While Saybil was busy checking his pulse, Los snatched the bag he'd slung across his shoulders and pulled it close. Peeking inside, she frowned. "Traveling a bit light, no? Art thou truly content with so little?"

"I, um...couldn't really think of what else to pack, aside from the essentials Holdem put together for me. Did I not bring enough?"

"Let me see... Books, canteen, some foodstuffs, a knife, and a lantern. Mm-hmm, not a terrible selection. After all, we shall travel by highway, and a light load is a welcome companion on such journeys."

"Would I need more stuff if we took another route?"

"Indubitably. To what other end dost thou suppose we support the highway's maintenance by paying the fare to tread it? Waterways and inns and perfectly suitable camping grounds line the road. The same cannot be said for a trek through fields and wilderness. One would need more vessels for water, not to mention a horse. Even a wagon, if it suited."

"I see..."

"But thou dost surprise me, I must say. I had thought the youth of today would seek comfort on such journeys, and overstuff their bags with trifles and trinkets," Los sighed, seeming somehow disappointed. She furrowed her brow and looked up at Saybil. "Thou art free to ask more from life, Sayb. A body pillow, for instance, would harm no one."

"The thing is, I just don't have that much stuff to begin with..." *Or memories, for that matter*, he wanted to add, but decided against it to avoid the odd look it usually invited. Having enrolled at the Academy with nothing but the clothes on his back, Saybil had hardly anything in the way of personal belongings. The Academy provided uniforms in addition to room and board, so it had never bothered him.

"You travel pretty light yourself, Ms. Los," he pointed out. His chaperone didn't seem to carry anything aside from a small bag hanging at her waist. The pouch looked about half the size of Saybil's bag, barely big enough to fit a bottle of water and a map.

"I have my staff, after all. And little Ludens is capable of almost anything," replied Los, puffing out her chest, when—

"Aaah! There you are! Found you! Oh good, I made it! Saaaybiiiil!"

—a voice called out. Saybil turned around and let out an, "Ah."

He knew that face—in other words, it belonged to a classmate. An oversized cap sat atop the girl's bright red locks, which bounced with her every step, glittering in the sunlight—and for some reason she was decked out for a journey. Los eyed her suspiciously as she ran over to them, but then her eyes widened with sudden understanding. She smirked and gave Saybil a light jab in the ribs.

"Well, well, well, quite the charming lass. Thy sweetheart, I presume?"

"No," Saybil said, in all earnest.

"Not one for jest, I see..."

"She's an upperclassman from the Academy. Everybody knows her... I think her name is...Hort or something."

"Dost thou know so little of her? The lass did not hesitate to call thee by name."

"Oh, good point. Why does she know my name...? We've never even talked."

The very next second, Hort came to a stop right in front of Saybil and shrugged off her bulging bag with a heave-ho. Then, whipping her head up and leaning in close, she said, "Were you introducing me?!"

"Ah, sorry. I know I shouldn't be—"

"No, no, I'm glad! That means you know who I am too, right? Thank Goddess for that! It would've been so annoying to explain if you'd been like, 'And you are...?'"

"I mean, you're practically famous. Everyone says you're the best student at the Academy..."

Hort's cheeks flushed bright red. "I-I-I'm not all that good! That's just a silly rumor my mediocre classmates made up to make our house look better!"

"A rather coy smile for such cutting words..." Los muttered, an

inscrutable expression on her face as she stared up at the blushing young girl frantically waving away the compliment. Finally noticing the witch, Hort's eyes sparkled as if she were a puppy discovering a new toy. "Who's this, Saybil? Your girlfriend?"

"No," Saybil said, just as earnest as when he had replied to Los.

Hort beamed from ear to ear. It was a dazzling smile.

Her facial muscles seemed to be alive and well.

*Now that's a well-honed smile. I wish I could do that.*

"Gotcha, gotcha. That's good to hear. I would've felt like a total third wheel if your girlfriend was coming with us. Well, whatever. So? Where's Loux Krystas? Isn't she supposed to be chaperoning us? She not here yet?"

"'Tis I."

"Huh? What'd you say?" Hort asked, smile still going full force.

An irritated-seeming Los thrust her staff in Hort's face and declared, "I said, I am thy chaperone, the selfsame Loux Krystas, thou bungling blockhead. I have no love for those slow on the uptake. A question posed again after a time I may oblige, but do not expect me to repeat myself mere seconds after my first explanation."

"No waaay!!!" Hort exclaimed. "But, you're even tinier than me!!"

"Height hath no bearing on leadership."

"But you're so adorable!!"

"What! How sudden! I am abashed!" Los cried, seeming genuinely abashed as a rosy pink bloomed on her cheeks, which in turn made Hort blush too, for some reason.

Suddenly, a looming black shadow fell over the flustered, mutually bashful pair. Beside them stood a lithe reptilian beastfallen wrapped in a pristine new cloak. The scales covering the tail that poked out beneath the long garment were black, while those around the beastfallen's bulging blue eyes were a glittering jade green.

"What's with the lady lovebird action? You two an item?"

"Kudo. Why are you here?" Saybil asked. The name associated with his face came immediately to mind, since this lizard beastfallen was in the same house as Saybil at the Academy.

Generally speaking, the Academy's students were of all ages and came from all walks of life. A pupil might just as easily be thirteen, thirty, or a centenarian witch. Only one, however, stood out clearly amidst the diverse tapestry of apprentice mages—Kudo, the only beastfallen student in the entire Academy.

"The hell d'you mean, 'why'? I got chosen, too, dude. For the special field program."

"Me too! I'm doing the program, too!" Hort chimed in.

"Huh? But..." Saybil trailed off. He'd assumed the special field training program was a last resort to help students like him, who were at risk of expulsion. But Hort was a shoo-in for the kingdom's armed forces once she inevitably graduated. It didn't make sense for her to be there. And while Kudo's speech and conduct admittedly left something to be desired, he also earned top-notch grades.

"Why would you two have to do the program...?"

"None a yer goddamn business," snapped Kudo.

"I applied for a spot," Hort said. "I'm a fourth-year now, which means I'm about to go on to year five, right? That'd leave me with just one more year before I graduate, but I've been thinking I *really* want to spend more time studying magic if I can, so I asked my Professor for advice. She was like, 'There's this special field training program,' and I was like, 'I'm in!' So she told me to follow after you. Oh, Professor, here's my letter of appointment." She handed Los a lambskin scroll sealed with wax.

"P-Professor...? Wh-What a lovely ring that has...! So be it, rejoice in my pardon! Hort, from this moment onward, I grant thee leave to venerate me as thy mentor. And, as a token of our fond acquaintance, I shall allow thee to call me Professor Los! I extend this invitation to thee as well, young Kudo or whatever thy name may be."

"Yeah, I'm not going with you." Kudo spat, slapping his tail against the ground. "I'm used to being on the road. I just came over to say you can count me out of this supervised shit. I'll get those two clowns as far as the village, too." He thrust his jaw toward the other side of the road, where two more students from the Academy were enjoying a last snack at a street vendor's stall. Los, Saybil, and Hort all craned their necks to see the clowns in question.

Saybil blinked. "I know them."

"No shit, moron. They're in our house. You telling me you don't know their names?"

"I've never needed to..." Saybil mumbled. "I mean, I would've remembered if they stood out as much as you."

Los batted her eyes in surprise. "In sum, young Kudo, thou didst march all the way over here simply to say thou wouldst not require my guidance? When I had not heard so much as a whisper of thee, so couldst just as well have been on thy merry way, leaving me none the wiser...? How conscientious of thee."

"Conscientious, my ass! I'm just not tryin'a get docked points for pissing off the professor by leaving without saying anything!"

"I see. So thou art a coward."

"Shut up!" Kudo shouted angrily, the scales from his face down to his neck turning a bright red. Kudo's scales changed color with his every mood. This fun fact made him a hopeless liar.

"And what about you, Saybil?" Kudo snarled, redirecting his anger to his classmate and poking him in the chest, hard. "Why the hell are *you* here? You do realize you're the only washout in our little group of straight-A all-stars, right? No amount of studyin' is gonna make your sorry ass a mage. Save yourself the trouble and just go let the headmaster kick you out already!"

With that parting shot, the irate beastfallen turned and lumbered off. He barked at the two snacking students and set off for the tunnel leading south out of the Kingdom of Wenias.

Scrunching up every muscle in her face, Hort stuck out her tongue at him. "*Blehhh!* What's *his* problem? I'd heard rumors, but he really is a jerk. Is he always like that?"

"Uh huh. I don't think he's actually a bad guy, though."

"Guess his parents just didn't raise him right, huh." Talk about cutting criticism. "But, like, he's a beastfallen, right? He looks scary enough as it is, why not try at least *acting* a little nicer, you know?"

"I don't mind. It makes him easy to read."

"You're just too nice!" Hort scolded him.

"Plus..." Saybil wavered for a second, then made up his mind and took the plunge. "I think it's kind of messed up to expect beastfallen to act nice all the time just because they're beastfallen. Honestly, I like that he couldn't tell a lie even if his life depended on it. It's actually kind of reassuring..." *I think he's fine the way he is. It's not like he chose to be born like that. It'd be cruel to force him to live a certain way just because of it.*

People said that beastfallen were the "epitome of depravation," violent and dangerous creatures—"everybody knows that." But Saybil had never met any beastfallen aside from Kudo and Holdem, and there were plenty of other students in the Academy who seemed a lot more dangerous than Kudo.

*I don't get it. Why should Kudo be the only one who always has to be on his best behavior, just because he looks like a lizard?*

Saybil knew that speaking up about it might make things awkward with Hort, whom he'd only just met, but he also knew that if he didn't say anything, he'd regret it later. Back when he'd started at the Academy, Saybil had run up against the phrase "everybody knows that" more times than he cared to remember. When he asked the other students to explain the logic behind this "common knowledge," most of them would get annoyed and walk off.

Saybil couldn't stand the silence any longer. He risked a sideways glance at Hort. She was studying Saybil carefully, until finally she broke out into another winning smile.

"You're pretty cool, Saybil."

"Wha?" he blurted foolishly, completely taken aback at the unexpected response.

"I think you're right! That feels right to me now! You know, you seem like the quiet type, but you really do speak your mind, huh? That's awesome! I feel happy all over for some reason. So, let me rephrase."

"Huh...?"

"Kudo shouldn't have talked to you like that! I don't care if he's a beastfallen or the hottest guy in the world, nobody should talk to people like that! Nobody!"

"Uh huh..." Saybil nodded. "You're right, he shouldn't have put it that way. It doesn't bother me, but that doesn't make it okay."

"You sure are tough!" Hort laughed and clapped Saybil on the shoulder.

"'Tough'? 'Indifferent' might be more apt, I dare say..." Los chimed in with a mildly exasperated air. "Ah, that reminds me. I had a question for thee, Sayb. Which subject has thy grades so dismally low? Thou didst have at least a passing grasp of history, and it seems thou dost pay close attention to thy lessons."

"I, um... See... It's magic..."

"Hmm?" Puzzled, Los rephrased the question. "I know full well we all have our strengths and weaknesses when it comes to magic. Is thy difficulty with healing enchantments, or combat spells, or...?"

"Oh, no, um... It's not like a particular kind or anything..." Saybil looked down at his hands. "The truth is, I can hardly use magic at all."

## 2

"Then perhaps 'twould be wise to leave the path of the mage altogether, lad."

"Professor! That's going too far!" Tears welled in Hort's eyes as she protested the witch's blunt judgment.

"No, I hardly think it goes far enough. Thy spells either fail or run out of control or elicit no response, I take it? Clearly, thou hast no control over thy powers. Were it my judgment to make, I would seal away thy magic this instant. 'Twould be better not to use it at all than to use it poorly. Whether 'tis sorcery or magic, to cast spells one cannot control is the most perilous pursuit of all."

"B-But...!"

"Kudo spoke truly. That confounded Albus! I cannot fathom what goes on in that head of hers... Return to the Academy, Sayb. I shall escort Hort alone to the village. As fortune would have it, my contract states that I must 'lead the designated students to the appropriate village.' Sending thee back should not run afoul of those terms."

"P-Please, give me a chance!" Saybil was frantic. "I can use a few spells...ones I practiced over and over again until I had them down. My professors wouldn't teach me a new spell until I could completely control the one I was working on. I'm confident the magic I know won't get out of control, seriously. It really is only a handful of spells...and they're all as basic as can be, but..."

"Hmph," Los snorted. "So to toil away day after day, year after year, gradually building a safe magical repertoire...is that thy intent? Interesting. A rather long-term goal, but not an unachievable one."

"So..."

"But why?"

"Huh?"

"Why dost thou wish to become a mage?" As she spoke, Los lugged Hort's massive bag over to the shade of a nearby tree and spread its entire contents out on the ground. It was crammed full of stuffed animals, nail-care implements, and sundry other unnecessary personal effects. Los began industriously culling the items, and Hort nervously watched her belongings being discarded as junk while she continued to listen to the conversation unfold.

"Magic is a technique that holds much appeal, a skill enjoyable to study, learn, and employ. Now that the world has come to know magic, there can be no thwarting its spread. However, trailblazers unfailingly confront trying hardships—tell me, hast thou heard this tale, young Sayb? There once lived an inventor who ingeniously revised an existing machine, such that what had before required three men to run now necessitated only one. Productivity increased, and the inventor was showered with praise—until the resentful men who had lost their jobs exacted a murderous revenge..." She paused. "Hort, what might this be?" Los picked up a rough metal file and shot the young mage a quizzical look.

Hort frantically snatched it out of her hand and turned beet red.

"A very personal feminine product!"

"...Why was the inventor murdered?" Saybil asked.

"That three-person machine turned into a one-man show, right? Why didn't they just make enough machines for everyone?" Hort reasoned. "Then no one would've had to lose their jobs."

"And if that new machine proved too difficult for merely anyone to operate?"

"...Ohhh." It all clicked in Saybil's mind.

*She's talking about magic.*

"So basically, we're the inventor...who'll get killed by the people who can't use magic...right?"

"Mages face all manner of trials the moment they set foot outside the Kingdom of Wenias. Curiosity, fear, hatred—and if you lash out at the people in return, the reputation of mages the world over shall plummet. But if you stay your hand, you risk a torturous death. You may instead choose to hide behind the kingdom's borders, yet even in Wenias, those who begrudge magery await the opportunity to raise a hue and cry and drag you all down to hell. Sayb, Hort, mark my words."

The two students flinched nervously as she said their names. Though Los was to all appearances a young girl, they could feel a searing power bearing down on them. Nothing about her expression or mannerisms had changed, but her intimidating aura was enough to leave them drenched in cold sweat.

"Would you still aim to be a mage, despite the risks? I do not know what you learned within the walls of the Academy, but the life of a mage is not an easy path to tread. 'Twould be far wiser to abandon your ambitions and remain powerless, relying instead on the magical prowess of others. If you rashly continue to pursue the accumulation of knowledge and power, somewhere along the way you may stumble, and see those mages you considered comrades take from you all you hold dear. Magic holds extraordinary power, and as such, 'tis a practice not easily abandoned simply because you grow weary of it. With that in mind, do you not think it prudent to turn back now whilst that road remains open to you?"

Saybil and Hort looked at each other.

"Professor, you...think we shouldn't become mages?"

At Hort's question, Los's demeanor softened somewhat. "Nay, I merely share with you the concerns of a kindly old woman, as one might caution an infant of the danger posed by the sword in its hands. A cheerful, intelligent lass such as thyself could surely find other employment, Hort. And thou, Sayb, hast a strapping physique that could enable a modest life as a woodcutter or some such."

"...The..." Saybil began apprehensively. "The truth is...I've never really...wanted to be a mage..."

"Huh?! Seriously?!"

"I mean, don't get the wrong idea. It's not that I *don't* want to be a mage... I've just never had any other option, so...I've never considered doing anything else... The thing is," he continued, "I don't remember anything from before I came to the Academy. So if I flunk out and my memories get sealed away, I'll be left with nothing... Which is why..."

*I have to become a mage. I've got no other choice. I can't even consider any other path.*

Most of the students at the Academy had eschewed other opportunities in order to pursue magic. Saybil, however, had never had the luxury of choice. That didn't exactly hang heavy on his heart, but having someone explicitly tell him after all this time that there were alternative paths did throw him for a loop.

*It's like, I've been human all my life. Someone could try to tell me, "You could've been a horse, you know," but I wouldn't be able to imagine what that meant. At most, I could conjure the image of pulling a cart or something.*

"You don't remember anything before the Academy? Does that mean you have amnesia?" Hort probed, leaning in close.

Saybil nodded. "I knew how to talk and eat and stuff...but I couldn't even read three years ago. I don't know if that means I forgot or just never learned how, though."

"Whoaa! That's wild! You're the first amnesiac I've ever met! How did you even get into the Academy? That's so weird! Oh, speaking of weird—" Hort suddenly switched gears as if a thought had just occurred to her. "You know how you get assigned to a house based on your magic proficiency? So that, like, you're grouped with people at your same level?"

"Y-Yeah..."

"Well, your grades are rock bottom, right? You're pretty notorious for it—that's how I knew your name," she said off-handedly, delivering this scathing remark with her winningest smile.

Saybil's expression remained stubbornly immobile, though he did manage to inch it slightly closer to a scowl. "Yeah... I've got the worst grades in the history of the Academy..."

"That's what's so weird. I mean, everyone else in your house is so good at magic. If you're that bad at it, you'd think they'd stick you in a lower group, right? So why did they put you with all those super capable students?"

"I figured it was just because I was a transfer..."

"That doesn't make any sense, Sayb! They could've just put you in a house that suits you better, couldn't they? Why would they go out of their way to match you with all those overachievers?"

Saybil noticed that Hort had adopted the "Sayb" nickname at

some point, but he didn't much mind, so he let it go without saying anything. His mind was more preoccupied with the mystery of his placement. With an extremely serious look on her face, Hort scooted even closer to him.

"My theory is, this must be some kind of experiment."

"...Wait, what?" Stunned by this entirely unexpected turn, it took Saybil a second to get the question out. "Sorry, what do you mean, 'experiment'...?"

"Just think about it—you have amnesia, Kudo's a beastfallen, I'm the most gifted student the Academy has ever seen, and we all got chosen to be in this special field program, right?! This has to be something they cooked up the moment we first walked into the Academy! We're setting off on a thrilling, pulse-pounding adventure, I just know it!" Hort half-shouted with excitement as she pumped her fists and waved them around wildly.

Though he had half a mind to point out that they weren't the only students in the program, and that Hort had volunteered for a spot, even Saybil had enough social sense to avoid pouring cold water on her enthusiasm.

After reveling in her notion for a moment, Hort beamed at Los and said, "Honestly, Professor, I think magic is the most wonderful thing in the world."

"So...it would seem," was all Los said in reply, though it was apparent from her face that she was thinking, *That much is painfully obvious*. It was very much the expression of an elder, equal parts exasperated and indulgent.

"I'm just dying to learn as many new spells as I can so I can help people with my magic. The truth is, I was hopeless at everything until I entered the Academy. But once I did, I started getting good at so many different things. It made me realize I had a talent for magic, and I actually began to like myself. That's why I want to be a mage!" Hort's eyes glittered. Her cheeks flushed with excitement, every iota of her being speaking to her love of magic.

"I grew up in the South, so it's not like I don't know how people treat mages and witches down there. But that doesn't bother me at all. I got *so* excited when I first heard what we'd be doing in the field program. You mean I get to spread magic in the South, help people get used to it, and get them to depend on it? That's, like, my dream job!"

"I see, I see... Thou carest that deeply for it? Very well, young Hort. I deem thee satisfactory."

"What about me?"

"Utterly unsuitable. Thou art too unmotivated and too ignorant of the ways of the world. If, with a full understanding of what exists beyond magic, thou didst nevertheless choose to follow the path of the mage, I would not object. But choosing magic because thou art ignorant of all other options is of dire concern. What if through this program thou didst learn more about society, and developed an interest in another profession—" Los caught herself. "Hmm? Ohhh, I see."

The witch stopped rummaging through Hort's belongings and looked up. By this point, the mountain of items deemed unnecessary dwarfed the possessions Los would allow Hort to bring with her.

"Perhaps therein lies the reason thou wert assigned to the program. 'Twould be unfathomably cruel to seal away thy memories and toss thee out onto the streets for naught but remedial grades. However, this experience could enable thee to expand thy knowledge of the world ever so slightly, such that thou mightest retain *some* memory should thy recollection of magic be thereafter closed to thee."

"You mean...Headmaster Albus put me in this program assuming I'd flunk out...?"

"Perhaps!" Los chortled. It didn't seem like a laughing matter to Saybil, but the possibility he could hold onto at least some recollection of the outside world did make the risk of expulsion seem a little less terrifying.

"Aww, it's not an experiment??"

As Hort pouted, Los thrust her bag—now less than half its original size—into her arms. "Well, I am not privy to that blasted Albus's schemes. Nevertheless, you two shall remain but apprentices until the moment you graduate. Keeping in mind that you may still elect to abandon this life until such time, use these days to try out the life of a mage... It will undoubtedly prove a font of rich experiences you might not otherwise gain."

"You really do talk like a teacher, Professor Los." Hort let out a ridiculous sigh as she gazed at Los in admiration.

"I do, don't I," Los conceded, looking mildly concerned. "The wise say people adjust their actions to match their titles. If this holds true, then perhaps you two have drawn out something professorial in me. You began to call me 'Professor' from the moment we met, which must have unwittingly inspired me to behave as such."

"In that case, I should start calling you 'Professor' *all* the time! That way, I can get you to teach me all kinds of things. I mean, you're the witch who made a pact with THE Staff of Ludens, like they write about in all the books! And there's never been a three-hundred-year-old ancient witch at the Academy!"

"I'm curious about that, too. I never did get a chance to hear more about your staff..." Drawn in by Hort's enthusiasm, Saybil turned his own expectant gaze at Los.

"Heh heh," Los chuckled. "Calm your twittering, my little nestlings. How much wisdom I impart to you rests upon how faithfully you fulfill your role as my pupils. But first, we must away. The next inn lies half a day's walk from here. If we do not arrive in time for dinner, we shall have no recourse but to sup upon the scraps littering the floor."

## 3

No natural light reached the interior of the tunnel, but the multi-colored lanterns hung all about made it dazzlingly bright. Throngs of people came and went, leaving the air somewhat stifling and a little muggy.

"Countless shops once crowded every inch of this tunnel, and lanterns of every imaginable color swung from their eaves. It was a truly fantastical sight," Los casually informed her pupils as their heads whipped back and forth, eyes straining to take in everything around them.

"But there are still so many lanterns," Saybil said.

"'Tis not half the number that once lit this place. They grew so numerous that the kingdom imposed a limit on how many each shop might have—but that, too, vanished with the war six years ago. That confounded Albus collapsed the tunnel to thwart invaders. Did your classes tell as much?"

"Oh, yeah, we learned about that! In Recent Wenias History," Hort said. "It freaked everyone out. Like, whoa, our headmaster's intense! Tens of thousands of Knights of the Church came and surrounded the kingdom, right? Supposedly we killed some noble's son in…umm, you know, some country, and that noble went to the Church and got them to send out the Knights to slaughter all the witches."

"An expedient falsehood," Los sneered. "The Church wanted to destroy Wenias at any cost for its embrace of magic. It needed a pretext to overrun the kingdom and quash the citizenry, whose hearts had begun to warm to this new technology.

"Strange are the twists and turns of history," she mused. "A mere decade ago, burning witches at the stake was not uncommon even in Wenias. The practice thrived, in fact. And yet, once the leaders of the kingdom saw the potential benefits magic could bring and realized all that witches and mages could contribute to the world, they resolved to cocxist with us. Now it has even become a sort of holy land for magic-users. Which is why, young Sayb, thou hast encountered no trouble trotting about in that rusticated robe, the very hallmark of a mage."

Saybil and Hort sized up one another's clothing. With her knee-length shorts under a scarlet waistcloth, leather tunic, and cape, Hort had the look of a true traveler. Saybil, on the other hand, still wore the robe provided to students at the Academy.

"Is it that bad?" he asked.

"Utterly dreadful."

*Man, I can't get anything right.*

"You weren't going to wear that the whole time, though, right?" Hort said. "I thought for sure you were gonna change at the next inn."

"But, I'm used to it...and it's comfortable... Plus, I don't have anything else..."

"Seriously?! C'mon, you are at least *book* smart, aren't you? You need to be more careful!" Hort frantically swung her fists about in the air. "You know how they feel about magic in the South! Those fossil-brained dum-dums can't get rid of the prehistoric idea that it's a sin for witches, mages, and beastfallen to even exist. You're basically *begging* them to attack you!"

"Quite the sharp tongue, young Hort..." Los remarked. "Nonetheless, 'tis just as she says, Sayb. I myself don this exceedingly adorable ensemble to likewise deceive such bloodthirsty fools."

*Oh. I thought it was just a personal preference.*

"It is, of course, also my personal preference."

"Wha...? Unbelievable, I didn't even say anything. How'd you know what I was thinking?"

"Not for naught have I lived these many long years. Indeed, this is not the last of my astonishing skills. My talents are many and varied."

"But Professor Los, doesn't that enormous staff just give you away immediately?" Hort asked. "It, like, literally stands out."

The witch just burst out laughing in the face of Hort's incisive observation, however. "None save for fellow practitioners or professional witch hunters could recognize my true identity by this staff alone, and the latter would perceive the truth even should I hide it from view. 'Tis already unusual to see a girl of such tender years journeying alone, after all."

To further accentuate her adorable persona, Los shot Saybil and Hort an exaggerated wink. The cuteness was enough to leave Hort's shoulders trembling with fear as she cried, "How could *anybody* resist that?!"

"In that respect, I, too, benefit from having you both as my travel companions. A girl of my apparent age would seem less out of place in a group, especially when thou art so tall, Sayb. Some might be successfully convinced shouldst thou claim eighteen years of age and profess to be my guardian."

"Hanh? You mean, you didn't choose to seem that young, Professor Los?" Hort asked. "I'm pretty sure I read that all the great witches could manipulate how old they looked..."

"'Tis a rather complex matter, I'm afraid." Los sighed, her eyebrows drooping. "My covenant with Ludens has stunted my growth. Unlike other witches who maintain a youthful appearance of their own volition, I did not choose this."

"You mean, you can't get any older...? You're gonna stay that way forever?"

"So it would seem. Several hundred years have passed since first I made my pact with Ludens, and in all that time I have gained not even the length of a pinky nail in height," Los admitted. "Ohh, I had almost forgotten. I promised I would tell you both the tale."

Los glanced up at the staff in her hand, and Saybil and Hort also felt their gazes instinctively drawn to it. A menacing weapon—or so it might have been described if not for the glass and gemstone adornments, which lent it an almost extravagant air. In fact, it looked more like a work of art than a witch's staff, albeit one rendered somehow humorous by the ribbons that matched those on Los's clothing...

"It must have been, oh, four hundred years ago, even before I had come into this world, that it became fashionable for witches to imbue the tools of their trade with the power of a demon. My master, an admirer of all that was novel, quickly decided to invest a favorite staff with such power, but inadvertently allowed the demon itself to enter...or so I have been given to understand."

"...Huh? I'm sorry, Professor Los, I didn't follow any of that."

"I'm not really sure what you're trying to say, either..."

Faced with Hort and Saybil's uniform incomprehension, Los pouted. "Those of my lineage have rarely taken disciples...and so I know not how to explain such things."

"I don't think *how* is the issue here... It's just all on, like, a totally different level... Right, Sayb?" Hort looked to Saybil to back her up, and he nodded vigorously.

"Hmm," muttered Los, tilting her head in thought. "What I mean to say is, a demon was unwittingly trapped beneath the many layers of protective barriers applied to this staff. One might try to destroy the staff and free the demon, but the staff's self-defensive instincts are far too strong. Any who should attempt to harm it will feel its wrath."

"Like, stealing magic power from witches or possessing them... right?" offered Hort.

"Indeed. Many are those who would destroy the staff, so it learned to automatically attack any who laid a hand on it. At wit's end, my master eventually sealed it away deep underground."

"What! That's so mean!" Hort exclaimed in sympathy.

"Wouldst not say?" agreed Los. "During those long years of confinement, the demon and staff fused into one inseparable being. Resigned to this inescapable fate, Ludens found a way to communicate, and, when we met nearly three centuries ago, proposed our covenant—so goes our history. I made a pact with the demon residing within my little Ludens, and here we are. And my darling is even capable of conversation. Say hello, Ludens."

As Los gently shook the staff, black tendrils emerged from the orb and twisted into a brief, cursive "Hi." This was so far removed from any magic or sorcery Saybil had heard about in class that he could hardly wrap his mind around it.

"So basically, if I touch the staff it'll suck me dry of all my mana?" Hort asked.

"Almost certainly."

"So then what happens? Would I, like, stop being able to use magic?"

"No, generally speaking, thou wouldst perish."

"Why?! Just 'cos I ran out of magic?!"

"Precisely. It would drain every last drop from thee. Make no mistake, 'tis not a matter of simply running dry of magic—thou wouldst lose even the minimal mana all humans require to survive. Mana is in essence one's soul, one's lifeblood. Though not everyone can convert theirs into the power of a demon, there is not a single human born without it. What? Does thine Academy not impart such basic wisdom to its pupils?"

"No, they covered it. I think it might've been my first day," Saybil said.

"No waaay! I never heard that!" Hort whined. "But then, why doesn't it kill *you*, Professor Los? Is it 'cos of your pact?"

"No. Taking the magical power from whosoever dareth to touch the staff is as instinctive an act as breathing for little Ludens, one which cannot be consciously controlled. I admit, what I am about to say contradicts my previous statements, but...I have no mana to steal. All that was within me I offered to Ludens when I broke the seal on this staff."

"WHAT?!" shrieked Hort, aghast. "Hang on, Professor. Does that mean you're, like, dead?! Have you been a ghost this whole time?!"

"Preposterous!" Los snapped. "No phantom could boast so young and fresh a body as this!"

"But you're the one who said you die if you lose all your mana..."

"Which is precisely the reason I rely on Ludens's magic power to sustain my body. And why I carry my dearest as a staff, in turn providing legs for one who would otherwise be inanimate. Such is the pact we have made."

"Huhhh," Saybil and Hort murmured in unison.

"So…if Ludens breaks…?" Hort asked nervously.

Without missing a beat, Los replied, "I would perish."

"What!!"

"The two of us are bound each to the other in body and mind, our fates forever linked." Los lovingly pressed her lips to the staff, which seemed to return the affection. "Yet another reason why I could not even dream of bending magic to evil ends, even should I read the *Grimoire of Zero*. Without mana, I cannot cast a single spell. And yet that dunderheaded Albus, surprisingly stubborn for one so young—but lo! All our chatter has brought us to the tunnel's exit. Feast thine eyes, young Sayb, upon thy first glimpse of the 'outside world.'"

Squinting against the blinding light that poured into the tunnel's mouth, Saybil raised a hand to shade his eyes and continued on until his vision slowly but surely adjusted. When at last the trio left the tunnel, a whole new world came into view. As expected, another bustling post town spread out around this end of the tunnel—though vastly larger than the one back in Wenias.

"Those waiting for their entry inspections built this community," Los informed her wards. "Once the process is completed, they have only to pass through the tunnel and head on to the town of their final destination, which is why the post town on this end is naturally much more expansive. Some among those unlucky merchants turned away at the border tearfully choose to establish their shops here as well.

"Now," began Los, striking her staff against the ground. "Let us embark, you two, on our merry journey!" The witch had just taken her first step southward, when—

Hort stopped dead in her tracks, then whipped around to look behind her. Her grand departure spoiled, Los followed Hort's gaze.

"What is it? Didst spot an acquaintance?"

"No... I felt this evil stare or something... Like, the hairs on the back of my neck all stood up."

"I had expected trouble would find us sooner or later, but...I had not imagined it would come the very moment we left the cover of the tunnel. 'Twould appear we have not a moment to lose in doing something about that raiment of thine, Sayb." Los scowled at Saybil's robe, and Hort joined her.

"Did I give us away?"

"Sure did."

"Indubitably."

"Sh-Should I take it off? If you don't mind me walking around shirtless..." Saybil began pulling up the hem of his robe, only for Hort to scream "Don't!" in an effort to cut his recklessness short.

"Walking about with a half-naked young man would only draw more unwanted attention. Nevertheless, it shall be more difficult to keep thine identity secret from here on. We have no other recourse. Let us purchase thee some new clothing before embarking on the next leg of our journey."

"Sorry." Saybil hung his head.

That malicious gaze—which Saybil had definitely felt too—had vanished at some point during their conversation.

## 4

"The kids from the Academy have come out of the tunnel, just like our source said they would. They split into two groups, though... Which should we pursue?"

The man threw a glance in the direction of the errand rider

who'd raced over on horseback to give him this news. He was in a corner of the forest, sitting up in a tree. While his well-worn cassock spoke of his connection to the Church, his muscular frame looked anything but priestly.

"Well, we're gonna hafta eliminate 'em all," he said, swinging a leg back and forth from the branch where he was perched. "Which group looked like they'd put up more of a fight?"

"One had a lizard beastfallen, and the other was all children."

"A beastfallen? Studying magic?" The man threw his head back in a full-throated guffaw. "Damn, that's rich! That is goddessdamn rich! You're tellin' me some monster that woulda lost its head to a witch's spell, what, last week, is using magic now?! You couldn't make this shit up!"

For ages, witches had used beastfallen heads as sorcerous offerings. They paid handsomely for them, too, leading some enterprising bandits to specialize in hunting beastfallen, despite the risks.

*Who woulda thought those same creatures would try to master magic themselves...?*

"So we'll start with the beastfallen's group?"

"Yeah, let's take 'em down. The runts can wait."

The man leapt down from his perch, then shouldered the enormous hammer that rested against the tree's trunk. One end of the head was flat, while the other boasted a vicious spike, and its haft was as long as a full-grown man is tall. Thick chains coiled around the handle, pushing the weapon's total weight well beyond what any human should've been able to heft single-handedly.

"We've gotta teach those Wenisian scum a lesson—show 'em the Church ain't never gonna settle for peace with the witches. Peace is weak talk. And the Church is *strong*. These witches strut around like this magic or whatever makes 'em so powerful, but we'll show the dirty bastards what real strength looks like!"

Brandishing the hammer high in the air, the man swung it with all his might straight into the tree against which it had rested just a moment before. The sturdy tree splintered into a million pieces, and sap gushed like blood from its pulverized trunk.

Emblazoned on the massive hammer the man wielded was an insignia: a wooden stake like the one a witch might be tied to, amid the flames in which she would be burned—the emblem worn by the murderous squad of specialist witch hunters operating under the aegis of the Church: the Dea Ignis Arbiters.

"Gather the troops! Set the traps! We're goin' lizard hunting!"

# Chapter Two

## 1

In his adventurer's garb—if that's what you would call the most innocuous of outfits Hort and Los had picked out for him—Saybil looked like the picture-perfect manservant accompanying his lady on a journey. That lady, of course, was none other than the glass-bead-bedecked, frilly-clothed Los.

"These plain clothes seem *so* much more natural on you than your robe, Sayb."

"Honestly, I'm surprised at just *how* natural..."

"Thou hast a true gift for concealing thy presence, young Sayb... Perhaps thy talent lies in spywork, not magic."

Say what they want—and they held nothing back—anyone would be hard-pressed to tell that Saybil was a mage by his appearance now. Even a seasoned witch hunter would no doubt look right past him.

"Another common means for fooling prying eyes is to clothe oneself in the garb of the Church," Los told the two. "'Tis nevertheless a gamble, as 'tis no easy task to explain it away to any who see through the disguise. When all is said and done, if seeking anonymity in a forest, the wisest course of action is to become a leaf."

Fortunately, Hort had been able to sell off everything Los had deemed unnecessary for their journey at the first post town. Her pockets lined with the temporary influx of coin, Hort splurged on whatever snacks or treats caught her eye, and left it to Saybil and Los to pick their share of the spoils. Stuffing their cheeks with bread, skewers of meat, and other fare, the three discussed the trip they were about to begin.

"Hey, Professor Los, how long does it take to get to the village?"

"Oh, not long at all. We journey by highway, after all, and shall hire a carriage to take us south. If the weather holds in our favor, ten days should be more than ample."

Los pointed her staff toward the passenger carriage waiting area. Horse-drawn wagons jostled for position as travelers boarded one after the other. Once a carriage reached capacity, it would set off on its way, soon to be replaced by the next, freshly arrived from another town.

Suddenly, every horse brayed in unison. A murmur shivered through the crowd until someone yelled, "The sky! Look!"

"It's the dragon of the Church and Mage Brigade! Whoaa, it's actually flying!"

"Hey, up there! We're rootin' for yaaa!"

"Huzzah for the Brigade!"

Craning his neck, Saybil looked up and caught sight of a dragon silhouetted against the sun. It was far off in the distance, but soaring their way at break-neck speed.

The Church and Mage Brigade was an armed force born of what had once been the Knights of the Church, and which functioned independently of any particular country. They were not mercenaries for hire, however; they were a neutral force that established outposts in towns throughout the various nations, ever on the move to preserve the peace and mediate conflicts.

"...The Church and Mage Brigade, is it?" Los murmured listlessly as her eyes followed the dragon, which had in no time crossed right over their heads. "A great transformation indeed…if only on the surface."

"Only on the surface?" Saybil repeated, curious about the tinge of derision in Los's tone.

"Even thou must know the Church and Mage Brigade was once known as the Knights of the Church, young Sayb."

"Oh, yeah. They're the force that was created to fight on behalf of the Church, since the clergy aren't allowed to take up arms…"

"Precisely. The Goddess's Sword they were called, valiant warriors entrusted with protecting the people and hunting down witches, who were the very embodiment of evil. After the peace accord with the witches, however, they took on a new name—or they were meant to. And yet, how very strange. Many in the South still proudly call themselves Knights of the Church."

"Oh my gosh, I *know!*" Hort agreed enthusiastically. "That's why when I heard people talking about the Church and Mage Brigade after I first came to Wenias, I was like, 'Huh? You mean the Knights of the Church, right?!' Everything's *totally* different down South. Literally *everything!*"

Saybil thought back to Los's explanation of the conflict between North and South the previous day, and how Church doctrine was deeply divided between those in the North who accepted witches, mages, and magic, and those in the South who rejected them. Evidently, that same division carried over to the Knights of the Church and the Church and Mage Brigade as well.

"As thou sayest, the ways of thinking in North and South are diametrically opposed. Perhaps 'twould be wise for us to limit our conversations aboard the carriage to subjects such as the weather and our health, that we may avoid mentioning any controversial topics. Still, no need to fret. Ours is but a jolly trip. Let us make merry as we go."

Los chomped down on one of the skewers Hort had purchased. Not wanting to take too much, Saybil chose the smallest skewer and took a bite. The moment he did, Hort cried out, "Aaah! Sayb, that one was mine! It's the only salted skewer! I was planning to eat that!"

"Oh, sorry. I already finished it."

*Come to think of it, I do kind of get the feeling it was set off to the side, apart from the ones that were covered in sauce.*

Hort turned pale. "In one bite?! Wow, boys are really... Wait, what am I saying? Sayb, you dummy! Spit it out!"

"Calm thyself, Hort. Thou hast simply to purchase another salted skewer to resolve the issue..."

"That's *not* the issue! Aaargh! Don't come crying to me if you get a stomach ache!" Puffing out her cheeks in anger, Hort whirled around and wouldn't even look at Saybil.

*They say words can carry curses. I don't know if Hort's hangry curse did this, but—*

"What's wrong, Sayb?! You're as white as a sheet!"

Not long at all after their carriage set off down the highway, Saybil's complexion turned deathly pale. Cold, clammy sweat left every inch of his body damp, and the pain in his head was enough to make him nauseous.

*I feel awful. Seriously, I feel like crap. Is this how I die? Yeah, could be. I'd certainly feel better if I did.*

His case of motion sickness was that severe.

"I'm sorry... I was totally fine in...Holdem's carriage... Why is it so bad this time...?"

"There is a world of difference between a noble's carriage and a passenger wagon, after all..." said Los. "If we liken Holdem's coach to a chef's herb-grilled specialty, our present conveyance would amount to a slab of raw meat on the verge of spoiling."

"What do we do, Professor Los?! This slab of spoiled meat's gonna kill Sayb!"

"In all my years, I have yet to see motion sickness claim a life..."

"But rotting meat kills! Like, no joke, you're dead!"

"'Tis true, putrid meat can in fact be lethal, but I mention it only by way of metaphor... Though I cannot speak for whatever thou didst eat before we boarded the carriage. Shall I provide thee some medicine?"

"Y-Yes, thank yo—*bleeeegh!*"

Even as Los handed Saybil the packet of medicine, he leaned over the side of the wagon and emptied the contents of his stomach onto the road. It was too late for medicine.

"Professorrrr! Sayb's not gonna make it!"

"Very well, very well! Yes, all right! Stop thine hollering! Here, young Sayb, a favorite handkerchief of mine. Use it to wipe thy mouth. Ho there! Driver! Stop this wheeled slab of putrid flesh and let us alight before we have a corpse on our hands!"

And so, the three were left to spend their first night sleeping under the stars. Still white as a sheet, Saybil lay prostrate, mumbling an unending stream of self-flagellation: *I'm sorry, I'm so sorry, Please, just leave me here, I'll just get in the way,* all of which Hort unfailingly answered with the patience and compassion of the Goddess: *It's okay, You don't need to apologize, We've gotta stick together, We've all been there!* This hellish scene continued to unfold with no end in sight until a single "Silence!" from Los shut it all down.

"Well, I was careless not to consider the possibility that the ride might make thee ill. Despair not, for the distance is not too great to be crossed on foot. Let us stroll to the village as if on a leisurely promenade."

Then, tapping her staff against her shoulder, Los sighed. "Good grief. In any event, tonight we slumber beneath the stars. I shall collect water from a nearby stream. Hort, be a dear. Collect some dry branches and prepare a campfire."

"Wh-What about me...?"

"Thou shalt stay exactly where thou art!"

Saybil wriggled about, vainly trying to be of some—of any—use. But having continued his vomiting spree ever since they got off the wagon, he'd since devolved into a strange being whose only purpose in life was to gush mysterious bodily fluids from his eyes, nose, and mouth. As he couldn't even keep water down, however, it was no laughing matter.

While the half-dead Saybil focused on nothing but breathing, Hort quickly gathered the twigs and branches Los had requested, and whipped up a fire with a little magic.

"*Charo rai*... Fire, ignite! Chapter of Hunting, Verse One—Rex. Heed this call by the power of my name—Hort!"

Flames shot forth from Hort's fingers, setting the pile of dry wood alight. Saybil scooched just a tiny bit closer to the welcome heat.

"...It's so warm."

"Does that help a little?"

Saybil nodded.

"Good, here's a little something extra." Smiling, Hort brought her hands together and closed her eyes for a moment. A small ball of light came to life in her cupped hands, then floated gently up to illuminate their camp.

"Whoaa," Saybil murmured in amazement. "That's Solm, right? You can already cast it without the incantation?"

One of the first spells all students at the Academy learned, Solm was used to bring light to dark places or keep warm in the frigid winter. Saybil could of course cast it as well, but not without the proper incantation.

"...You're incredible, Hort. Seriously."

"Wh-Where did that come from?! I'm not the only one who can cast Solm at will—plenty of other kids at the Academy can, too! They say it's so simple, even non-mages can cast it, right?! You're, like, the only person who'd compliment me on something so basic!"

"Maybe, but I can't do it without the incantation... You've mastered this thing I can't do at all, so it's amazing to me, at least."

"I mean...I-I guess that makes sense, but...I feel sorta embarrassed for some reason..."

"Plus, c'mon. Look at me."

Saybil was currently so far from anything amazing, trying to spell it out in words was more trouble than it was worth. Forget not being amazing—he was a complete disaster.

"I just got lucky the carriage didn't almost kill me! And you never know, I might get food poisoning at some point, too, so... we're not so different!"

"Just the fact you can even think like that is amazing..." Saybil mumbled. "You're super smart, and so nice..."

"I'm not all that nice, you know! I'm just a good people-pleaser! And I never did well in school until I enrolled at the Academy, so..."

"Oh, right... You mentioned that earlier." *Something about how she wasn't good at anything before the Academy. Hard to imagine now, looking at the star student she's become, but...*

"I used to get chewed out all the time, every day. No joke. But here, check out this smile." Hort gave Saybil a top-shelf, full-throttle smile.

"...Adorable."

"Right?! You're so honest, Sayb!" Chuckling, Hort puffed out her chest. "That's my secret weapon. It's a little easier to get people to like you if you give them a nice smile, right? Well, I've always smiled with everything I've got, ever since I was little. People'd get mad at me if I didn't, and I'd barely get anything to eat..."

"...Hort."

"So I was, like, totally shocked when I first started at the Academy. I had a dorm room with a fluffy bed, all the yummy food I could eat in the cafeteria... I felt like I'd woken up and become a princess or something. But I get the sense pretty much everyone at the Academy has some kinda baggage, you know?" Hort gripped her oversized cap with both hands. "We come from all over the land, leaving our families behind to become mages, right? I mean, especially the teenage students like us... We want to change ourselves... We want the power to change something... so we go and take the entrance exam. At least, that's how it was for me."

"...Sorry."

"What for?" Puzzled, Hort looked over at Saybil. "You've got full-blown amnesia. That's, like, the epitome of baggage. See, we're in the same boat!" she reassured him, waving away his apology. "Anyway, your turn! So, how far back do you remember? Like, do you remember how you got into the Academy? The curiosity's been driving me crazy!"

"When I came to, I was talking to Headmaster Albus. We'd already signed the contract..." That's how Saybil knew he hadn't taken an entrance exam. He had no memory of it. "I'm pretty sure... someone brought me there... I've got this fleeting memory of a really beautiful woman..."

Hort's eyes sparkled. "What? Who, who?! What kind of woman?! What's her name?"

Saybil shook his head. "I don't know. My memory cuts in and out... When I asked Headmaster Albus about it, she told me not to chase after my past... That I'd remember if I needed to..."

"Whaaat?! So the headmaster knows everything?"

"Yeah, I think so..."

"That's so shady! Wow! Now *that's* baggage!" Getting more fired up by the second, Hort inched closer and closer to Saybil, who scooted away to keep some space between them. "That's definitely not normal. It's so, like, mage-ish!" she exclaimed, smiling ear to ear.

Saybil had never really thought of himself in a positive light, but hearing her made him just the tiniest bit proud of whatever it was that set him apart from others.

"But," Hort continued, "who was that woman, anyway? You must be dying to meet her!"

"Umm..." Saybil hemmed.

"Huh? You don't want to?"

"Well... If possible, I think I'd rather wait until I can use a little more magic first..."

Hort burst out laughing. Just then, the two heard footsteps in the grass.

"What's this? Thou art much livelier than I'd expected!"

Los had returned from the river. She'd walked off empty-handed, and Saybil had been wondering how she'd bring back any water. Then he saw that the Staff of Ludens had shifted into the shape of a cooking pot and was filled to the brim.

"Wha?!" Hort cried. "P-Professor, you're not using *the* Staff of Ludens as a pot, are you...?!"

"Watch thy tongue, young Hort, or it may be thine undoing. I simply set off to fetch water with little Ludens, who is now kindly carrying it for me. I have no intention of using anyone as a pot," insisted Los, nevertheless setting the pot—or rather, the Staff of Ludens—directly on the fire. She then began tossing in ingredients for a stew.

Hort let out a shriek. "Professor, are you actually cooking in the Staff of Ludens?! Forget *like* a pot—that *is* a pot!!"

"Must thou bewail mine every move? My little Ludens's power knows no bounds. Such power aids me in my travels, and I in turn serve as Ludens's legs. Wouldst thou claim that Ludens is merely using me as a mode of transport? I think not."

"But... But, are we really gonna eat dinner out of the 'Witch Eater'...?! Doesn't that kind of give you cannibal vibes?!"

"Preposterous! Arrgh! Now I cannot rid myself of the image!"

Hort's "cannibal vibes" comment had evidently struck a chord. Grumbling all the while, Los stirred the barley, vegetables, and dried jerky floating in the pot. After letting it all stew for a while, the witch served Saybil and Hort each a bowl. As soon as they took a sip, they both had the same thought:

*Is it just me, or is this restoring a little bit of my magic?*

## 2

By the next morning, Saybil was once again able to walk well enough to keep up with Los and Hort, and before midday they had made it to the next inn along the highway without incident. The first floor of the inn doubled as a tavern where the many travelers who passed through quickly filled their hungry stomachs. Saybil and his companions happily merged with the bustling scene and savored their lunch.

"I'm sooo full... I couldn't eat another bite..." Having wolfed down an entire fresh-baked pie all by herself, in addition to a hearty helping of chicken and bread, Hort slouched back in her chair and patted her bulging stomach.

"Wow, you're like a bottomless pit..."

"You're just starving yourself, Sayb! Everyone else eats as much as me!"

"Mages are generally rather gluttonous, 'tis true," Los remarked.

"Huh? Really?" *Never heard that before.* Saybil, for one, was a modest eater.

"Such behavior derives from the desire to recover from food whatever magical power they had used up in sorcery or spellwork. Though a simplified form of sorcery, magic still consumes vast amounts of mana. Witches who have other means to replenish their stores may not eat anything at all, however, as magic can fulfill all their physical needs. Conversely, budding practitioners are more likely to have near-insatiable appetites—though for some 'tis merely a matter of taste."

"But, I don't eat much at all..."

"Thou art the exception to the rule. As are witches such as myself with no magical power of their own." The unstated implication being, *Why would someone need to restore their mana when they almost never cast spells?* Inwardly hurt, Saybil nursed a quiet air of bravery in the face of despair.

"Nevertheless, young Hort, 'twould be wise to take care when dining in public. Even a meal of average size for a mage can draw attention, for our enemies are surely aware of the appetites of magic-users."

Hort flinched. The enemy to which Los referred was none other than the anti-witch faction. If it was well known that one could efficiently screen for mages by the amount of food they consumed, magic practitioners with ridiculously loaded plates were sure to attract attention, like it or not.

"Wh-Why didn't you tell me this sooner, Professor?! Did I stick out that bad?!"

"Well, a single pie could easily enough be attributed to the hearty appetite of a growing youth. As luck would have it, we are a band of three, one of whom is a strapping young man. I imagine that helped blunt the impact somewhat… However, it did nothing to dampen the attention thou didst draw to thyself in savoring every bite with such ecstatic relish."

"I–I'm so embarrassed…! Argh! This is all your fault for not eating enough, Sayb!"

"Huh? S-Sorry…" Saybil apologized to his classmate, who was now covering her bright red face behind both hands, then took a quick glance around the room. His eyes landed almost immediately on a pair of diners chomping their way through a conspicuously large feast.

*Ah, yeah. That does stand out. Guess they must be mages, huh?*

As soon as the thought occurred to him, Saybil stood up.

"Oh." The scrape of his chair drew the mages' attention to him as well, and their eyes met. "Those two were with Kudo…"

"Whew! Saybil, man am I glad to see you! You're traveling with the chaperone, right?" said one of the students who had apparently been obliged to join the field program. He was one of the two guys Kudo had bragged about leading to the village, but there was no sign of Kudo himself. The two apprentice mages stuffed the last scraps of bread into their mouths and ran over to Saybil's table.

"Take us with you! Please!"

"We got attacked by bandits last night. Now we don't even have a map, and there's no way we can get to the village just the two of us. We were just about to give up and head back to the Academy."

"Huh? Your things got stolen?!" Hort asked with surprise, but the two shook their heads.

"Kudo had the map. But he ran off by himself."

"...Kudo? Ran off by himself?" Saybil repeated.

"Yeah, man. He talked big about taking responsibility for us and leading us to the witch's village, but then he just bolted at the first sign of danger. Unbelievable, right? Our fault for ever trusting a dirty beastfallen."

Saybil let out a dubious grunt. Something felt off.

"Wow, that's so awful!" Hort exclaimed.

As he listened to the two's chorus of "I know, right?" Saybil looked over at Los. She noticed his gaze, and cocked her head.

"Yes?"

"No, it's... I'm just having a hard time believing all this..." Saybil muttered under his breath.

"Huh? You calling us liars?" The two exploded with indignation.

Los checked them. "...And yet, 'tis rather an odd tale. Kudo fled, yet you have not a single scratch between you. And your belongings were left untouched?"

"Yeah. We got lucky."

"Oh, no, no, no, my lads... No one escapes a bandit attack unscathed without good cause. The most prominent possibility would be that the culprits saw no value in robbing you... But 'twould be easy enough to find a buyer for two young men such as yourselves, looks notwithstanding. No halfway decent bandit would brook your escape."

Los tapped her fingers on her crossed arm. "Furthermore, Kudo is a beastfallen, and therefore a naturally skilled fighter. Logically speaking, it would be easier to leave him be and capture you two instead. The real question is, what kind of bandits would even dare assault a group which included a beastfallen in the first place? The risk of counterattack should have been too great, but conversely, if it were the beastfallen they were after, the two of you would not have escaped with your lives. Beastfallen hunters are a villainous sort who specialize in sneak attacks. They are not prone to leaving survivors.

"So—" She turned to study the two students who claimed Kudo had abandoned them. "How, then, did you two escape in perfect health, while the bandits pursued only young Kudo?"

"H-How the hell should I know? We got attacked, Kudo ran off, and the bandits chased after him! It's the truth, we're not lying!"

"Yeah! Kudo said we were just dead weight! That there was no point trying to protect a couple of worthless losers who can't even use magic!"

Los thrust her staff at the two resentful young men. "'Worthless losers who can't use magic,' is it? He said this of you, two students at the Royal Academy?"

"Yeah! And his grades aren't even that much better than ours!"

Los raised her eyes toward the heavens. "I see... Yes, it's all quite clear now."

"Professor Los? What's going on...?" Hort inquired nervously.

Though her expression remained unchanged, Los was obviously acting strange. The witch peeled her gaze away from the ceiling and locked it back onto the two apprentice mages. Then—

"'Tis a witch hunt."

"What?!" the students all cried in unison.

"Young Kudo must have intuited the truth forthwith and intentionally trumpeted your incompetence to signify that *he alone could use magic,* thereby providing you two an avenue of escape. Brave, but reckless. While perhaps not praiseworthy, his actions certainly have not earned such abuse from his fellows."

This clearly unnerved the two mages who'd so adamantly insisted Kudo had abandoned them.

"How did you know, Sayb? That Kudo didn't just run away?" Hort asked.

Saybil tilted his head. "I didn't *know,* exactly...but Kudo once told me he started studying at the Academy to protect people. He said he wanted to join the Church and Mage Brigade. And once, when the other kids in our house were kind of bullying me for falling behind, he stood up for me... He's really not a bad guy."

Hort shut her mouth, gripped the edges of her cap, and pulled it down a little further onto her head.

"Still... If that's true, then there really *was* nothing we could've done! Maybe if we go back to the Academy and tell the professors about the witch hunters, they can handle it, but... Speaking of, where the hell's that chaperone?"

"Fool. She sits right before thine eyes." Los let out an aggravated sigh and got to her feet. Even at her full height, she was shorter than anyone else there, and couldn't have looked less like a professor or a chaperone. Nevertheless, she did not appear to be merely a girl their age as she announced, "I shall go." Even the two students who had no inkling of her situation didn't laugh or venture a "Don't be ridiculous." They could tell that her frippery, so out of place for a child her apparent age, did indeed befit a witch.

"'Twas my misjudgment to grant Kudo leave to travel without me. Hort, Sayb, recalling the malicious gaze you felt, we can assume the witch hunters have had their eyes trained on us ever since we left the shelter of the tunnel. They presumably thought students from the Academy would prove easier prey, and a particularly powerful means for delivering their murderous message."

Saybil was aghast. He'd been the only one wearing an Academy uniform, and he was the one Kudo had called out to. His careless dress had clued the hunters in to the fact that they were all mages.

"It's my fault, Professor… Let me go with you! I've got to help Kudo!"

"M-Me too! Let's go save him!" Hort volunteered.

"Absolutely not," Los said curtly, pouring cold water on her two charges' enthusiasm. "Should our foes in fact be witch hunters, they will unquestionably have countermeasures in place to deal with sorcery or magic. Two greenhorn mages would be naught but an impediment."

"But…!"

"Silence! Should anything nefarious happen to young Kudo, the blame shall lie with me. Likewise, Albus will have my head and that third-rate butler Holdem will stave it in should injury befall any of you. No, I will not have that. We shall take a room here tonight, where you are to wait patiently."

## 3

Saybil and Hort sat facing each other on the edges of their respective beds in the room Los had rented for them at the inn.

"Can you believe she left us behind, Sayb?"

"...Nope."

"But we can't just sit here and do nothing, right?"

"...Nope."

"I guess it's a good thing divination is a required subject for all us 'greenhorn mages.' For it to work, we need a personal item the person we're trying to find has kept on them—the longer the better. And it just so happens we have Professor Los's favorite handkerchief, which she so kindly lent to you while you were vomming your brains out yesterday."

Hort's presentation felt a little too perfect, and she was just a little too ready to break the promise they'd just made.

"You'd better not. I'm tellin' you, we should just stay here like she said," one of Kudo's traveling companions cut in, trying to stop Hort and Saybil from divining Los's whereabouts. "We're not tryin' to get kicked out just 'cos *you two* decided to go rogue!"

"Hey! Are you saying graduating is more important to you than your friend?"

"Friend?? Gimme a break, Kudo's a beastfallen."

Hort narrowed her eyes and glared at them. "Kudo, you dummy... You never should've wasted your breath trying to protect these losers."

"Yeah, seriously. If we'd stuck together, the three of us probably could've fought off the witch hunters, but he just had to play the hero, *and* get the Professor caught up in his shenanigans," the other one said. "Beastfallen really are stupid. He looks like a lizard—

maybe he's got a lizard's little pea-brain, too."

Hort opened her mouth to retort, but settled on turning away from them with an icy expression, facing Saybil as if to say she refused to have anything more to do with Kudo's one-time traveling companions. "I guess this kind of crap must be why Kudo acts the way he does."

"You don't know the half of it." Saybil shook his head. "This is what he gets on a good day."

Kudo endured pointed bullying as regularly as the daily lessons given at the Academy. Some students even felt no qualms about telling him to keep out of their sight because they couldn't stand to look at reptiles. But Kudo let all the abuse slide off his back. He always sat at the most visible table in the library or up near the front of the classroom, his tail swinging idly back and forth.

Once, after some others made fun of Saybil for his failing grades, Kudo had told him, "I don't know why you're killing yourself over this shit, but you're not cut out for it, dude. Just give it up." While it may have seemed like Kudo was adding insult to injury, he had actually meant to cheer Saybil up. He'd probably meant to convey that "magic isn't the only option for you out there. You may not be great at this, but don't let it get you down," but trash talk was the only language Kudo spoke.

"And I do hear what you guys are saying. If Kudo hadn't run off, you might've stood a chance fighting as a team. We're still just outside Wenias, and it's possible you could've found help if you all escaped together. But Kudo ran for it without even talking it over. It was—what'd Professor Los call it? Reckless?"

"Whose side are you on, Sayb?" Hort demanded sullenly.

Saybil didn't know how to respond. "I don't think...I'm on anyone's side..."

"Hmph," Hort snorted, glaring at him through narrowed eyes, then shooting a sideways glance at their two fellow apprentices standing awkwardly nearby. "Well...I guess you do have a point. But, you know, I've been thinking. Maybe this is all part of the special field training program—like, maybe it's already started?"

Saybil blinked in the face of this jarring possibility. "What do you mean?"

"Doesn't this all feel a little too convenient? We're only on our second day, and Kudo's already been attacked by witch hunters, the two kids he was traveling with are totally fine, and Professor Los has gone out to rescue him. If we just stand around staring at our shoes or run back to the Academy, don't you think they'd just view it as a total lack of initiative?"

"...I see."

"Like, what else did we get permission to use magic for? If we just sit on our hands, maybe they'll brand us as useless wastes of space—and kick us out! Maybe Kudo's the only one who'll get to graduate, since he stood up for his friends."

It was here that Saybil remembered Hort was the school's top prospect. Discerning the deeper meaning behind people's intentions came to her as naturally as breathing. She could suss out what others were after, what they wanted from her, and conform her behavior to their demands. It was one of her greatest strengths, and it probably gave her a leg up in exams, too. That said—

"What if it's not a test? What if we go off on our own and get expelled for *that?*"

"That's also possible," she readily admitted. "But if we're gonna get kicked out either way, wouldn't you rather do it in style? I'm going after Kudo, but I won't ask anyone to come with me—gimme a second to concentrate."

Hort laid out a map of the area she'd borrowed from the inn's proprietress, over which she dangled a pendulum made from animal bones. Taking Los's handkerchief in hand, she shut her eyes and breathed deeply for a few seconds.

Then her eyes flew open. "Found her!"

*Yup, she's definitely the real deal.*

Saybil couldn't stop marveling at Hort's amazing talent. Scrying in and of itself was not a very accurate art. Even practiced witches were known to misinterpret the results of their divination much of the time. And yet, Hort had predicted where Los—still on the move in search of Kudo—would be with incredible precision. It felt almost like a miracle.

"Man, I've really been on a roll since we left Wenias," Hort remarked as she lit a tiny flame on the tip of her finger and blew it out. "It's like, I feel all this power welling up inside me—like I can do anything! The scrying came through way clearer than usual, and I can cast spells without concentrating at all."

"Maybe it's because we're outside the barrier around Wenias?"

"Yeah, maybe. There *is* a magic seal surrounding the entire kingdom. D'you think that might be why it's harder to cast spells inside? How about you, Sayb? Do you feel anything?"

"No, not really..." *I've still got to concentrate like my life depends on it just to set some kindling on fire. I don't think I even have enough magic power for a barrier like that to make a difference in the first place.*

"Right now, I feel like I could take on anyone! I'm sure I could pull off even a kind of complicated spell without much trouble. You can count on me, Sayb! I'll make sure you're nice and safe!"

Saybil didn't know whether to feel thankful or pathetic. What he did know, though, was that it was a great relief to have Hort beside him.

"...Those two didn't end up coming along, huh?" Hort noted as they turned off the highway and into the woods. Almost immediately, their footing grew treacherous. Hort's voice carried a tinge of disappointment as she forged onward, pushing branches out of the way.

"Did you want them to come?"

"I mean, the more of us the better if it comes to a fight, right?"

"Then you probably shouldn't have talked to them like that." They might not have refused if she'd enticed them with one of her winning smiles.

"Aw, come onnn," Hort pouted, her cheeks puffed out. "What kind of monsters abandon a friend like that?! And after what he did to protect them? Even if I turned on the charm and convinced them to come with us, anyone who'd bail on their friend like that might do the same thing again when it mattered most.

"You know," she continued, turning to look at Saybil, "I don't put on a smile for just anyone. Only when there's something to be gained from it. Pretty messed up, right?"

Saybil cocked his head and gestured toward himself. "But, you smile at me all the time."

"That's what's so weird! It just kinda happens when I'm with you! I'm not even doing it on purpose! I think I must like you, Sayb."

"Ugh."

"Wait, did you just 'ugh' me?!"

"Sorry," Saybil said in a panic. "I just didn't see that coming at all." His expression didn't change, but his heart was pounding.

"Oh, don't get me wrong, though! I mean I like you as a friend! You know...the same way I like Professor Los! Hanging out with her is super fun."

"Ah...I get that," Saybil nodded. "Yeah... She's really something."

"D'you think she'll get mad at us for going after her?"

"Probably."

"But, like...don't you get the feeling she wouldn't be *that* scary even if she did?"

Saybil pictured an angry Los flailing her little arms and legs and her enormous staff around in a furious rage. Strangely enough, it filled his heart with fondness. She had threatened Saybil with a halberd mere moments after they met, but the witch known as Loux Krystas was so unscary that even then Saybil had never feared for his life.

"Wait, hang on." Ahead of Saybil, Hort raised her arm, motioning for him to stop. "There's a cliff..." She dropped to her knees and peeked over the edge. "It's a pretty big drop... I wonder if we can even get down here..."

Hort scanned both directions to see if there were any paths leading down the precipice, but the cliff seemed to go on forever.

"Oh! Look, Sayb. That branch is broken."

The two jogged over to check out the snapped branch, only to find its tip drenched in blood. A closer look revealed black scales glimmering amid the blood.

"These..." Hort caught her breath. "...are Kudo's. He's hurt."

Saybil nodded with conviction. A scattered trail of blood led toward the cliff's edge. The beastfallen mage must've gone over right there. But all Saybil and Hort could make out at the bottom were treetops, with no clear sign of Kudo.

"Aaaah!" Hort suddenly shrieked. "Sayb...look! I-Is...Is that...?" She pointed away from the cliff, back toward the forest.

Saybil's breath caught in his throat. A single glance was all it took to see the destruction: broken branches, trampled bushes, and a fallen tree, its trunk smashed to pieces. But nothing caught the eye more than the sheer volume of blood spattered over everything. The fallen trunk was so saturated with blood that what they'd seen on that first branch was nothing in comparison. And there, at the base of the tree, they found something covered in black scales—a tail, or at least the end of one. The end of Kudo's long, slender tail was just lying there on the ground.

"...Cut himself shaving?"

"Sayb!! Now is *not* the time for jokes!!"

"Sorry, couldn't help it... But, either way, I don't think this was a training exercise."

"D-D'you think Kudo's...dead...?"

"No, I'm pretty sure he can grow a new tail..."

Saybil had seen the beastfallen pick up a pinky he'd cut off by accident and stick it back on. Still, Saybil's heart was pounding like an alarm bell.

"If he can s-stick it back on...then I guess we should take this with us...?" Hort's fingers trembled as she reached out to touch the dismembered tail, which was about the size of a human arm. "Ew! It's cold! And hard! And freaky!" But she somehow managed to master her quaking hands, wrapping the tail in a bit of cloth and stashing it in her bag.

"Ewww... It's heavy...! I've used lizard tails for spells before, but when it's Kudo's, it feels heavy... Like, in an emotional sense, too...!"

"Hort, check out the ground," Saybil said, lightly tapping her on the shoulder as she trembled under the weight of Kudo's tail. "There are three sets of bloody footprints. These small, fresh ones must be...Professor Los, right?"

"I-I think so..."

"From the shape, these must be Kudo's, so I guess the other ones belong to...one of the witch hunters...?"

"Hold on, Sayb, how are you so calm?!"

"I'm not. I may not look it, but I'm scared out of my mind. See? My palms are sweating." Saybil turned both hands face up and presented them for inspection.

Looking at his drenched palms, Hort exclaimed, "Wow, it's true!" then quickly wiped them dry for him. Still holding onto Saybil's hands, Hort fell silent. Then, she looked up. No smile brightened her face.

"Hort...?"

"It's not your fault, Sayb... That Kudo got attacked, I mean."

"Huh?"

"So...let's turn back. I think what we're doing is insanely dangerous."

"Everything we've been doing has been dangerous, though..."

"No! This is totally different! Don't you see? There's only three sets of footprints! Don't you get what that means?"

Saybil cocked his head.

"It means there's only one witch hunter!"

"Isn't that a good thing?"

"No, it's the opposite of a good thing! Kudo was up against a single enemy, but he chose to run instead of fight! That must mean whoever was after him was way, way stronger!"

"...Right."

"Don't you remember what Professor Los said? That witch hunters have ways of protecting themselves against magic? I was thinking we could probably take on a bandit or two if we outnumbered them, but..."

Hort's whole body was shaking. Her trembling fingers squeezed Saybil's hand.

"Hort?"

"You learned about them in school, right? About the Church's professional witch hunters?"

Saybil blinked. "Yeah... They gathered a bunch of criminals who were condemned to death and put them through special training to fight witches, right?"

Hort nodded. "I met one once. When I was really little... Back when witch hunting was just a fact of life in the North *and* the South... I...went to a nearby village to play with a friend. But when I got there, this man in clerical robes was getting ready to set fire to a wagon heaped with dead bodies."

Saybil could feel anxiety and fear flowing through Hort's fingers and into his hand. He could almost see the gruesome scene the tiny girl had stumbled upon, smell the stifling stench of burning flesh—

"And that guy, he said to me, 'You got a friend in there? If you do, you'd better be able to prove she ain't a witch or I'll hafta burn you, too.' So—" Hort grabbed the edges of her cap. She had a habit of reaching for it whenever she felt nervous or was discussing something serious. "I ran for it. I told him I didn't have any friends there... That I'd come on an errand... But the truth is, I saw it—my friend's favorite teddy bear...burning on the wagon...! But I was so scared, I..."

"Hort... There wasn't anything you could've done. I mean, by that point it was—"

"I'll never forget it, that emblem—the stake and flames of the Dea Ignis Arbiters."

Several hundred years prior, the Church had established a specialized unit to protect civilians from the threat of malicious witches. This battalion of "disposable pawns," drawn from convicts destined for execution, was dispatched to uncover witches posing as holy women and burn those hiding amongst the townspeople, to save the Church from having to send a thousand soldiers whose lives would be forfeit in the attempt. These condemned convicts endured grueling training to prepare them for taking on witches alone, and for discarding their lives in battle. That was Dea Ignis, the Goddess's Purifying Flame.

As time passed, the world settled down and the population of witches dwindled, but even with its raison d'être diminished, Dea Ignis remained as a deterrent force. Public opinion turned against the abject cruelty of its practices, however, leading to its dissolution once peace was reached between the witches and the Church.

*That's right—it's not supposed to exist anymore.*

Saybil was about to reassure Hort by reminding her of this, but the words died in his throat. The organization itself had without a doubt been dismantled. *But that didn't mean its members had suddenly disappeared.*

"If…If Kudo got attacked by an Arbiter…then we're not going to do anything but get in the way. So c'mon, Sayb! Let's turn around! Let's leave this to Professor Los—I'm sure she'll bring Kudo back safe and sound…!"

Just then—

*"Gaaaaaaaaaah!"*

—a bloodcurdling scream echoed through the trees. Saybil and Hort looked at each other.

"…Sayb, was that…?"

Together, the two began unwinding a sturdy ivy vine coiled

around a large tree. Once it was loose, they tossed it over the side of the cliff and made sure their makeshift rope reached all the way to the bottom. They looked at each other again.

"Hort, I think we should run for it, too."

"Right?!"

"We're probably just gonna get in the way."

"I think so, too!"

"But—"

"But we've gotta do this," Hort finished. Though her body quivered and tears threatened to spill out onto her cheeks, it still made Saybil feel safer having her by his side. "We...We can't pretend we didn't hear that scream. If we turn back now, I just know it's gonna haunt me for the rest of my life. I mean, I still regret running away as a little girl, even now."

"We'll get to him in time, Hort," Saybil said. "And about that Arbiter attacking the village... I bet if your friend had been alive, you wouldn't have run. You would've held back your tears and did all you could to save her—just like you're doing now."

Hort bit her lip and nodded, her expression full of a determination Saybil could not even begin to measure. The two rappelled down the vine until they hit the ground, then peered through the darkness in the direction from which the scream had come. A split second later, a deafening boom resounded through the woods. A battle was on—somewhere in the forest.

"Let's go!"

They ran.

# Chapter Three

## 1

*You that beastfallen that plays with magic?*

The attack had clearly targeted Kudo. He'd recognized immediately that there was something very off about this burly man in clerical garb who'd approached his group as they prepared for another night of camping. Not only did this stranger know Kudo could cast spells, but he'd gone out of his way to speak to them and confirm his target, rather than catching them unawares. This hinted at the man's absolute confidence that he could kill the lizard beastfallen even if he was on his guard.

Kudo sprinted into the forest to give his two companions a chance to flee and retaliated with magic, but for some reason, his attacks had no effect. He had narrowly managed to shake off his pursuer by severing his own tail when the man grabbed hold of it, then leaping down off the cliff.

His relief didn't last more than a few seconds, though; Kudo quickly realized he had no idea how to get back to the main road. He surveyed the towering precipice—if he rashly climbed back up, he risked leaving himself open to another attack. The thought froze him to the spot.

"You're all right, it's gonna be fine... You've got food, and this forest is big enough for the both of you... He'll never find you... You got this."

Giving himself a pep-talk to keep his mind off the pain and encroaching despair, Kudo found a hollow in one of the trees and tumbled inside. The cold ate at him, but he restrained himself from starting a fire out of fear it might draw too much attention. Though a reptilian beastfallen, Kudo was warm-blooded like a mammal. He wrapped his cloak tight around himself and rolled into a ball to keep his body temperature from plummeting. The scales on his body, which usually shone with vivid color, had darkened to a uniform black, the defeated hue of a cowering target hiding from his attacker in the darkness. Try all he wanted to deceive himself, Kudo's scales would always remind him of how frightened and uneasy he truly felt.

Kudo clicked his tongue in frustration, then forced himself to buck up, until finally he saw a reddish tint return to some of his scales.

*So, what's my move?*

The beastfallen mage lay inside the hollow hugging his knees to his chest, and collected his thoughts. Help would eventually come if his two companions could inform the Academy of what happened. And, given that Kudo had the group's only map to the far-off village, the likelihood his fellow classmates had turned back was exceedingly high.

*But what if they didn't?*

Images of Saybil, Hort, and their chaperone flashed into Kudo's mind. He clicked his tongue again.

*What if those two join up with Saybil and them? And what if they don't bother going back to the Academy, but just keep heading toward the village?*

He couldn't deny the possibility. Kudo was, after all, a reviled beastfallen; it wouldn't be the first time someone had turned their back on him.

*Should I try to get as far away from here as I can while I've still got the cover of night? Or should I wait and see if that guy puts some distance between us on his own?*

No sleep came to Kudo as he awaited the morning. He nibbled on some dried jerky from his bag, then cut a length of vine and sucked out the moisture within to moisten his throat. The beastfallen strained his ears and listened to the forest. There was no sign of anyone approaching.

*So, no one's coming to help me?*

Chuckling grimly, Kudo left the shelter of the hollow. If his two companions had met up with Saybil's group and continued on to the village, there'd be no witnesses to attest to the witch hunter's attack. Kudo could say whatever he liked, but no one would ever believe him. So he was sure to be expelled. For three long years he'd worked his ass off at that Academy—and he hadn't endured the social misery, poured blood, sweat and tears into overcoming his illiteracy, and learned a bunch of spells only to get kicked out over something as stupidly anticlimactic as sitting around inside a tree.

Kudo glanced at the stump of his tail. The wound had stopped bleeding, and a scab was already starting to form. It hadn't hurt. Or maybe he was just used to it by now.

As far back as he could remember, Kudo had been kept in a cage and put on display at a freak show. It wasn't every day you saw a reptilian beastfallen, much less one with a skill as unique as Kudo's: his ability to regenerate. Long spears shoved through the bars of his enclosure would stab him in the stomach, and Kudo would crumple to the ground, hollering in pain—but his wounds would close in a matter of seconds, drawing roars from the astonished crowd. His arm would be chopped off, only for a new one to start growing a few days later. The severed arms themselves he was ordered to eat—he knew the taste of his own flesh. This world of torture was all Kudo had known as a child.

"Compared to that…this ain't shit."

Kudo walked for a bit, keeping the cliff on his right, then paused, listening. "Is that running water? Must be a river…!"

The beastfallen broke into a run. He didn't know when he might come upon another water source. He'd drained the last drops from his canteen the previous night, and he needed water if he was going to continue his journey. But the very next instant, a chill ran through Kudo that froze him in his tracks.

The river tumbled down the precipice, carving a wide, open path through the trees. If the witch hunter hadn't actually given up on Kudo, if he was waiting to ambush him by the bank, Kudo would be spotted the instant he showed himself. Slowly, quietly, Kudo crept backwards until his back was flush against a tree, and there he halted.

Ahead lay the river—and, if his memory served, it curved around behind him as well. In that case, should he climb back up the cliff and return to the highway?

No. He'd be defenseless during the ascent, and try as he might to keep a low profile, he would stand out starkly against the bare rock face. Kudo had no way of knowing how dedicated his pursuers were, but given that the big man had hand-picked the beastfallen mage as his quarry, odds were slim they'd call it quits that easily.

Just then—

"Oiii!"

—a voice called out, and Kudo instantly dropped to the ground.

"Didja find him? Wouldn't be surprised if he hit the river any time now!"

"Nah, no trace of 'im!"

"Keep your eyes peeled! If we let him slip, Master Arbiter'll have our heads!"

Kudo shuddered.

*I knew it—they're still after me. And now there's more than one. They definitely would've caught me if I'd run out to the river. It's a miracle they didn't find me in that hollow last night.*

Kudo found a tree with good climbing branches and scrambled up, careful not to make a sound. From this higher vantage point, he could see two sentries sitting by the banks of the river. Unfortunately, they were too far apart to take them both down in one go. As soon as he went for one, the other would yell for "Master Arbiter" or whatever. Kudo suppressed a sigh and looked up at the sky above him.

*An Arbiter, huh? It just* had *to be Dea Ignis, didn't it?*

"Weren't they disbanded, though...? Shit, just my luck..."

*Guess I'll have to follow the river downstream, away from the highway. He can't possibly have enough minions to cover every inch of it.*

"What the...?" As he was about to make his way back down, Kudo spotted something and stopped short. "...Twine?"

There were lengths of twine tied around the branch on which he stood, stretching out to other nearby branches. He touched one; it was taut. An ominous feeling came over him.

The branch beneath him creaked loudly. It had been partially sawn through at the base, almost as if they'd known Kudo would climb this particular tree. It was—

"A trap—?!"

The branch gave way beneath Kudo's feet, snapping all the twine wound around it and unleashing arrows at the mage from all directions. A bell began to ring, set up to alert the hunters when their prey had fallen into the snare. Kudo leapt from the tree to escape the onslaught of arrows—only for something sharp to impale his feet.

He howled, collapsing to the ground. A closer look revealed sharpened wooden stakes buried all around. Some straw had been strewn over them and topped with loose dirt, presumably to hide them from anyone jumping down from the tree.

They'd predicted his every move.

*That all you got...?!*

Kudo could regenerate torn-off limbs; a measly stake in the foot would barely even slow him down. He bolted, desperate to get away from there at all costs. His panic, however, blinded him even further to his surroundings. Unable to lift his injured feet very far off the ground, Kudo tripped over something and fell flat on his face. A cord had been tied from the base of one tree to another, a simple trap to trip anyone running carelessly through the forest.

"Shit! Now they're just making me look like an asshole!" Kudo cursed, scrambling to his feet. That's when he saw the figure standing directly in front of him—an enormous man clad in a clergyman's robe, holding a hammer as tall as a person. Kudo gasped.

"Well, well... We meet again, lizard boy."

The man grinned cheerfully. His tan skin had a healthy look that seemed made for the light of day; whether the same could be said of the stench of blood, the putrid smell of death, that rose from his every pore was another question entirely.

"You're Dea Ignis... An Arbiter—!"

"Guess we can skip the introductions. But damn, boy, you really walked right into those traps. Ha! They were kid stuff!" The man—the Arbiter—guffawed as he approached. "Bet you're wishin' you hadn't climbed up that tree, huh? Well, forget it—wouldn'ta made a lick of difference. If you'd come up to the river on the ground, you'da found more traps waitin' for ya. Same goes if you'd just scrapped the river and made a run for it. Thing is, I'm a full-time witch hunter now, but I used to be a trapper—hunting humans, you get me? And I never overlook nothin'. These are my huntin' grounds. The second you stepped into these woods, there was never any chance of you gettin' out again."

Kudo ran through a mental list of the spells he could cast immediately. The Arbiter was close, too close.

*What can I get off before he's on me? The shortest incantation I've got is Steim, the arrow of light. No, that's not gonna cut it. I used a way stronger spell on him last night and it didn't do shit. Maybe I should give up on the physical attacks and try to create some kind of diversion, or—*

"Soooo," the Arbiter began, swinging the massive hammer up to rest on his shoulder, "your best move here's to just lay down and die like a good little lizard." Kudo heard the hunter's voice whispering right into his ear.

The guy had been at least fifteen paces away, but he'd closed the gap in less than a second. Kudo's reflexes kicked in and he tried to jump out of the way with all the speed he could muster, but the Arbiter's hammer slammed down on his toes, pulverizing them. Suppressing the instinctual urge to fall to the ground screaming, Kudo thrust an arm toward the man and called on the only spell he could cast without an incantation, the most basic of all beginner spells.

"Solm!"

Light shot forth from the mage's palm. The Arbiter leapt back from the sudden, blinding flash, dropping to one knee and covering both eyes with his hands. Kudo seized the brief opening and booked it.

"Shit! That's right—you're a tough bastard, ain't ya? The kinda monster who'd cut off his own damn tail to get away. A few crushed toes don't mean shit to you, do they?"

Opening and closing his dazzled eyes a few times, the Arbiter got to his feet and shook it off. Then he flashed a wicked smile, enthusiastically baring his teeth.

"Now that's rich! Awright, let's see how far you can run in a forest full up with booby-traps! You hear me, little lizard mage?!"

Spurred on by the specter of death pressing close behind him, Kudo sprinted as fast as he could, not even risking a sideways glance. Ever since the moment he was born, Kudo had been in a constant fight for his life. Even after he escaped from the freak show, it had taken everything he had to overcome the malice that reared its ugly head to stand in his way, continuously protecting himself from the ruthlessly unjust fists that fell on him.

He instantly knew an enemy when he saw one. So an enemy he stood no chance of defeating, he didn't even need to see to know. The one after him now was clearly in a different league. Kudo couldn't possibly beat this guy in a fight—even the odds he could successfully escape from him were outrageously low.

*Why me?*

*Why is it* always *me?*

Including him, five students had been in the special field program, yet this man had come after Kudo first. And Kudo knew why. He was both a beastfallen and a mage—the two things the Church reviled most. Even so, he couldn't help but wonder why.

"Those boo-boos on your feet slowin' you down? Or you just scared of fallin' into another trap?"

Suddenly, the Arbiter was running right alongside Kudo.

*Impossible!*

No sooner had this crossed his mind than a vicious blow struck Kudo's body and sent him flying through the air. He actually heard his ribs shatter and his flesh rupture. The searing pain told him he'd been hit with that enormous hammer before his thoughts even had time to catch up.

"Ahhgah... Nghh...!"

Blood spurted from Kudo's mouth as he lay writhing on the ground.

"Aah, sorry, am I too fast for ya? You gotta understand, though, my line of work puts me up against witches who've been honing their skills since long before I was born. Been a while since I took on one as weak as you. Guess just bein' a beastfallen mage don't necessarily make you much of an adversary, huh. I mighta gone a teensy bit overboard."

The Arbiter leisurely strolled over to Kudo and crouched down directly in front of his face. "Hey, lemme ask ya somethin' before I kill ya. You buddy-buddy with those other little shits?"

Kudo's head whipped around like he'd been slapped in the face. He thought for sure leaving those two behind like that had gotten them off the hook. In which case, who were the "other little shits" this guy was talking about?

"You split up into two groups, right? The way I heard it, there were three other little brats who went off without ya. I was hopin'

I could dangle a little lizard bait to lure 'em in and make my life easier, but..."

Tilting his head to the side, the Arbiter burst out laughing. "Sorry, sorry. If they didn't even want a dirty beastfallen travelin' with 'em, they sure as hell won't give a shit what happens to you. Forget bait—they'll probably thank me for takin' out the trash."

The Arbiter howled with laughter. Kudo had nothing to say. He knew better than anyone that it was the truth.

"Awright then, better make myself a lizard pancake an' get movin' on to the next—is what I *would* say, but...that wound's already gone an' closed up, hasn't it? If nothing else, you've got a first-rate power of regeneration. Just how good is it? Could we keep ya alive forever so long as we leave your head intact and give ya a little food 'n' water? The Church is crawlin' with folks who'd lose their shit over havin' a little bastard like you to do their experiments on. And they say there's no such thing as a perfect souvenir— Oiii! Someone get a cage!"

Kudo's blood ran cold. A vision of his younger self appeared beside him, eyes dead and hollow—his arms and legs had been severed so they could grow back for the amusement of the audience.

The Arbiter grabbed what was left of Kudo's tail and got to his feet, dragging the injured beastfallen along behind him. Kudo clutched at some tree roots, trying to stave off the inevitable.

"Hey... Y'ever heard of 'futile resistance'? Don't gimme any trouble—boy!"

The Arbiter swung the massive hammer high above his head and brought it down onto the roots, crushing Kudo's hands right along with them. Robbed of both hands, Kudo instantly dug his teeth into the next root he could find.

*No.*

*No. Not again. I'm never going back in a cage again.*

Just yesterday he'd been a student at the Academy of Magic. Sure, he'd faced some low-level discrimination, but Kudo had been granted the same right to study as everyone else, and had enjoyed a relatively normal life.

*I take one step outside Wenias, and this is what I get?*

Kudo had been caught completely off guard. His success at the Academy had given him an inflated sense of his own abilities, and a misguided certainty he could protect himself—and others.

Something Headmaster Albus had once told him came back to Kudo.

*Listen, Kudo. The world will always be cruel to you.*

She'd been trying to get through to Kudo when he said he didn't need a chaperone.

*But you don't need to carry the burden of that cruelty all on your own.*

"Just shut up!" Kudo had spat, before proceeding to insult the snow-white beastfallen wolf who stood behind the headmaster, telling him he was nothing but a weakling who'd gotten where he was by riding on a witch's coattails.

*Remember this: as long as you are a student at this school, I will never abandon you.*

*Loux Krystas may be somewhat eccentric, but she really is a good witch.*

Kudo had slapped away the helping hand that he'd been offered. Would anything have been different if he'd joined that witch with the enormous staff, that Loux Krystas? Would she have been able to fight off the Arbiter and lead them all safely to the village? Would Hort, the most talented student at the whole Academy, have turned the tide of the battle?

"Gimme a break, kid... Even *you* can't survive havin' your head bashed in. Aaah, forget it. I'm tired'a this shit. So, what? You tryin' to tell me you'd rather die?"

The Arbiter stared down at Kudo, his teeth firmly clamped onto a gnarled root, and let out a sigh. Then, raising his gigantic hammer, he said, "Have it your way. Guess they're gonna hafta settle for your flattened corpse as a souven—"

"Haaalt!"

A shrill cry pierced Kudo's and the Arbiter's eardrums. The sharp *swish* of a blade slicing through the air followed immediately after, and the Arbiter took a huge leap backward. The trunk of the massive tree Kudo had been clinging to groaned as it split cleanly in two.

"Whoa-ho! Now here's a nasty one...!"

A grin spreading across his face, the Arbiter readied his weapon. In the next instant, a small girl appeared without warning atop the hammer's head. She must've hopped down from a tree branch, but she moved so lightly and with such terrifying grace that even the Arbiter, who had undoubtedly been watching for his opponent with every fiber of his being, could only gape in amazement.

"Hunh?" was all that spilled from his open mouth.

The girl atop his hammer—Loux Krystas—thrust her enormous staff at the Arbiter. Then—

"Say hello, Ludens."

Black sludge instantly began flowing out of the staff. It morphed into the head of a wild animal, which opened its maw wide to clamp down on the Arbiter's head.

"Oh—Ah...Aaaaah!" the Arbiter screamed, swinging his hammer with all his might. The momentum sent Loux Krystas flying through the air, but she merely alit on a nearby branch. Her movements were breathtaking, unlike anything one might expect from a witch, and more like the expert maneuvers of a battle-hardened soldier.

"It's...you... Why...?" Kudo's voice was trembling.

Raising an eyebrow, Loux Krystas peered down at the reptilian beastfallen from her perch high above his head. "I'll have none of this 'why' nonsense. I was entrusted with thy care as well as thy classmates'. Is it not natural, then, that I race to the rescue when one of my wards has a witch hunter hot on his tail?"

"But—!"

"Enough! If thou canst move, withdraw at once!" she snapped. "Now, as for thee, Arbiter, 'twould seem I have thee to thank for my pupil's predicament. My, my, how far Dea Ignis hath fallen. Never did I imagine a day I'd see one of you scrambling after a defenseless fledgling that strayed from its nest."

Her seething face suddenly broke into a smile.

"Ah, but forgive me. Dea Ignis has been plummeting to the depths from the very start. And yet, how very strange. Was thy band of curs not disbanded by official decree...? So why dost thou still don thy soiled robes and engage in the dishonorable task of hunting these budding mages? Perhaps thou didst fall into destitution, bereft of any talent save for murder, and thus accepted an offer of employment from the extremists of the anti-witch faction? Poor soul!"

Los's clear, uninhibited laughter echoed through the forest, blowing away all fear, anxiety, and even pain.

"You… That staff…! Don't tell me that's actually the Staff of Ludens…?!"

With a dramatic flourish, Loux Krystas rested her staff on her shoulder and lifted the hem of her flowing dress in a small curtsy.

"The very same! And I am she who is oathbound to the Staff, the Dawn Witch, Loux Krystas. And, for the moment, I am also chaperone to these fledglings from the Academy of Magic." Loux Krystas's sweet smile quickly took on an overwhelming sense of menace. "Now begone! Thou art naught but a rabid dog whose Church masters no longer hold his leash! I have no love of battle. Leave now, and I shall spare thy life!"

The Arbiter took a step back. Evidently he could sense he was no match for her. All the arrogant confidence was gone from his eyes as he searched frantically for an escape route, though that didn't mean he had given up searching for an avenue to victory as well.

Just then—

"Professor Los!"

"Kudo! Professor Los! Where are youuu?!"

—that avenue presented itself in the form of two greenhorn mages.

## 2

Saybil and Hort raced through the forest following Kudo's bloody trail. It had stopped at a hollow tree, then started back up again near the river where a trap had evidently been triggered. Assuming the witch hunter must have caught up to Kudo, the two grew even more anxious, and finally began to call out for him and their chaperone.

"Professor Los!"

They knew they were close. Hoping beyond hope they could help in some small way, Saybil and Hort yelled at the top of their lungs.

"Kudo! Professor Los! Where are youuu?!"

Kudo's blood was still fresh. They figured he had to be somewhere within earshot—and they were right. In the same moment they realized that heavy footfalls belonging neither to Los nor Kudo were rushing toward them at an unbelievable speed.

As if chasing after the footsteps, Los's angry voice rang out: "You fools! Why have you come?! RUN!"

But it was too late. Something like a tempest stirred by dark, murderous intent bowled into them before they could take their first steps. Saybil pushed Hort out of the way just in time to take the full brunt of the man's body, which sent him toppling to the ground.

"Ah—kh!"

The impact knocked the wind out of him. But before he could catch his breath, someone pressed a knee down hard on his chest and began choking him, making it impossible for Saybil to stand or speak.

"Thanks, little man. You showed up just in time."

"Sayb!" Hort shrieked.

"Don't move!" With a single look, the man froze Hort where she stood; the incantation she'd begun to recite died on her lips. "Won't take more than a second to snap your friend's neck. If that don't bother you, then by all means, use that fancy magic of yers.

Not that it'll do shit to me..." he snarled. "Ain't that right, Prof!"

Los had arrived a moment too late; she stopped short at the sight of the man holding Saybil by the throat.

"...And? What dost thou intend, Arbiter?" she inquired, displaying no emotion. "Wouldst thou snap the lad's neck and crush the heart in the lass's chest just to die by my hands? For I warn thee, the moment thou dost slay these children, thy life is forfeit."

"Or, we could take the easy way outta this, where nobody dies...*Professor Los.*" The Arbiter bared his teeth in a smug smile. "Drop the staff. I'd say the Staff of Ludens along with its contracted witch would be more than enough to pay for three mage pups. I'd even have some change comin' to me, I expect."

"Preposterous... Why should I expose myself to harm for the sake of some younglings I have only just met? There is not sufficient coin in all the realm to pay out that change."

"You sure about that?" The Arbiter clenched his fist, cutting off Saybil's windpipe. The young apprentice writhed and clawed at the man's wrist, but to no avail. Struggling served only to leave Saybil more breathless than before, and his consciousness quickly began to fade.

"Desist!" Los cried. She eyed her staff with a pained expression, and let it fall to the ground with a deep sigh. "I have done as thou didst ask. Now release Sayb."

Saybil gasped as the Arbiter's grip loosened ever so slightly. Panting and spluttering, his chest heaving, Saybil took in the situation. The Arbiter let out a full-throated cackle.

"Whoa-ho, you shittin' me?! I never thought you'd go for it. But seein' as you came all this way for a beastfallen mutt, I figured it was worth a try... You tryin' to tell me the witch bound to the Staff of Ludens is *actually* playing teacher? Gimme a break! The bishop is *never* gonna believe this!"

Los shrugged. "Such things are beyond the reckoning of a mad dog."

"Professor Los!" Hort screamed. "Don't worry about us! Pick up the staff and teach him a lesson!!"

"Shut up, brat. Another word outta you and your friend's neck goes *crack*. Then you'll be next." A dark look in his eyes, the Arbiter glared at Hort, who began to tremble and curl up into a ball, pulling her cap down over her head further than it'd ever gone before. Satisfied he had the situation completely under control, the Arbiter gave a leisurely nod. "As for you, *Professor Los*, back the hell away from that staff. You're comin' with me." Grabbing Saybil by the neck and pulling him to his feet, the man dragged his captive along behind and flung him down beside the staff. Then he loosened the cape he had draped over his priest's garb and put it over the Staff of Ludens.

"Pick up the staff, boy."

"Huh...? But..."

"Don't get your panties in a twist, you spineless little slug. It's made of special consecrated cloth. Even the Staff of Ludens ain't more than a scrap of wood with that wrapped around it. Now hurry it up!"

Saybil grabbed the staff.

"See? Nothin' happened, right? Hort, tie up your precious Professor," the man ordered. Hort didn't move. "...Oi, don't gimme any a that rebellious bullshit, little lady. You can drop the act now."

"Wha?" Saybil was baffled.

Her face downcast, Hort said nothing.

"...Her name..." All of a sudden, it clicked. The Arbiter had called Hort by name—a name *no one had said* since the moment they first encountered him. The man let out a chuckle.

"C'mon, your friend needs a little help here. Go on, Hort, introduce yerself!"

"Stop it!" the girl pleaded. But the Arbiter didn't care.

"There's nothin' to hide, kiddo, the cat's outta the bag. No point cryin' about it now. C'mon, tell them! Tell 'em how the Church sent you to infiltrate the Academy of Magic as a spy for the anti-witch faction!"

## 3

*Everyone called me a "devil child" when I was growing up. There were horns sprouting from my head pretty much as far back as I can remember, and eventually they grew too big to hide under my hair.*

"Don't ever stop smiling. The Goddess will be your salvation," Hort's mother had told her when she gave her daughter up to the Church.

As their first order of business, the Church had held Hort down and sawed off the offending horns against her will. While it didn't hurt, the awful sound of the saw's teeth grinding back and forth above her head terrified Hort. She remembered crying through the whole traumatic ordeal.

The following year, Hort discovered that she shed her horns (which were actually more like deer antlers, thrusting toward the sky) every twelve months or so, only for them to regrow. It wouldn't do for Hort to wait for them to fall off on their own, though; they attracted too much attention. So she quickly learned to shave them down to a manageable size. Hort was always careful to wear a cap as well, just in case, to prevent anyone around her from finding out.

*Restrain yourself,* they told her. *Be kind to all, and perhaps your good deeds will wash away some of the sinful curse that has tainted your soul since birth.*

Then, one day, all the other orphans like Hort—though she was the only one with horns—were corralled together and ordered to enroll in the Academy of Magic. They were to take the entrance exam and, if they passed, surreptitiously feed the Church information about the Academy. And if they were placed in positions of power after they graduated, they were to work secretly for the benefit of the Church. Told this was the only way unfortunate, cursed, useless children such as themselves could ever repay the debt of gratitude they owed the Church, many orphans were thus sent to infiltrate the Academy of Magic.

But the only one to ever pass the entrance exam was Hort. From then on, her talents blossomed. Her fellow students showered her with admiring gazes, words of praise, and embraces of respect. Never having experienced such things before, Hort doubled down on her studies, and before she knew it, she had earned a reputation as the most talented mage in the Academy.

"What do you want to do after you graduate?"

When people asked her this fateful question, Hort never knew how to respond.

"I'll bet you could do *anything*, Hort. You could even work at the royal palace! You could be the strongest mage in the whole kingdom—I just know it!"

"Aw, you're too kind," Hort would hear herself say with a smile, her voice seeming to come from somewhere far off. She knew that the more important the position she was entrusted with after graduation, the further the Church would encroach on the kingdom's weakest points.

After all that effort, after striving to help the Church dismantle the kingdom from within, would her tainted soul be cleansed of all sin? Would the Church faithful accept her as one of their own? The answer was a glaringly obvious no. In that case, should she come clean and tell the Academy everything? What if that got her expelled? Hort would have nothing left.

Finally, Hort resorted to looking for ways she could fall behind her peers. However, a talent once blossomed cannot be returned to its bud. The special field program provided the perfect way to postpone her graduation even a little bit.

*I just need to put it off until I can find a way out of this.*

Or so she'd hoped.

"C'mon, quickly now, tie up the professor. I'll give you all the credit you deserve when I report back to the higher-ups. I'd a been in deep shit if you hadn't showed up with this kid in tow."

Hort had convinced Saybil to come with her to rescue Kudo—but she'd never imagined it would lead to this. The ominous gaze she'd felt as soon as they left the tunnel had been enough to make her suspicious that someone had leaked to the Church the details of their insignificant trip. She'd even gone so far as lightly poisoning some of the food she'd bought, in an effort to disrupt their plans. Unfortunately, Hort hadn't considered the possibility Saybil would eat the poisoned skewer instead…

She'd only meant it as a precautionary measure. Hort had even chided herself for being too paranoid. That was why she hadn't objected to Kudo and the others traveling on their own. Even if she didn't manage to delay their journey, Kudo and his group wouldn't have gotten all that far ahead, in which case Los might realize the danger and be able to protect them.

Hort had told Saybil it wasn't his fault. And she'd meant it. In truth, the blame for everything lay on her shoulders. Her selfish attempts at self-preservation had led to disaster.

Her cap still pulled all the way down, Hort asked, "If I tie up Professor Los...are you still going to kill Sayb?"

"Hey, don't go spillin' the beans. You're just makin' it harder for me." The Arbiter grinned.

"...That's your style, isn't it?" Hort whispered.

The image forever burned into her memory: stacks of dead bodies, her friend turning to ash—and a giant of a man surveying the gruesome scene with obvious enjoyment, an Arbiter wielding a massive hammer, the one they called the Tyrant. A man who would murder an entire village of innocents just to kill a single witch.

"It's okay, Hort." Saybil broke in on her thoughts. Hort looked up. "This isn't on you."

He was smiling. Saybil, the boy whose frozen facial muscles didn't normally have the capacity to form any expression at all, was putting on an awfully awkward smile just to reassure Hort.

*You traitor!* he should've shouted at her. He should've berated her with the angry curses appropriate to the situation. *I can't believe you'd stoop so low as to trick me into coming here!* It was definitely not the time for him to give Hort an encouraging smile that seemed to say, *Don't blame yourself, even if this gets me killed.*

Hort clenched her jaw. She'd made up her mind. At least, she thought she had. The moment she decided to set out with Saybil, she'd promised herself she wouldn't run away from anything. Not this time.

The young mage reached into her bag. When she brought out her hand, though, it held no rope; instead, her fingers were wrapped around the end of Kudo's severed tail, which she'd found in the forest—a piece of flesh that, having come from a beastfallen, would serve as a powerful offering for spell activation.

"Wait... You little shit, what are you—?!"

"*Bahg doh gü Laht!* Hellsfire, rally to me! Blast and burn!"

The severed tail in Hort's hands was reduced to blackened ash, which then scattered to the winds. From the ashes rose a blazing serpent that slithered its way up the mage's arm.

"Chapter of Hunting, Final Verse! Flagis!"

The flaming serpent bared its fangs and shot out toward the Arbiter. Flagis was a spell designed to immolate the target, and was the most powerful and dangerous enchantment taught at the Academy of Magic. It latched on and engulfed the designated victim in flames that raged only long enough to burn them to nothing. Hort had sicced the blazing snake on the Arbiter. Now that he had removed the special consecrated cape in order to handle the Staff of Ludens, he would be vulnerable to attack.

But the Arbiter was too quick. He snatched the Staff of Ludens from Saybil, ripped off the cloth, and used it to dispel the serpent mid-strike. In that split second, the battle was lost. Her magic repelled, Hort's face drained of all its blood and she froze in place, while Saybil lay face down on the ground.

"...The hell was that?" the Arbiter demanded, staring daggers at Hort as he bitterly brushed burnt hair from his shoulders. "You turnin' on me?"

"Ah... Uh..."

"Awright, I see how it is. So you're a dirty traitor... Not that I'm surprised, comin' from a *devil child.*"

Hort staggered back a step. She hadn't thought about what to do if her attack failed.

"Right then, time to die," the Arbiter growled, raising the mighty hammer above his head and setting his sights on Hort. Just then—

"Nay, Sayb!" Los shrieked. "Touch it not!"

Locked into their bitter staring match, neither Hort nor the Arbiter understood what Los was talking about. They simultaneously turned to look at Saybil.

"No way," Hort murmured, aghast.

Saybil's bare hand was wrapped around the staff—the Staff of Ludens, the notorious Witch Eater that devoured all the magic of any who touched it.

"I'm sorry, Professor Los." Saybil turned to her—smiling once more. "For only getting in the way."

Never before had Saybil cursed his own impotence as bitterly as he did now. He'd always nursed the hope deep in his heart that he'd find a way to contribute, that maybe there was something he could do.

*But what has that ever amounted to in reality?*

Hort had just seen the secrets of her past unwillingly exposed, and yet still she had risked her life to save Saybil with the strongest spell she knew. And now she was in serious trouble.

*Meanwhile, what am I doing?*

Suddenly, Saybil's eyes flitted over to the staff he'd held under that piece of cloth just a few moments before—the Staff of Ludens.

*—Use me.*

The words flowed directly into his mind. All at once, the solution to this impossible puzzle raced like a shock of electricity through his body.

*The staff... That demon in the form of a shape-shifting staff... Only Los can wield it.*

*—Preposterous.*

A staff that turned magic power—life force—into strength.

"Nay! Sayb!" Los screamed.

Saybil hesitated for a brief second, then took hold of the staff.

*At least I managed to apologize. For following after her when she'd told us to wait. For letting the Arbiter capture me and make her drop the staff. For forcing Hort into a life-or-death battle. I can't think of anything to apologize to Kudo for, though, so I guess that's something*—so went the ridiculous thoughts marching through his head.

A deafening roar pierced Saybil's ears. The black globe embedded in the staff ballooned and began to spill over, erupting into a violent gale of darkness that wrenched the branches from the surrounding trees.

Saybil felt his clenched fist, then his wrist, his elbow, and finally his whole body seem to meld and become one with the demonic staff. He had lost all control.

"What in—?! The hell is goin' on?!"

"Ludens! Thou mustn't! Release the child, Ludens!"

The Arbiter's irate shouts and Los's desperate plea were the last things to reach Saybil before all sound grew distant. The whirling, writhing ebon gale converged for a split second on the staff, then exploded outward. Blown away by the detonation, Saybil's body twirled through the air before crashing backwards against a tree and collapsing to the ground in a crumpled heap.

*Woops. Dropped the staff.*

This was the last thought Saybil had before it all went black.

# Chapter Four

# 1

Eyes opened that by all rights should never again have seen the light of day. The deep red staining the sky looked like blood, but was in fact nothing more ominous than a placid sunset. Saybil heaved himself groggily into a sitting position. As he did so, the cloak that had been draped over him slid down and he found his face mere inches from Hort's, who'd been peering down at him with concern.

"Gaah—ah!" he yelped unwittingly, scrambling backwards.

"Sayb! You're alive! He's aliiive!" Hort exclaimed joyfully as she threw her arms around him. Still not grasping what had happened, Saybil scanned his surroundings.

They were in what looked like a field razed by wildfire. The surrounding trees had been blown out of the dirt, roots and all. They lay scattered in piles, their branches broken and the earth that had held them upturned. Saybil and the others sat in the very epicenter of the destruction.

"...Um... What happened...? Are we all dead?"

"We are very much alive, thou bumbling fool!" Los shouted with a sharp whack to the top of Saybil's head. The confused mage curled into a ball, clutching his head.

"Ow... Th-That hurts..."

"Proof that thou art yet among the living!"

"Professor Los? Sorry, but what happ—"

"Later."

"But, what about the Arbiter?"

"Later, I said! First, takest a seat right there. Hort, Kudo, you too."

Saybil withered in the face of Los's fury. Hort and Kudo sat down on either side of him, looking very uncomfortable. Kudo had lost both hands and looked absolutely exhausted, but didn't seem to have any life-threatening injuries. Los's anger had him shrinking in fear, too, but the sight seemed almost comical after the hellish experience they'd just been through. Hort seemed relatively unharmed. Saybil let out a sigh of relief.

*Good. Nobody died.*

"Wipe that look of cretinous enervation off thy face! Dost thou not recognize thy current straits?"

"Huh...? Umm..."

"I'll have none of thy *umm...*s! Thou art in for the reprimanding of thy life! I, thy professor and chaperone, am mere seconds away from castigating thee to high heaven!" Los swooped in so close, her forehead almost bumped Saybil's. He drew back reflexively.

"And yet here thou art, with *Thank goodness, no one was hurt* written all over thy face! Must someone be slain before thou wilt reflect upon thy deeds?! If so, I will gladly oblige so that thou might recognize the weight of thine actions!!"

"I-I'm sorry... I really am!"

"Each and every one of my wards—reckless, reckless, reckless! These fools all want to be the hero!" Los poked Saybil violently, then thrust her staff in turn at each of the students cowering on the ground. "This one uses himself as bait in some overblown attempt to protect his companions, while these two rashly disregard direct orders to wait for my return! This one then rushes into a foolhardy magical offensive against an opponent who *clearly* has the means to nullify it! And this, this suicidal lad insists on taking up a staff he well knows will kill him at a single touch!"

"I mean... Seems like I'm least at fault here," Kudo grumbled under his breath. Instantly Los pounced on him, latched onto his head, and brought her forehead right up to his.

"If *thou* hadst not first *insisted* on such *reckless* behavior, I might have been spared the task of setting out to *rescue* thee, no? In faaact, if thou hadst not affected such *pretentions* and refused my protection at the outset, we could have *avoided* this whole *ordeal*, yes? Get that through thy thick skull, or even *I* shall no longer be able to contain my wrath!"

"Gyaaaah! Too close! Too close!"

"P-Professor, calm down! Kudo's injured! And he's sorry!" Hort frantically tried to appease Los, even though she herself was also currently an object of the witch's wrath.

Los moved on to Hort, glaring deep into her eyes from less than an inch away. "To be quite frank, I had not considered the possibility thou mightest possess the ability to track me. Indeed, the greater the prodigy, the more dangerous the misuse of their power! Perhaps it would be wise to seal away all of that talent once and for all!"

"E-Eeek! So close! Seriously, way too close! Give me some space, Professor...!"

But Los just plowed on, heedless of Hort's protestations. "And another thing: I'll have thee know I had a proper counterattack planned! Didst think I was rendered helpless without my staff? Didst convince thyself, 'I must save Professor Los or she'll be killed'?! What pompous overconfidence, and from a fledgling barely out of the nest! Hast thou any idea the scenes of carnage and devastation I have survived, and most magnificently, to boot?! Of *course* I had plans in place should my staff be stolen!"

"Ooh! Like what?!" Not even a severe scolding could dampen Hort's curiosity.

After a period of silence, Los mumbled, "...Feigning death?"

"That's not a counterattack!"

"Silence! 'Twould have been but the first step of a brilliant plan to make him drop his guard that I might unleash a raging rebuttal! If hadst not stolen the spotlight and invoked whatever thou didst call that incantation, I would have performed a majestic one-witch show of revenge!"

"Eeep! I'm so sorryyyy!"

"And finally, I turn to thee, Ludens!" Her cutting tone taking on an even sharper edge, Los roared at the staff and thrust it into the ground, lodging it deep within the soil. "How darest thou cast a wandering eye toward Saybil, when I am thy sworn partner?! What, art not satisfied with me alone? Dost require more than I can provide? Mark my words: if young Sayb had perished, I would have smashed thee to flinders! As punishment, thou shalt spend the day sealed within a linen prison!"

To any ignorant passersby who happened on the scene, Los would have probably seemed more than a little unbalanced. But given that the staff responded by extending tendrils of its unique black substance to spell a cutesy "Sorry" in the air, those witnesses might just as well have questioned their own sanity instead.

"A-About that... Professor Los?" Saybil asked with trepidation. "Why am I not dead...? I touched the Staff of Ludens."

While busily wrapping the staff in a piece of cloth, Los shot Saybil a glare that seemed to say, *Dost not recognize thy precarious position? How darest thou presume to ask anything of me now?*

Nevertheless, she evidently judged some explanation necessary, and said at last, "'Tis a simple affair," before dislodging the pitiful staff from its earthen hold. "Thy inner store of mana surpassed the amount my little Ludens could absorb."

"Oh... I see," Saybil replied, though he very much did not see what that actually meant. Hort and Kudo did, however.

"Wait, this clown had more mana than the staff could handle?!"

"Too much mana...?! How much would that even be?! Is that normal?!"

"Nay, 'tis an entirely unprecedented store of magical power, as I'm sure thou dost realize. Not even the fabled 'Witch Eater' could handle it all, so it was forced to release the excess in a dizzied frenzy. Meanwhile, young Sayb shows absolutely no signs of magical depletion. He must indeed possess a bottomless well of the stuff—he cannot invoke magic? But of course. Should Sayb use the full measure of his magic without restraint, most spells would transform into wild, unmanageable forces of unimaginable might. Conversely, restraining himself in fear of this, he might suppress his own power overmuch and thus be unable to invoke any spell at all."

Saybil looked down at his hands. She had a point: he'd always either put everything he had into a spell, or tried to squeeze out only the tiniest bit in fear of it spiraling out of control.

"Furthermore, excess from this extraordinary trove of mana flows out of Sayb's body and affects those around him."

"Affects... So you mean Sayb's the reason my magic's been so on point since we started this trip?!"

"'Tis quite likely. Thou must have an inkling of this, too, young Kudo, as didst study in the same class as he."

"H-Hell no...! I just...worked my ass off...!" Kudo muttered, but the lack of conviction behind his denial made it clear Los's words had hit the mark.

Saybil, on the other hand, was the least convinced of all. "But, I've never felt...like I've got this huge supply of magic or anything..."

"I, too, found it difficult to believe. Granted, I had thought thee a promising young man, but never did I expect it would prove true to this degree... And yet, thou didst place thine hands on the staff and live to tell the tale."

Sighing, Los looked up at her staff, now completely wrapped in cloth. "Gracious... After three hundred long years of expending magic, little Ludens once again has a full belly. When now shall my life reach its end...?"

Saybil blinked at the troubled tenor of Los's tone. But before he could ask about it, the witch turned her back to the three mages-in-training with a twirl.

"A quick survey of the area has not turned up the body of that Arbiter. Given that none of us has even a scratch to speak of, we can safely assume the fiend has likewise escaped unharmed."

"What?! But then—!" Hort shot up, but Los quietly pushed her back down.

"His attack failed, and now we are on our guard. I sincerely doubt he has the reckless courage to attempt another attack under such circumstances. Nevertheless," Los continued, letting her gaze fall on Kudo, "that will only hold true so long as we stay together. Thou shalt come with us, young Kudo."

"What...?! No, I can take care of—"

"Thyself?" Los cut him off before he could finish, grabbing his cheeks and once again bringing her smiling face right up to his. "Pray tell, how exactly dost thou intend to journey to the witch's village bereft of both hands and tail? Go on, convince me of thy reasoning. If canst not, prepare thyself to—"

"Aaaah! Too close! Get outta my face! All right, all right! I'll go with you, okay?!"

"Very well," Los snorted, then released the beastfallen from her grasp.

"Shit, man... Well, guess I better go back up to the top of the cliff and find the other half of my tail before some wild animal—"

"Oh!" Hort blurted out, followed only a few seconds later by Saybil's own, "Ohhh..."

Kudo had not been close enough to see when Hort invoked her spell. So he had no idea she'd used his severed tail to activate Flagis.

"What?"

"No, um... The thing is... See, I actually did pick up your tail, but..." Hort chuckled nervously. "I used it! Sorry!"

Hort delivered the news with her most adorable smile yet, but Kudo's scales instantly turned pitch black in horror.

## 2

"Can't sleep, Sayb?"

Saybil sat outside their inn later that night, idly gazing at the stars; when he turned around, he found Hort walking toward him with two steaming mugs.

"Heh heh heh. I commandeered the kitchen for a sec. Here, it's warm milk."

"Thanks." He took the mug from her hand, and with his first sip he felt the sweet warmth of honey and milk spread throughout his tired body.

"Rough day, huh?"

"Yeah... It still doesn't feel real, you know?" Kudo had been attacked by an Arbiter, Hort had turned out to be a spy sent by the Church, and Saybil had learned he possessed an unlimited trove of magical power. All these unbelievable things had happened in such quick succession that Saybil was left feeling dazed, like he was floating in a dreamworld.

"...Um."

"Yeah?"

"You know how the Church sent me to the Academy to spy for them...?"

"Oh yeah, you mentioned something about that."

"H-How can you brush it off like it's no big deal?!"

"I mean, because it isn't... You're the one who said everyone at the Academy had baggage, remember?"

"Well, sure," admitted Hort, pouting. "But...weren't you suspicious?"

"About what?"

"That I'd brought you to the Arbiter on purpose... That I put Kudo and Professor Los in danger..."

"But...you didn't, right?" Saybil shot her a puzzled look. "You did everything you could to keep me from going. And Kudo chose to travel on his own. That had nothing to do with you. Plus, we've been together every minute since we left. When would you have had time to coordinate with the Arbiter?"

"Th...That's true, but..."

"So how would I doubt you? Professor Los didn't blame you either, did she?"

"...No." Hort shook her head. "I tried talking to Kudo about it, too... He gave me this real nasty look, and was like, 'So what? Don't go thinking you're the shit just 'cos you used to be in the Church'..."

"Yup, sounds like him."

"Argh! You're all just way too nice! Magekind is doomed if everyone's gonna be such a softie!"

"It's not really about being nice... More like indifferent, I think..."

"You should care more about the people around you!"

"Huh...? Did you want me to yell at you?"

"No, but still!" Hort puffed out her cheeks.

*Phew. I thought maybe it was some kind of kinky thing.*

"Well, anyway, I guess we can cross one mystery off the list. You weren't put in an all-star class—your classmates just got really good at magic because you were there."

"Guess so... It still doesn't feel real, though. And, I mean, *I'm* still a total washout."

"Doesn't it make you happy?"

"I...guess? At least you and Kudo will have an easier time doing magic if I'm around... But it's not like I'm actually *doing* anything." Saybil fell silent, his head hanging dejectedly.

Suddenly, Hort pulled off the cap she always wore. Released from the hat's weight, the locks that usually looked so long sprung up and stuck out every which way, seeming much shorter.

"...Can you see them?" she asked.

"Hmm? See what?" asked Saybil. Hort took his hand and brought it to the top of her head, placing his fingers on a certain spot.

*It feels hard, and pointy. Is this—*

"...Huh? A horn?"

"Yeah."

"Huh? Wait, what?"

"I just showed them to Professor Los, too. Turns out I'm a

beastfallen."

"No way..." *Beastfallen are supposed to look different from humans, like Kudo does. But Hort looks perfectly normal—if anything, she's way cuter than most people.*

"People called me a 'devil child' because of these—it's why I was left in the care of the Church. My whole life, they told me that the more kindness I showed to others, the more my sinful soul would be cleansed. Over and over, they told me to be nice to everyone. But then, when we first learned about beastfallen in class, I was like, *Huh? Wait, am I...?*"

Beastfallen are the *mere shadows* of powerful warriors created a thousand years ago to increase the military might of the power-hungry aristocracy. Witches imbued human bodies with the souls of ferocious beasts, creating half-human, half-animal monsters, which they called beast warriors—but whenever the witches and beast warriors died, the beasts' souls were left with no place to go, and they would find a host among the witch's bloodline. That's how babies born with monstrous appearances came to be known as beastfallen.

A great many beast warriors and witches fell in the war five hundred years prior, as well as in the witch hunts that followed. Countless wayward beast souls found themselves adrift, and the resulting beastfallen were unjustly persecuted without ever understanding why they were born into such bodies.

Hort touched the horns hidden beneath her locks and gave Saybil a shy smile. "They say the wandering soul of a beast warrior finds a new place among the witch's descendants. But apparently, if the witch's bloodline ends, the soul disappears. So, what do you think happens when the witch's bloodline gradually thins out over generations of marriage with normal people?"

"You get...*those*?" Saybil glanced at Hort's horns.

"Yeah, the beast's soul gradually gets more and more diluted, too. Professor Los said there's actually quite a lot of us, and people just don't notice. Some have a really good sense of smell, others have super sensitive hearing... A lot of us don't even realize what we are ourselves, and discriminate against beastfallen—like I did."

Hort smiled grimly. Branded a devil child at birth, handed over to the Church and raised by its members—Hort never stood a chance. She was destined to have held those prejudices.

"But today, when Professor Los told me, 'Thou hast the soul of a beast in thee,' I felt this weight lift off my shoulders. It was such a relief. I was like, thank Goddess, I'm just a beastfallen. And it's all because of you, Sayb."

"Me?"

"Yeah, I mean, you never, ever say anything bad about Kudo. You said it shouldn't matter if he's a beastfallen or not... Every time you stood up for him, it made me smile a little inside."

"No, but that's...nothing special... I just said what I was thinking, that's all..."

Hort smiled gently. "Hey, Sayb. Remember when Professor Los called me your girlfriend by mistake?"

"I don't know if that was a mistake so much as a joke..."

Hort leaned close to Saybil. She must've just taken a bath; Sayb could smell the scent of soap. Then:

"Next time someone makes that mistake, you don't have to correct them."

For a second, Saybil froze up completely. The next word out of his mouth was "...Huah?"

It was actually more of a dumbfounded grunt, well removed from anything one could call a word. Hort hastily grabbed up her

cap once more and whirled around, turning her back to Saybil.

"I'm going to sleep! You should get to bed soon, too!"

"Hey, hold on a—"

But Hort had already begun scampering off. Saybil had the sense that she was blushing, and couldn't bring himself to call her back. All that remained was the now-lukewarm mug of milk and honey in his hands. He drank it all down in one gulp. Wondering how the heck he was going to get to sleep when he felt more awake by the second, he tilted his face toward the heavens, a rush of blood leaving him blushing, too.

Then, behind him—

"Thou wert meant to kiss her, young Sayb!"

"Aaaaah!"

—Los appeared without a sound. Cackling at the scream that escaped Saybil's lips, she perched sprightly atop her staff where she'd thrust it into the ground. Seated up there, the normally diminutive Los looked down at Saybil for once.

"H-How long have you been there?"

"From the very start. I left the inn alongside young Hort."

"That's impossible..."

"Any witch worth her salt can hide her presence at will. 'Tis perfect for spying on the first flutterings of young love."

"Whoa... What a creep!"

"You have only yourselves to blame for putting on such an interesting show for me." Saybil's insult had slipped out before he could stop himself, but Los let it go without comment, seemingly unfazed. "She is indeed a lovely lass. Wherefore didst thou falter after such a blatant profession of affection?"

"Umm... I didn't exactly 'falter', I..." Uncomfortable, Saybil rubbed the back of his neck. "I just...don't really get it..."

"Get what?"

"...Love and stuff."

"Gaaaaah! The purityyy!" Los squirmed atop her staff. "Well, such is the lot of youth. 'Twould be most displeasing were the younger generations instantly knowledgeable of romantic affairs. It warms the heart to see such unadorned, uncontrived emotion. Well, lad, worry, suffer, and flail thy way forward! The greater thy struggle, the more delicious the show."

"That's really twisted..." Saybil grumbled as he gently brushed Los's hand off of his head.

## 3

The next morning, a mage purporting to be sent by Headmaster Albus appeared at the inn where they were staying and led away Kudo's two erstwhile traveling companions. At a loss as to what was going on, the three remaining students went down to the dining hall and found Los waving her staff wildly back and forth to beckon them over.

"Those two going back to school? They droppin' outta the field program?" asked Kudo. But rather than answering, Los merely responded with another question.

"Young Kudo, didst thou not sense anything amiss during thy time with those lads?"

"What do you mean?" Kudo took a seat, then ordered a whole roast bird that could just as easily have been listed on the menu as a giant meatball. He reached out to take a sip of water, only to click his tongue in frustration when he remembered he'd lost both his hands. Sitting next to him, Hort noticed his plight and brought the glass to the beastfallen's lips.

Just then—

"They were moles."

—water exploded from Kudo's mouth.

"Careful!" Hort exclaimed.

"Sorry! But didn't you hear what this lady just said...?!"

"It's 'Professor Los,' Kudo, not 'this lady'!"

"I don't give a shit! Were they really...m-moles...?"

"They sent the Church a helpful tip—that a group of greenhorn mages were about to leave Wenias for a special field program. And apparently, they intended to continue passing to the Church such information regarding the Academy. Young Kudo here came under attack, yet those two managed to escape. Thy ploy to act as a decoy notwithstanding, this struck me as most strange. So I surreptitiously installed in their room a means to listen in on their conversations."

The witch tossed a seashell onto the table. "Put it to thine ear."

Kudo reached out to grab it—only to once again realize he was handless. "Oh, come *on!!*" he groaned.

Hort picked up the shell, and the three apprentices leaned in close and pricked up their ears.

*—Dude, we're in deep shit. That professor's gone after 'em.*

*—What's our move? If the Arbiter thinks we snitched on him, we're as good as dead.*

*—Shit...! That chump change isn't worth all this!*

*—Nah man, we're good. As long as the professor takes the Arbiter out, we're just innocent victims.*

*—Yeah, but then who're we gonna sell our information to...?*

*—We'll just find another contact! Anybody in the Church'll jump at the chance to buy dirt on the Academy.*

That was all they needed to hear. The three mages pulled away from the shell and looked at Los.

"What'll happen to them?" Saybil asked.

"Their memories will be erased. Thereafter they'll be banished, I expect."

"They'd hang, if I had my way," Kudo growled with bared fangs, his scales turning a rusty brown.

"I wouldn't go that far... Though it does kinda feel like they're just getting off scot-free. I feel like they should get, I dunno, a hundred lashes or something! Right, Sayb?"

"...So they'll lose all memory of their time at the Academy?"

Los shrugged. "Presumably."

"Then I bet they'll try to enroll again...and they'll never get in, but they won't know why. That sounds like a plenty bad punishment to me."

"Ngh... When you put it that way, it does feel pretty harsh..."

"I don't give a shit. Not my problem. Kill 'em, I say."

"I wish you wouldn't say it like that, Kudo, even if my heart's right there with you!" Hort clutched her cap and squirmed.

"In any event, that matter has been settled. The rest of us shall henceforth travel in a merry band of four. But first, young Kudo. Thou wilt be hard pressed to do much with those stumps of thine. How long will they take to regenerate?"

"Who the hell knows." Kudo let out a long sigh and looked down at his nubs. "They'll probably start sprouting in, like, three days...but I'm guessing it'll take maybe twenty to get all my fingers back."

"Much too long. Let us hasten the process."

"Like it's that easy! They're not bean sprouts, ya know!"

"Dost thou not practice healing magic? As far as I am aware, you mages study magic divided into four chapters: the Chapter of Hunting, useful for trapping prey and the like; the Chapter of Harvest, which assists with agricultural pursuits; the Chapter of Capture, employed to maintain peace and security; and finally, the Chapter of Protection, for treating ailments and afflictions."

"Amazing! You're, like, an expert, Professor Los!"

"Not idly have I yearned for the *Grimoire of Zero* these many long years. As I understand it, the textbook from which you study is a defanged, simplified version of the *Grimoire*... Regardless, they must have taught you a spell or two for how to treat wounds, yes? I cannot help but think a little magic could help thy regenerative capabilities hasten thy recovery, even if only by a little..."

"Not gonna happen!" Kudo hissed. "Spells from the Chapter of Protection use up the most mana of all. You're basically bleeding yourself to heal someone else. I'd run outta magic and hit the floor long before I got to my fingers."

"Rubbish. Thou shalt have enough mana and to spare."

"Who's talking 'rubbish' now—?" Just then, a thought hit Kudo. His mouth clamped shut and he looked at Saybil, following Los's gaze.

Hort took in the scene and said, "Oh, I get it. We've got unlimited magic as long as Sayb's around! Sayb, you're amazing!"

"Now then, who amongst you is most adept with the Chapter of Protection?"

"Probably Kudo. He was the best in our house at it," Saybil replied, pointing at the beastfallen. Instantly, Kudo's scales turned a bright crimson.

"Bullshit! I'm way better at the Chapters of Hunting and Capture!"

"But the Chapter of Hunting was your worst subject. I remember people making fun of you for it during our first year," Saybil insisted. "They were like, 'How is he so bad at hunting when he looks like *that*?'"

"Don't you have better things to remember, washout?!" Kudo went to raise his fist—but alas, his arm ended at the wrist. "Shit! Fine, how do we do this? Do I just cast the spell like normal?"

"'Twould be more efficient if thou wert in physical contact with Saybil. Thou hast heard of people plundering mana from a dead witch by gripping her left hand, I presume? 'Tis the hand closest to the heart, you see. So likewise, young Kudo, hold Saybil's left hand in thine. Though the transmission can be made even more effective through contact with a mucous membrane, where blood vessels can be felt directly... Through a kiss, for instance."

"I'm good with the hand."

"Let's stick with hands, please."

Kudo and Saybil rushed to get the words out, each speaking over the other.

"So I just hold Kudo's hand?"

"Indeed. That shall remain thy sole focus. The very thought of allowing thee to share magic power with Kudo without any sense of how to regulate or control the flow invites disaster."

"Disaster?"

"Recall that Sayb doth possess a store of mana great enough to set little Ludens's head spinning. Any mere mortal mage exposed to such an overwhelming volume of magic would instantly begin spewing fountains of blood from every possible orifice, and ultimately disintegrate entirely."

Kudo quickly pulled back the hand—technically, the stump—he'd offered to Saybil. Los caught his wrist with one hand, however, and clasped Saybil's with the other.

"Do not fear, young Kudo. 'Tis much like assaying a meal when thou art famished. Art likely to overfill thy stomach to the point of distress, no? One must simply know one's limits. For the moment, I shall regulate the flow of mana thus. All thou must do now is cast the spell from the Chapter of Protection on thyself—can you both feel it?"

Kudo and Saybil nodded.

*Yeah, I feel something.*

The wrists Los held tingled with the flow of magic. Kudo anxiously opened his mouth, then shut it.

"What's the matter, young Kudo?"

"...Hey, I'm not the only one, right?" He glanced at Saybil and Hort in turn. "You guys get a little...e-embarrassed...doing incantations in front of other people, too, doncha?"

The two erupted:

"For sure. It's embarrassing."

"Why'd you have to bring that up?! I've been trying so hard not to think about it!"

"I mean...! It's fine when it works or whatever, but I feel like crawling into a hole whenever the spell doesn't activate! It's not just me, right?!"

The vast majority of Saybil's spells failed, so he knew a little *too* well what Kudo was talking about. It was the first real roadblock everyone who attended the Academy ran into: the embarrassment that came with reciting incantations. At the same time, a half-assed reading would never get you anywhere. Many spells also required gestures on top of the spoken formula itself. As a result, everyone at the Academy began their first year just going through the motions, getting used to conducting themselves like real mages.

Kudo took a deep breath and refocused himself. "*Ēa doh Kūha*—Flow, Blood! Become as flesh once more!"

In that moment, Saybil felt a huge stream of magic rush out of his palm.

"Chapter of Protection, Verse One—Chordia!"

"A-Ah... Amazing! Your hands, they're growing back...!" cried Hort.

"Shut up! I'm tryin'a concentrate!" Kudo barked angrily. Then, to finish the spell, he intoned, "Heed this call by the power of my name—Kudo!"

Chordia, the most fundamental spell in the Chapter of Protection, was used to restore the wounded body to its original state, closing up lacerations or setting broken bones. And—it could also regenerate pulverized hands and severed tails.

Looking down at his hands after he had completed the incantation, Kudo was dumbfounded. "...Damn, it really worked."

The next moment, the whole tavern burst into cheers. Only then did Saybil and the others remember where they were—a regular dining hall at a nondescript inn on the side of the highway. Not exactly the most inconspicuous place to work a spell powerful enough to restore both of someone's hands.

"Whoaa, didja see that?! He just grew a new pair o' hands!"

"That what they call magic?? What a sight! Guess you must get the chance to see a lot of mages this close to the Wenisian border."

"Wish I could study magic, too..."

An overwhelming chorus of praise erupted from every mouth, to the point that it was difficult for the mages to process. It left Saybil and his friends, fresh from their nearly fatal encounter with the Arbiter the day before, completely baffled. Los, on the other hand, climbed onto the long dining table and welcomed the riotous applause as if it were her due.

"P-Professor Los...? What are you...?" Saybil asked in a fluster.

Los smirked and turned toward her three pupils. "To focus on naught but the challenges of life as a mage would easily dampen the fiercest of ambitions. In truth, half the population will despise you, while the other half will meet you with adoration. Acclaim on par with the threat to your lives awaits the three of you."

"But...weren't we supposed to keep a low profile?!"

"So as to avoid attack from the Arbiters, yes. But what good would such caution do us now? You have already endured the most treacherous of dangers, so you have earned the right to seek acclaim in equal measure! Think of it as a rehearsal for the field program! Show the world your worth as we make our merry way!"

The witch rapped the tip of her staff hard against the table. "Ho there, bard! Play! Sing! Give us a song in praise of mages!"

As the tune began to flow out from among the cheers, Los hopped off the table, clapped her hands loudly, and led her charges toward the door. "Now off we go, my little ducklings! Lift up those heads! Straighten those shoulders! Make way for the mages of Wenias, pride and joy of the kingdom!"

# [ Interlude ]

"A cityyyyyy!" Hort cried, thrusting her fists triumphantly into the air.

It was a city indeed. After leaving the Kingdom of Wenias, camping out, fighting off an Arbiter, staying at an inn by the highway, then walking along the road for half a day, they had crossed the border and finally come to a bustling town.

"It's huge...and there are so many people," Saybil marveled.

"Oh, you think? It's super small compared to Plasta," Hort said. Plasta was the Wenisian capital, home to the Academy of Magic.

"I never really left the Academy..." Saybil didn't even have a working knowledge of the city he'd been living in. And since Holdem had driven him from the Academy to the tunnel in a wagon, Saybil hadn't gotten more than a fuzzy notion of what some of the main roads were like.

"Does that mean this is basically your first time walking around a city?"

"Yeah. At least, as far as I can remember."

"Shit, talk about livin' under a rock!"

"Move! Outta the way! Yer standin' in the middle of the street!" The angry shout set all three apprentices' hearts racing. They quickly scooted out of the way just in time for a horse-drawn carriage to race past, dousing Saybil with mud. He stood there gaping.

"...Huh? Wait...what?" Shooting a glance at Hort and Kudo, he saw that they had nimbly avoided the mud shower and were now both giving him looks that screamed, *Daaamn.*

Los cackled. "Tell me, young Sayb, how dost thou feel after being baptized into city life?"

"Umm... I feel like I want to wash my face."

"Indeed, indeed. Come along, my little ducklings. Stay close and don't go astray. My usual inn comes equipped with a grand bathhouse."

"B...Bathhouse?" Hort repeated nervously, her face tight. "Do... Do you think they'll let me in...?"

"But of course. Why would they not?"

"Really...? Really really?"

Saybil cocked his head. "What's wrong, Hort? We had a big bathhouse at the Academy, too."

"Well...yeah, but..." Hort spluttered, uncharacteristically at a loss for words.

At which Kudo cut in: "Dumbass! How's she gonna take a bath with a buncha other people when she's tryin'a hide her antlers? I bet back at the Academy she just snuck a barrel into her room and took her baths there."

"Oh...right."

Hort chuckled bashfully, pressing her cap firmly down atop her head. "No, I mean, sometimes I'd wrap a towel around my head to keep them out of sight, but yeah, I never could really relax..."

"You just went in like normal, huh, Kudo?"

"Sure. It's not like I've got anythin' to hide."

"Whaaa? I've gotta say, I respect that about you," Hort said.

Los's "usual inn" turned out to be a luxurious establishment in the wealthiest part of town. Los brazenly stepped through the front doors with Saybil and the others following nervously behind. The elderly owner of the inn popped out of nowhere and led them to the best rooms in the place.

"A dear old friend," Los said by way of explanation. "I pulled her back from the brink of death when she was but a child, and gave her a few lessons on how to survive in this world. The next time I dropped in to see her, she was running the best inn in the city. Human development is a fearsome wonder to behold. She urged me to stay as her guest whenever I liked in repayment for saving her life, and I've been gratefully taking her at her word ever since."

*Fair enough, but I'm pretty sure letting four people take over the best rooms in the house without paying is going a little too far.*

Though one room already felt unbelievably large to the young mages, the owner insisted on providing them with two, saying, "This is a little tight for four, I'm sure you'll agree."

"I'd be fine with an empty stable..." Saybil offered.

"Yeah, this place isn't exactly my vibe..." Kudo agreed.

But Los just waved their grumblings aside. "Turning away a kind gesture is naught but disrespect. Save your humble abstentions for when they are truly needed."

Left with no other option, the three mages resigned themselves to a night of luxury. Nevertheless, Saybil was still covered in mud. He wasn't about to sit on one of the silk sofas or compromise the featherbed with his filth.

"We should probably hit the bath first, right...?"

"Ya think?"

That settled, Saybil and Kudo tossed their belongings into the room and headed straight for the baths. After undressing in the changing room, a butler appeared out of nowhere and collected their soiled laundry, informing them as he departed that he would wash and press it for them.

"Huh? Then what are we supposed to wear back to the room...?" Saybil fretted, but the manservant quickly put two sets of loungewear in a basket and handed it to him.

*They've really thought of everything.*

The vast bathing room seemed to go on forever, but was empty save for Saybil and Kudo. The shallow circular tub had been dug into the earth itself, and pipes sprouting from the walls continuously filled it with fresh hot water.

Saybil looked at Kudo.

Kudo looked at Saybil.

"Let's make sure we're nice and clean before we get in."

"...Yeah."

They were too faint of heart to stand the thought of dirtying the pristine baths in any way. The two filled wooden buckets with warm water and got to work scrubbing down every inch of their bodies with washcloths. Kudo washed his scales in much the same way Saybil laved his skin.

"Kudo, you don't sweat, right?"

"Nah, I shed scales instead. You know, like molting. It's easy for dirt and stuff to build up in there." The beastfallen carefully scrubbed all the way down to the tip of his tail. His feet and his tail tended to get dirtiest, since they were closest to the ground.

A somewhat awkward silence passed between the two. They didn't have much to talk about in the first place.

"...So, me and Hort were talking with Professor Los before you joined up with us."

"Yeah?"

"Yeah, about why we wanted to be mages. She was telling us how dangerous it is...and I got a pretty good feel for that yesterday...

but, what made you want to go for it?"

"So I could join the Church and Mage Brigade."

"Do you have to be a mage to do that?"

Kudo clicked his tongue. "You seriously don't know shit, do you? Only the best of the best warriors get to be in the Church and Mage Brigade. It used to be called the Knights of the Church, where all these knights renounced their worldly goods to get together and protect the Church and the people."

"That much I knew..."

"So, the Church hates beastfallen, right? You know, the whole 'epitome of depravation' thing? So obviously, there wasn't a single beastfallen in the Knights of the Church back then. But once it became the Church and Mage Brigade, they made a beastfallen battalion—the real cream of the crop. You can't just be physically strong; you gotta be smart as hell, too. Like the knight who serves the headmaster."

"Ohh, you mean Holdem."

"Don't you dare toss his name around like that! He's not your BFF, asshole!" Kudo snarled and bared his fangs. Saybil shrunk down into his shoulders. "...So...anyway, the thing is...I'm not strong enough to be a knight," the beastfallen mumbled, reluctant to admit the hard truth. "Being a mage is my only ticket in."

"So that's it," Saybil whispered. *Guess Kudo had a really good reason, too. Just like Hort.*

And unlike Saybil.

"What drew you to the Church and Mage—"

"How deep you tryin'a dig here?!"

"S-Sorry. If you don't want to talk about it..."

"They saved my life. The Church and Mage Brigade." Apparently he didn't actually mind discussing it. After that terse answer,

Kudo's face softened a little. "I mean, not the whole battalion, but... You ever heard of the Dragon Conqueror King?"

"Umm... Is that the guy who rides on a dragon?"

"That's the one. I used to be part of this freak show, and we got mixed up in the whole Disasters of the North thing. I didn't get more than a few scratches, but the building collapsed and I got trapped in my cage. The assholes from the troupe who survived just left me to die, I guess... But anyway, I managed to keep myself alive for a while, eating whatever I could reach, but just as I was thinking, *This is it, I'm gonna die,* someone started clearing away the rubble. It was him. He was all in black armor," Kudo whispered, then went on to explain how he grew to hopelessly admire the Dragon Conqueror King, that black-armored knight mounted on his silver steed. "I was just a beastfallen, the so-called epitome of depravation, a dirty freak show attraction buried under bricks and rubble... Even after he noticed me, he could just as well've left me there to die. Nobody was about to give him a medal or whatever for saving someone like me. But when he saw me, he smiled, and said, 'Good, you're still alive.' That's when I decided I wanted to be like him. Someone who saves people, protects people, whether anyone praises them for it or not."

"I see."

"So? What's your story?"

"Huh?"

"Why'd you wanna be a mage? This ain't a one-way street."

Saybil hesitated. He figured Kudo would blow his top if he told him he'd never wanted to be a mage. That said, he didn't have what it took to make something up out of whole cloth. Just then—

"How are you finding the baths?! Spacious, are they not? Outstanding, no? I often pop by this city for no other reason than to relish their magnificence!"

—Los's voice suddenly echoed through the room. Startled, Kudo and Saybil turned their heads in the direction from which it had come, only to immediately whip them back around in the exact opposite direction.

She was naked. Not a stitch of clothing. Not even a towel to cover her bits and pieces—just her full-on birthday suit (plus the staff in her hand). The steam just baaarely sufficed to hide the sensitive areas they had absolutely no business seeing, but on second thought, Saybil wasn't sure there was any part of a woman's naked body he had business seeing in the first place.

"P-P…P-Professor Los…?! What are you…?!"

"The hell are you thinking? Seriously, the *hell* are you *thinking?!*"

"No need for such hysterics, lads. Did you not say the Academy had communal bathing facilities as well?"

"Yeah, but not mixed!"

"Oh hoh? Not but a hundred years ago all baths were mixed as a matter of course… Though come to think of it, I do recall seeing only other women in the baths of late. That must be why," Los mused, as if letting old memories wash over her while she strode confidently toward the panicked mages.

"W-Wait, why are you coming over here, Professor?!"

"Why? That I might wash thy back for thee…"

"Back off! Nobody asked fer that, you nympho!"

"N-Nympho?! Why must I be subjugated to accusations of sexual perversion simply for not wearing clothing into the bath?! How unspeakably rude of thee to foist thy morals on me, and then berate me for violating them!" the witch fumed, wildly swirling her staff around as she briskly strode past the two and leapt into the water with a splash. "I care nothing for the trifling changes of this world! And in any event, this bath is currently reserved for our exclusive use. We may mix and frolic freely without a soul to criticize."

"*We're* criticizing!"

"My, what innocent young lads you are! All in a fluster! Are your nethers roiling at the sight of my exquisite physique? Is that what drives this bashfulness? Well, rejoice in my pardon! I have a great love of human instinct. Roil to your hearts' content!"

"The hell I will, dumbaaaass!"

But Los's attention had already left the explosively irate Kudo.

"Young Hort, thou shalt catch cold afore long if dost linger in the changing room forever. Cease thy squirming and come join us."

"I-I caaan't! You didn't tell me we'd all be bathing *together!*"

"Wait, you dragged Hort into this too, you freak?!"

Saybil looked up at the ceiling. Poor Hort. Being lured into a joint bath with a couple of dudes had to be hell for a girl her age. What was this crazy witch thinking? Even Saybil, with no memories to draw from, knew better than to go peeking at naked girls.

"Hey, Hort! Saybil and me are gettin' out! Just take cover somewhere 'til we're gone!"

"W-We'll close our eyes, okay...? I promise we won't look—I promise!"

The two left the tub and scurried over to the changing room—but.

"W-Wait! Gimme a second! Don't come in yet!!"

They stepped into the changing area. Their timing was impeccable: Hort was smack in the middle of putting on her lounge dress. She had raised her arms to slip the loose gown over her head, leaving absolutely nothing to cover her body. Every single thing they had no business seeing was on full display, without so much as a

wisp of steam to obfuscate the view. The boys saw the curves of her bulging breasts, the mole next to her bellybutton, her soft-looking, voluptuous thighs—everything.

*Crap, gotta close my eyes!*

But Saybil's eyes remained wide open.

"Aaaaaah! Sorry! H-Here, take this!" Kudo screamed. Panicking, he grabbed the closest thing he could get his hands on—which turned out to be the towel wrapped around Saybil's waist—and offered it to Hort.

"Huh?" Petrified by this sudden turn of events, Saybil stood stock still as his own nether regions were exposed for Hort to see.

For a moment, time stopped. As soon as Hort's eyes fell below Saybil's waist, her face turned a bright, burning red.

"Eeeaaaaaaah! A monsterrrrr!" she shrieked, pulled her gown on quicker than the eye could follow, and sprinted out of the changing room.

"...I mean, to be honest," Kudo began, clearing his throat as he handed Saybil the towel he'd grabbed a moment ago, "I'd call *that* a monster, too."

"You might want to hold off on the snarky comments 'til you give me that apology you owe me," Saybil shot back with uncharacteristic coldness, snatching his towel back out of Kudo's hands.

# Chapter Five

## 1

The rest of the journey proceeded so smoothly that its tumultuous beginning started to seem like nothing more than a nightmare. Every innkeeper along the highway knew Los, and happily provided extra rooms upon learning she was traveling with company. The witch had every spring, river, and stream along their path committed to memory, and would playfully teach her charges how to hunt whenever they camped outside for the night.

Los disclosed to every injured person they chanced upon that her wards were mages, and had the students treat the wounded strangers. If they ran into a carriage stalled by a fallen tree in the road, she would instruct her charges to remove the obstacle with their magic. The profuse thanks they received bolstered Hort and Kudo, who had been persecuted since childhood, and filled Saybil, who had no memories to speak of, with pride. They had for years lived at the Academy in the course of their studies, but had never felt so strongly and thoroughly protected as they did during this journey.

"You know, you kinda give me mom vibes, Professor Los," said Hort.

"Whence such sudden words?" the witch frowned. "First thou callest me 'Professor,' and now 'Mother'? Art regressing to a suckling babe?"

"No, but I know you'd baby me if I did. I think I like you better than any of the professors at the Academy," Hort declared, squeezing Los in a tight embrace.

She could call Los "Mother" all she liked, but Hort towered over the witch, and to all outward appearances would be the big sister of the pair. And yet, as Los struggled to pry the young mage off her—not quite so displeased as her words might suggest—she did in fact look something like a mother at her wits' end dealing with her daughter's clinginess.

"Mother, huh...? You know she's just gonna up and leave once she's done her job, right?"

"Did you have to bring that up?! I've been trying not to think about it! Now I'm gonna cry!"

"Cry all you want, dumbass. So, Professor, what's your plan after we get to the village?"

"Ah yes, you and Hort were not privy to the details of my contract with Albus, were you?"

"But you were, Sayb?" Hort asked.

Saybil nodded. "I was there when they signed it."

"Albus vowed to grant me an audience with the Mud-Black Witch, author of the *Grimoire of Zero,* once I safely escort you all to the village. As such, I shall set off to meet her after my duties are discharged."

"And do what?"

"Talk."

"I don't get it." Kudo's scales flashed yellow.

*Based on what I've seen so far, it seems like Kudo turns yellow whenever he's feeling something negative. When he's embarrassed or angry he blushes red, and when he's scared, his scales go all black. Kudo's facial expressions are hard to interpret since he's a beastfallen, but I think overall his scales make him easier to read than other people.*

"Pish posh. 'Tis simply an attempt to stave off boredom," Los replied off-handedly, her voice tinged with drowsiness. "I'm bored, bored, bored. So bored I can hardly stand it. After three hundred long years, I've almost grown weary of breathing itself. Yet so long as I have little Ludens with me, there shall be no end to this life of mine. A witch who sustains herself with magic has no need even of sustenance. Pray tell, young Kudo, dost thou grasp what this means?"

"It's crazy convenient."

Los laughed. "Indeed. Convenient it is, without question. But the vast majority of every animate being's life is devoted to securing food. They must eat to survive. And to eat, they must hunt, they must labor. The same holds true even for plants, which strive day after day to acquire as much sunlight and water as possible. And yet, once one is released from the fetters of such 'sustenance,' every other natural undertaking loses its purpose."

"Say what?"

"Let me put it this way," Los began, pointing her staff at the beastfallen. "Lack of sleep shall not kill me. Therefore, sleep holds no meaning. Starvation shall not kill me. Therefore, eating serves no purpose. I shall not die, so I have no need for descendants, which renders procreation, and as a result love and lust, pointless. Now, tell me. What remains to fill my life?"

"Huh? I mean... What...?" Drawing a blank, Kudo turned to Saybil and Hort. The two looked at each other, then joined Kudo in his hemming.

"...Fun, I guess?" Hort said finally.

Los snapped her fingers. "Precisely!"

"Ooh, I got it right?! Yaaay!"

"Enjoyment is everything to me. I have no need of sustenance, sleep, sexual desire—in other words, all the pursuits necessary for sustaining life, which you three require. The sole endeavor left to me is the search for entertainment: books I have never read, stories I have never heard, people I have never met, dangerous exploits—! Even the destruction of the world had my heart dancing with excitement. That day, as I gazed upon the surging hordes of demons intent on laying waste to the human race, I thought:

*"Ahh, how wonderful it is to be alive."*

Saybil's breath caught in his throat. He felt like he'd gotten his first real glimpse of the true nature of the witch Loux Krystas—whose life had long ago deviated from any normal human sense of meaning.

"You've seriously got a screw loose..."

"Remember this, young Kudo—and you too, Sayb, Hort: such is the nature of a witch. As the ages pass, the 'norms' of the world change with them. Witches who live for hundreds of years are thus exposed to all manner of 'norms,' and fittingly lose sense of what is strange and what is not. In time, as you three master the arts of the mage and proceed to the work of witches and sorcerers, you shall also lose this connection to what is 'normal.'"

"...But," Saybil began shyly, "I think...you're still...a good person..."

"Wh...What an unexpected declaration! 'Tis enough to make an old witch blush!" And indeed, Los turned bright red even as she said this. The way she squirmed with embarrassment, her hands clapped to her flushed cheeks, looked nothing like a hedonistic witch divorced from all sense of "normalcy."

"Hrm... Ahem... Well, I admit...I have also recently come to a new discovery," Los began, clearing her throat and fishing around in her bag for a map to hide the awkwardness she felt at not having anything to do with her hands. "Spending time with others is quite amusing. No person is exactly like another. Better yet, new lives are born into this world every minute. Since I realized that my encounters with them provide more entertainment than any other venture, I have not known boredom as I once did."

"Is that why you decided to chaperone us?" Hort asked.

"Indeed. This journey with the three of you is a special pleasure. And how could it not be, when each of thou hast the finest 'baggage' there could be."

Had anyone ever bestowed such high praise on them for the issues they brought to the table? Saybil, Hort, and Kudo shot each other indescribable looks and shrugged.

"But this journey, like all things, must come to an end erelong. According to this map, I believe we have not half a day's walk before we arrive at the—"

"What're you doing?! Hide! Get out of there!"

A shrill voice pierced the forest. They heard the sound of someone approaching through the bushes at a run, and then a child leapt into view—a little boy shorter even than Los, no more than five or six years old.

"And who might you—"

"Doesn't matter, just hide! Hurry! If he finds you, you're dead!" The boy grabbed Los's hand and yanked. Los instantly grasped that something was amiss and let the boy pull her along without another question. Saybil and his friends naturally followed suit.

"Hurry, hurry!" he urged the group, leading them to a tree whose roots protruded dramatically from the deeply gouged earth. A curtain of vines hung down, creating an almost cave-like burrow. The little boy pushed everyone else inside, then jumped in after them. Then—

"Caterpillar, Thunder, Eye of Bird—Door, I bid thee shut."

—after spouting a list of disjointed words, the boy placed a hand on the ground to complete his *incantation.* Los and her wards stared in disbelief at the child before exchanging glances to confirm they weren't seeing things or misreading the situation.

"Tell me, child. Didst thou just…perform *sorcery*?" Los asked, but the boy cut her off with a sharp *Shhh!*

"You're too loud… The only thing this barrier doesn't hide is sound."

*He just said "barrier." So it really must've been—*

"Professor Los, look," Hort said, pointing to one of the countless roots dangling down from the ceiling of the burrow. Too short on her own, Los clambered up onto Saybil's shoulders to get a better look at the roots. A grim expression crossed her face.

"This barrier… 'Tis impeccable. The ritual has been intentionally left incomplete so that a designated phrase can activate it."

"H-Hey, little guy. You said the only thing the barrier doesn't block is sound. Does that mean it conceals everything else? Did the village witch put this up, by any chance?"

According to Albus, a witch with the power to decimate the entire world dwelt in the village that would play host to the special field program. The barrier's masterful execution wouldn't be so surprising if she'd been the one to create it. The boy shot Los and the others an irritated look for refusing to shut their mouths, then nodded once.

At that very moment, they heard footsteps crunching through the fallen leaves outside. They could tell just by listening that whatever approached was unbelievably heavy, its wild, powerful footsteps sinking deep into the loamy soil.

"C'mon, you little brat. Where're you hidin'?" a booming voice called out. The little boy shivered and shrunk down even further, leaving the young mages tense and edgy. "Come on out, boy. I ain't gonna eat ya. Come out now and I'll let this all slide."

*Crunch, crunch.* The footfalls grew closer. Anyone who bent down could easily peer inside the enclave beneath the tree roots where the small group hid. Saybil felt utterly exposed. There they cowered, powerless to do anything but huddle together while the encroaching footsteps and menacing voice sent chills through their bodies.

"Now look, kid. If you don't show yourself, the other little kiddies you abandoned are gonna take the punishment in your place. You run, and I guarantee they'll all come down with a case of broken legs."

The boy flinched. Hort silently wrapped her arms around him from behind. No one said a word. They all simply shook their heads to say, *Don't go out there.*

*Crunch, crunch.* The footsteps were almost upon them. An enormous shadow darkened the ground outside, followed by a hulking white figure.

*It's a beastfallen. And he's…massive.*

Saybil and his friends held their breath. A colossal, fully armored carnivorous beastfallen stood before them. White fur with light grey stripes covered its body, claws as sharp as knives protruded from its hands and feet, and razor-sharp fangs lined the mouth of a feline head held up by a neck as thick as a log. Sinister scars scored the beastfallen's nose, while the sword in its hand seemed as heavy as a full-grown man. Everything pointed to the fact that this beastfallen made his living as a warrior.

*But why would someone like him be in the village—*

"—Odd. Pretty sure I hear heartbeats coming from somewhere around here..."

Saybil immediately clamped his hands to his chest. Hort and Kudo followed suit, trying desperately to subdue their racing hearts. The beastfallen turned its head in their direction. Ears twitching, the carnivorous warrior paced back and forth in front of the exposed tree roots—evidently, he hadn't actually seen them yet. The enormous creature then hoisted his sword to rest on his shoulder, tapping it pensively up and down.

The next instant—

"RAAAH!"

—he brandished the sword and brought it around in a vicious sideways slash. The tip of its massive blade blasted away several of the roots belonging to the tree under which Saybil and the others hid, the resulting gust whipping their hair about.

Saybil almost screamed in spite of himself. Though he knew the beastfallen couldn't see them, an ominous chill slithered down his spine just the same. He himself had only just barely managed to suppress his fear; it was too much for a small child to endure.

"A-Aaaaaah!" the little boy screamed. He wriggled out of Hort's arms, which were stiff with fright, and dashed out from the safety of the rooted hollow.

"No—don't!" shrieked Hort, jumping out after the boy. Saybil and Kudo raced out of the barrier, hot on her heels. Kudo was the fastest. He grabbed the boy and scooped him up in his arms as Saybil and Hort stepped out in front to protect them. For a second, all was silent.

"What do we do now, Sayb?! We're totally out in the open!" Hort cried, on the verge of tears.

"I-I-I-I don't know! We should probably run for it!" Saybil yelled back. Behind them, Kudo clicked his tongue.

"Idiots! He's just a beastfallen! We can hold our own with our magic! Hort, get him! Saybil's right there!" Meaning she could cast spell after spell with no problem.

The beastfallen waited patiently for the three youngsters who had appeared before him to finish their little chat before once again hoisting his sword up to rest on his shoulder.

"Three little mage brats, eh...? Right. You must be the... What was it? 'Special Field Training Apprentices'?"

The three were stunned.

"H-How did you—!"

"I have my ways." The beastfallen smiled, baring his teeth. "So? What's your move? If you're plannin' to come at me with magic, you're much too close. That little lady's head'll go flyin' the second she begins chanting. You messed up big time, jumpin' out all at once. One of you shoulda hung back and cast at me from my blind spot."

"Gracious—my thoughts precisely, large one."

The air crackled with violent menace. It emanated from directly behind the beastfallen—where Los stood, brandishing her gigantic halberd. The massive warrior swung his sword as he whipped around to face her, powerfully rebuffing her attack. The impact sent Los flying backwards toward a tree, but with a light kick against its trunk, she propelled herself up to squat on a high branch. The witch glared at Saybil and the others.

"Run, you fools!"

And run they did.

The beastfallen didn't chase after the fleeing mages. Los hopped down from her perch and squared up against her foe.

"Wilt thou not give chase?"

"What kinda fool d'you take me for? The second I turn my back on you, I can kiss my sweet tail goodbye."

"'Twould seem *thou* hast taken *me* for the forgiving kind. Thy tail would not nearly suffice; wouldst bid farewell to thine entire bottom half."

The beastfallen lowered his sword.

Los continued. "What's this? Dost thou intend to retreat?"

"I'm a mercenary. I don't pick fights I can't win. How's about we make ourselves a little deal? Let me go, and I'll hold off on killing those brats—for now, anyway."

"What cowardly nonsense is this? I need only strike thee down to ensure their safety—forever."

The hulking beastfallen swished his tail back and forth. After staring him down for a moment, Los let out a sigh.

"I see… Kill thee, and those behind thee would spring into action—is that it?"

"Always nice to do business with people who catch on quick. There's a little village up ahead. A village my master controls. If I don't come back, one of the townspeople'll pay for it to teach the others a lesson."

He went on: "All I wanted was for the runt to go back to the village. And those 'field program apprentices,' they went running straight for it, you follow? No point fightin' to the death with you just to chase after 'em."

"Hmph." Los tapped her halberd against the ground, transforming it back into a harmless staff, thereby signaling that she'd accepted the truce. The beastfallen accordingly sheathed his mighty sword.

"Interesting staff you got there," he growled, grinning.

"Is it not? A fine staff, indeed."

"Sure is—the Staff of Ludens, huh."

Los's eyes widened. "How dost thou—?!" But the beastfallen turned his back to her before she could finish her question.

"You better go after your precious students. Until we meet again."

With that, the mercenary vanished deep into the woods. Los watched him disappear, then studied her staff. Nothing about its appearance should have revealed its true identity to a piddling mercenary at first glance. The only ones who would know were witches as long-lived as Los—or those who made their living hunting witches...?

## 2

"Father! I'm baaack!"

"Laios... You had us worried, running off without a word like that."

After fleeing from the beastfallen, the three mages-in-training had followed the boy—Laios—until they arrived at a small chapel on the outskirts of a village. It was surrounded by cultivated fields, and a herd of cows rested lazily in their pen.

In the chapel's front garden stood a young priest. As soon as Laios caught sight of him, he broke into a smile and raced up to the

clergyman, throwing his little arms around him.

The three apprentices looked at each other before cautiously approaching the priest. None of them had particularly warm feelings toward the clergy, thanks in no small part to the Arbiter who had attacked them during their journey. But once they saw that the priest, who seemed sincerely pleased at Laios's return, wore a blindfold over both eyes and was leaning on a cane, their wariness naturally abated. The priest's neatly cut shoulder-length hair was a striking jade green, and though his eyes were hidden, it was clear he was a very handsome man.

Jumping up and latching onto the priest's waist, Laios pointed at Saybil and his friends. "They say they're mages from Wenias, Father."

"Wenias? Then you must be the special field training students..."

"Wait, you know about us, too?!" Saybil was flabbergasted.

The priest cocked his head. "Headmaster Albus sent you here, did she not? In which case it's only natural for the inhabitants here to have a working knowledge of the program, wouldn't you say—how dimwitted are you?" he explained, tacking on an unnecessary insult. The priest quickly caught himself, however, and covered his mouth.

"Forgive me. After many long years of holding nothing but rancor for witches, I accidentally lashed out at you mages as well."

"W-What an asshole..."

"Shh! Quiet, Kudo!" scolded Hort.

"These guys saved me. The mercenary went all *slash!* with his sword, and they got me outta the way!"

"...Oh? So you stood your ground against the mercenary? A somewhat reckless decision, one might say." The priest turned toward the apprentices.

"E-Excuse me…Father?" Hort began, ever so timidly. "What in the world was that all about? That beastfallen—"

"Leave this place." The clergyman pointed in the direction they had just come from. "This village is not fit for the field training program, not anymore. I urge you to return to the Kingdom of Wenias."

"What…?! But, um, I'm sure we could help in some way. We can use magic, you know, so if you tell us what's going on, maybe we can do something about it…" Hort insisted.

"Magic…?" The priest smiled grimly. "Your trifling sleight of hand won't mean anything to her. You met the mercenary, did you not? His master is the witch who has this village in her iron grip. None can oppose her."

"But," said Saybil, "Headmaster Albus said an incredible witch with the power to destroy the world lives here… What happened to her?"

Letting out a long sigh, the priest gently shook his head. "Witches are above all else self-interested and capricious creatures. Two years ago, another witch arrived and demanded control of the village. Our resident witch balked at the thought of battle and surrendered it to her without a fight."

"That's awful…" *How could she hand it over so easily? She just abandoned the village, like it didn't matter at all?*

"In any event…our situation is not all that dire. As you can see, we were spared our lives. And we've been promised peace, so long as we do not rebel."

"You're tryin'a call a mercenary chasing after a kid and threatening to snap his friends' legs 'peace'?"

The priest said nothing. Kudo continued his tirade. "If it's really so peaceful here, why'd that kid try to escape? What was he runnin' away from?"

"That is not something an outsider would understand."

"I was trying to get to Wenias," Laios spoke up, taking over for the evasive priest. "I thought maybe if I found that Albus lady, I could get her to fight the witch for us."

"Th-That's a great point, Father!" Hort smiled. "Y-You're right. We're total outsiders who only just got here, and we don't know exactly what happened. But, we *were* attacked by a beastfallen. That's not normal—and it's definitely not peace. So, maybe if we explain the situation to Headmaster Albus, she'll—"

Again, the priest sighed. "Do you...really think Headmaster Albus is unaware of our predicament?"

"...Huh?"

*I've had a bad feeling about this ever since I saw that summons on the bulletin board. If Albus already knew what was going on here... If she knew, and just let it happen—and deliberately sent us into the middle of it...*

"Headmaster Albus herself approved the 'changing of the witches.' Evidently she isn't interested in the particulars of village governance so long as it continues to function and has a resident witch. I imagine Headmaster Albus might be moved to intervene should the witch shed the blood of the villagers... However, this witch intends to sustain the village in order to extort taxes from its inhabitants. In that, hers and Headmaster Albus's interests align."

"But then," Hort began, her lips trembling, "are you saying... the headmaster sent us to the village knowing we'd never be able to actually do our field training? Knowing we were doomed from the start? If she did...and if we just give up and go back, we're gonna be..."

"...Expelled...?" Saybil was the one to drop the bombshell, but they were all thinking it.

Kudo exploded with anger. "You saying the headmaster was tryin'a get us expelled from the very beginning?!" He hoped someone would refute the possibility.

But the priest simply answered, "I'm afraid so." In validating their fears, he drove a stake deep into the hearts of the three youths who'd journeyed through so much to arrive at this place.

"And we're supposed to just accept that and go, 'Well, if you say so'...?! Why don't we just do somethin' about that witch who's taken over the village? What about the Church and Mage Brigade? Their whole thing is being the shield to protect witches and the sword to defend the Church, right? I bet they could sort this out."

"Why would they?"

"Huh?"

"What reward would they reap for saving our humble, insignificant village, when they could conceivably lose a thousand soldiers in a battle against such a powerful witch? The ends do not justify the sacrifice."

"Who gives a shit about rewards?! The Church and Mage Brigade aren't a bunch of greedy mercs! They're virtuous knights whose work is supported by alms and donations!"

"Quite the devoted admirer, I see..."

Kudo sneered. "Once I graduate, I'm gonna join the Brigade's magical battalion. It's been my goal since before I ever started at the Academy."

"My, my. That is a commendable ambition—however," the priest continued, "around here, they call themselves the *Knights of the Church*. Furthermore, our village was built at a witch's behest. The plight of such a village, now subjugated by another witch and her beastfallen mercenary though it may be, will inspire no more than derision. They won't stake their lives for our sake."

*In order to spread understanding of the benefits of magic in the South, I have created a village with its own witch,* Albus had said. *Go to this village, where witches receive equal treatment, and find a way to help its inhabitants.* But despite all that, Albus had abandoned this place in its time of need, and, to add insult to injury, used it as a tool to relieve herself of a few burdensome students.

*She's terrifying.*

Rumors Saybil had heard about Albus rushed back to him, rumors he had put no stock in at the time. *What's so scary about her?* he'd thought. *She's actually really nice.*

And yet.

"Why do you believe this man?" a voice called out from above. Saybil looked up. There was Los, sitting on a branch, swinging her legs as she peered down at her wards. Saybil had no idea when she'd gotten there.

Hort shouted with joy. "Professor Los! Oh, thank Goddess you're safe!"

"Our beastfallen friend proved to be a sensible sort. We did not so much as engage," the witch replied drolly as she leapt down from her perch. Without a pause, she marched right up to the priest and began circling him like a shark. "But never mind that. Do you not find this man rather suspect? Without evidence proving the contrary, how can you claim with any certainty that he is not in league with the beastfallen?"

Saybil glanced at the priest. "Well, um... He just doesn't look, you know..."

Timidly, Hort added, "He's, well, his eyes..."

This priest—blind, supported by a cane, and dispatched to a village promoting co-existence between humans and witches—seemed to be the very symbol of misfortune, the archetype of weakness.

But Los simply snickered at the suggestion. "His eyes? What of them? What difference does it make if he can or cannot see? To all appearances I am but an adorable young lass, while in truth I am a witch of great renown. In the absence of sufficient justification for trust, I shall maintain my skepticism—whether faced with a cherubic child or a blind priest."

"How very discourteous, especially for one dropping in unannounced... Given your insistence on sufficient reason for trust, I presume you must have adequate cause to view me with suspicion?"

"Of course," Los replied curtly. "That beastfallen mercenary—he knew I was the escort for these students here."

"Huh? How?!"

"Odd, is it not? As you can all plainly see, I appear to be naught but an innocent child. I would have forgiven him mistaking me for another student, but how did he discern I was your guardian?"

Saybil considered the question. If appearances didn't provide any real information, there was only one explanation. "Someone... told him ahead of time?"

"My thoughts precisely. Still, the question remains: who? And to what end? Wait, I do believe I have an inkling—a certain Church-affiliated individual who attempted to murder my precious students during our journey."

"Ah!" Kudo exclaimed. "That Arbiter...! You sayin' the bastard blabbed about us after he got away?!"

Los continued to elaborate on her theory. "Let us say the Arbiter reported to the Church, which then shared this information with the clergyman before us. If we furthermore assume the priest then passed this information on to the witch in order to protect his standing in the village and exploit the villagers in concert with her, it gives us a simple explanation for how our beastfallen friend knew of me. What sayest thou? Sufficient cause for suspicion, wouldst not agree?"

"...Hmm, it would appear so." The priest heaved a deep sigh. "Just to clarify, an Arbiter of Dea Ignis attacked you and your students on your way here?"

"And a vicious attack it was, too. A behemoth of a man swinging an enormous hammer. One of our number lost both his hands, while another's maiden secret was revealed."

"Professor Los! 'Maiden secret'?! Don't make it sound so gross!"

"An enormous hammer... The Tyrant, then," said the priest. "I see... It's a wonder you escaped."

"Rather coy, aren't we?" Los remarked, making an exaggerated show of turning her face to the heavens.

"I trust you can no longer say with confidence that your deductions about me are correct. If you believed me so firmly to be your enemy, would it not be wisest to kill me straight off? Since you cannot bring yourself to do it, I presume you are not entirely certain of your suspicions."

"'Twould be child's play to kill thee. However, I have a great love of closely considering proclamations of innocence. If thou dost insist I have misapprehended the situation, then thou wouldst of course gladly guide us to the village, yes? If we see for ourselves how the villagers behave around thee, or what they say to thee...it may yet dispel our suspicions."

"I'm not good enough?" pouted Laios, still glued to the priest's side.

Los swooped in uncomfortably close to the boy's face and said, "Even the most disgraceful fiends have devoted followers. Who is to say this priest is not in fact thy father?"

"He's not! My papa's waaay bigger!"

"Well then, take us to him. I should very much like to speak with thy father."

"But..." Laios looked up at the priest. He seemed to be watching the man's reaction closely.

With another deep sigh, the priest conceded: "...As you please." And with that, he nudged Laios to lead the way, and they set off down the path toward the village.

**3**

The motley gang followed the path from the chapel until they came to a gate constructed of stout logs stood on end, which marked the entrance to the village. As soon as he spotted the burly man standing beside it, Laios broke into a run.

"Papaaa! See? *This* is my Papa!"

"Laios!" The man started to run, too. The two rushed toward each other like charging boars, and when they slammed together, the man lifted Laios high up into the air, spinning him round and round. "Laios! I'm so glad you're okay!"

"He's quite unharmed," the priest quietly reassured the other man.

Tears welling in his eyes, the man nodded, an amiable smile stretching across his face from ear to ear. "Thank you so much, Father! I was so...so worried...!"

"It is not me you have to thank. He came back all on his own… with these youngsters in tow."

"Ohhh? And they are?"

"The special field training apprentices, evidently."

"What?! You didn't tell them to turn back?!"

"I did, in fact." The priest looked to the sky with an exhausted air. "They apparently suspect I work under orders from the mercenary and the witch who controls the village."

"Ahhh! Well, can't blame 'em! You do seem mighty shady!" the man said with a hearty guffaw. Laios laughed loudly along with his father. The man brushed past the silent priest and strolled up to Saybil and the others. They could almost feel his passion for life warm the air with every step closer he took.

"The name's Uls. Thanks for bringing my son back to me. But, hmm… So you're the field training students, huh…? Talk about a raw deal. I get it, though, it must be hard to believe. Can't feel good to hear that the head honcho of the school you've been studying at all these years was hoping for you to fail out."

The pity in the man's eyes made Saybil's heart twinge. Neither Hort nor Kudo knew exactly how to react either, and awkwardly let their gazes fall to the ground.

"Well, don't let it get you down! There's plenty o' things you can do with your life! Hey Father, mind if I take these young'uns to one of the vacant houses? Must've been a long trip from Wenias, and I'll bet they could use a good night's sleep before they head back."

"I have no objections, but…" The priest turned his blindfolded eyes in the direction of the group.

Los spoke for them all. "I thank thee for thy kindness. We gratefully accept the offer."

"Yay!" Laios hollered. "I'm coming too! Let me show them around!"

Los urged her crestfallen pupils along and followed Uls into the village. True to his word, Laios peppered them with facts as they walked along the main road.

"We're all working together to build up the village. And guess what? I'm the *only* kid that was born here. That's why I'm everybody's favorite," he declared proudly.

His father gave him a light rap on the head. "There you go again, you little braggart. We love all the children here equally! The only ones who treat you special are me and your ma!"

"That's not true! The witch lady put a spell on me when I was born so that everyone would like me, remember?" Laios insisted, before catching himself with an, "Oh!"

"Um...I mean the *last* witch lady. Not the one we've got now. 'Member that barrier in the forest? She's the one who set that up for us, too. She said some bad people might try to come after us someday since there's a witch in our village, so we needed someplace safe to hide."

"And a magnificent barrier 'twas indeed. Not often in my long life have I come across a witch who could create one such as that, and leave it intentionally incomplete to boot."

Uls nodded. "Right you are. She was an incredible witch. The pride o' the village."

"If she was really that incredible, why the hell did she just give the place up without a fight?" sneered Kudo. Hort elbowed him in the ribs.

A troubled look clouded Uls's face. "Hard to know how to answer that. I wonder myself. Who knows what goes on in a witch's mind? She was with us from the very beginning, building this place from the ground up, but..." He trailed off, surveying the village lovingly.

It was a small settlement, seemingly built on the ruins of a previously abandoned village, such that old, dilapidated houses leaned unsteadily amidst newly renovated dwellings. The town square had a well in the middle, and was surrounded by a clinic, a shuttered tavern, and the like. A hush enveloped the entire village. Still, that didn't mean it was uninhabited. Sayb noticed people nervously peeking out at them from behind their curtains.

"Remarkably quiet, this village," Los observed.

Uls nodded. "We don't get many visitors round here, so people get skittish and hole up at home. We're a pretty small village as it stands... Then again, more people means more mouths to feed, so it's not as easy as askin' more to join us. Laios here's the only child born in the village these last five years. All the others're orphans. It takes a village to raise 'em, and that we do. When Laios came, they were all jumpin' for joy that they had a new 'baby brother'...and he let it get to his head."

Uls ruffled his son's hair. "It was a difficult labor, and we almost lost both my wife and the baby. But thankfully we had a witch in the village. She really was somethin'. She could heal any injury or illness right quick. And in the winter she'd use her scrying to tell us where the good huntin' was. That's the only reason we made it through without starvin' to death.

"But," he went on in a slightly more hushed tone, "things aren't all that different now compared to two years ago. We just can't leave the village anymore. That, and now we have to pay taxes to the witch. 'Bout half the villagers are pretty unhappy about it, and the other half don't seem to mind too much."

"So thy son falls into the former group...?"

Uls forced a smile. "Thanks for bringing him back. People fleein' the village is the one thing the witch and her mercenary won't abide. Well, here we are. This here's the finest vacant house in the village."

The house was in a nicer area on what seemed to be the main road, just a short walk from the town square.

*Why is there a vacant house in a spot like this?*

The thought had hardly crossed Saybil's mind when he looked up to find something dangling down the wall of the two-story house.

"Hey, check that out." Hort pointed at the dangling figures blowing gently in the wind—human figures.

"Ahh, don't mind those. They're just dolls." Uls smiled at Hort, who had gone white as a sheet. "One for each o' the people who lived here last. I'm not at liberty to say what happened, but this house opened up when they tried to make a run for it. The dolls're there to discourage anyone from gettin' the same idea. Anyone except the kiddos who can't remember two years back, 'course."

Saybil craned his neck to study the dolls. Upon closer inspection, he could see they were just straw-filled bags dressed in human clothes. Even so, the effect was painfully ominous.

"I'll bring over some bread and wine later in the evening. It's not exactly fine livin', but...I hope you'll be able to get comfortable and relax."

With that, Uls took his son's hand and walked away. Los watched them go, tapping her staff on her shoulder.

"Interesting," she muttered under her breath. "Hmm... Very interesting," and so on, as she crossed the threshold into the empty house. Scanning the neat and tidy space, she continued her chorus of "Interesting, interesting."

The three apprentices followed her nervously into the house, at which she whirled about to face them.

"Right," she declared. "We shall kill this witch."

"What?! Where the hell did that come from?!" Kudo shouted.

"While we're at it, we shall do away with Albus as well." Los was smiling—and dead serious.

"C-Calm down, Professor Los!" pleaded Hort. "Killing the headmaster won't solve anything!"

"Is it not thoroughly vexing, though? The contract I signed stipulated that I lead the students to the village and hand them over to the care of the witch who would supervise them. And yet, such a witch does not exist. That cursed Albus deceived not only you three, but she dared dupe me as well!"

"So...you did all this work for nothing?"

"Indeed. The same goes for you three, does it not? No field program can be conducted in a village bereft of the designated supervisor. You three shall be expelled, and all memories of magic wiped from your minds."

Los took a deep, deep breath. Then, after a very pregnant pause, she erupted. "Graaaah! The more I think of it, the greater my wrath at that incorrigible brat grows! My forbearance is at its end! How dare they make such a fool of me! I shall hurl her *and* her third-rate servant into the furnace together, smelt them down, and mold them into a new staff!" Los ranted, stomping around like a child in the throes of a tantrum.

"I have made up my mind, little ducklings! I shall finish this job if it be the last thing I do. They have yet to see the true fury of the Dawn Witch! Bwaha, bwahaha, bwahahahahaha!!!"

"...Dude, what do we do?"

"Hmm... This is a tough one, huh, Sayb?"

"I mean, I really don't want to get kicked out and lose my memories, but..."

Los's exaggerated maniacal laughter did little to get the three apprentices on board with her plan.

"Youths these days! So disappointing. Utterly lacking in zeal. Do you intend to give up all for lost, simply because your headmaster deems you unworthy?"

"You don't think I'm pissed off outta my mind?! But...I'm just tryin'a live to see another day. Kill the witch who runs this town? Just the four of us? No way in hell we can pull that off."

"I hate to admit it," Hort said, "but I think Kudo's got a point. Maybe there's another way, though? I know the priest said the Brigade doesn't really cooperate with witches and mages in these parts, but...if we go back to Wenias and explain the situation to the battalion there, maybe they could help?"

Saybil considered the situation.

*Kudo may have gone total pessimist, but Hort's way too optimistic. And, most importantly—*

"We haven't met the witch yet."

"So what?" Kudo demanded.

"Are we really going to ask the Church and Mage Brigade to kill a witch we haven't even laid eyes on? Uls and the priest both said that things aren't that bad here, that nobody has to die as long as they follow the rules. But what would happen to this place if we brought the Brigade here?"

Hort caught on. "It'd probably...turn into a battlefield. If the witch fights back...she might even use the villagers as hostages."

"So—" Saybil began.

"I think we need to do this on our own."

In other words, he agreed to Los's plan. They would kill the witch. But they had to do it on their own.

"Let's find the witch and talk to her. If she really is evil, we'll fight. That's what I think we should do."

Baring his teeth, Kudo shouted, "Who the hell do you think you are?! Seriously, don't you get it? You're a washout—the biggest failure the Academy's ever seen! I get that you might be feelin' all high on yourself 'cos you've got this never-ending supply of mana or whatever, but that doesn't change shit! You still can't even use magic!"

"But if I'm around, you and Hort can cast all the spells you want. Plus, we've got Professor Los, and I could probably stun the witch if I grab the Staff of Ludens again. If we get her with a sneak attack while she's dazed, maybe—"

"That's not gonna work, dumbass!"

Kudo's livid cry pierced Saybil's eardrums. But for once he didn't back down.

"So you want us to just sit back and let them kick us out of the Academy? If that happens, we'll be abandoning this village. We'd be pretending we never saw anything, and choosing to forget everything. I don't want that."

*I don't want to forget. Not about magic, or about this journey, or about Los, or Hort, or Kudo.*

Kudo grabbed Saybil by the collar and got in his face. "Get off your high horse, you stupid fuckin' washout! The only reason you can run your mouth like that is 'cos your head's in the clouds! Do you even hear yourself? You're telling us to go into a battle we know we can't win. You're telling us to die!"

"Kudo! Stop it! That's not what Sayb was trying to—"

"I don't give a shit what he was *trying* to say! He said what he said!"

"I...!" Saybil choked out, barely able to breathe. "I'm going with Professor Los, even if it's just the two of us."

"Wha—"

"I realized something. Back when the Arbiter was trying to kill us, when I went to reach for the Staff of Ludens... I—" Saybil grabbed Kudo's arm and threw it off him. "I'm not afraid of dying."

When he took hold of the staff, determined to lay down his life if he had to in order to protect Los and the others, Saybil had felt an overwhelming sense of...calm. He didn't fear the end of his life. In fact, deep down inside, he probably—

"...*I'm* afraid," came the reply, though not from Kudo.

Saybil turned to Hort. "...Sorry. Of course. Most people are. That's why I won't ask you to come with me. You and Kudo can find a safe spot away from the village and wait. If we take the witch down I'll send someone to get you, and if nobody comes after a while, you can just head back to Wenias."

"What are you talking about...?" Hort said stiffly. "That's not what I meant. I'm saying I don't want *you* to die, Sayb!!"

"Huh? Why?"

Hort was left utterly speechless. She stared at Saybil in dismay, tears welling in her eyes, but Saybil had no idea what was making her cry.

"Huh? What? Wait, why are you cryi—"

"It's your fault, dipshit," said Kudo, striking the follow-up blow.

"'Tis thou who art to blame, young Sayb." Los broke her silence to finish him off.

To make matters worse, Hort dashed out of the house, still rubbing the tears from her eyes.

"Hort!" Saybil tried to run after her, but Los tripped him with her staff and sent him sprawling.

"What dost thou intend if dost catch her, young Sayb?"

"Huh...? I mean, apologize..."

"For?"

"For making her cry...!"

"No, no, no. 'Tis the worst response thou couldst have given. Unclear as to what thou hast done to offend, didst think she might regain her cheery composure if thou didst but apologize? 'Tis the epitome of a terrible apology."

"What a total moron."

"Excessively low regard for thyself can at times hurt others—young Kudo, educate this numbskull on the subject of what brought Hort to tears."

"I mean, she's your friend, dude," the reptilian beastfallen said without hesitation.

Saybil froze. "...Huh?"

"Hort's over here tryin'a tell you she doesn't want her friend to throw away his life, and you look her straight in the face and say, 'You're in no position to feel sad about my death,'" he went on, imitating Saybil's voice perfectly.

Saybil looked out in the direction Hort had fled.

*My friend—*

Just as Saybil had hated the thought of losing his memories of Hort and the others, Hort had hated the thought of losing Saybil.

*She didn't want to lose me. I'd never even considered that. Dammit—!*

Saybil was fed up with himself for how little he understood others.

"I...I'm going to go say sorry!"

Saybil got up, and this time he really did run out the door.

"Oh hoh, what it is to be young."

Los watched fondly as Saybil chased after his friend, then took staff in hand and began inspecting the house.

Kudo watched her putter about for a bit, then called out, "Hey."

"Yes?"

"You really think…we can win?"

"Who can say…? We may. Then again, we may not."

"Which is it?!"

"Not even I know all, young Kudo. There are some things I cannot determine with any real certainty."

Los poked around in the cabinets until she spotted a good-sized pot, then grabbed a few herbs she found in a drawer and tossed them in.

Though it did strike him as pretty strange that there'd be such things in an uninhabited house, Kudo turned back to the more pressing issue at hand: Los's evaluation of the situation.

"In other words, we could lose, right? We might die?"

"'Twould stand to reason."

"How is that worth the risk?! We're fighting for our futures here, but you're just messing around. You could walk away from it all, even the contract with Headmaster Albus, if you just gave up on the *Grimoire of Zero*. You don't have a single dog in this fight."

Los walked over to the kitchen in search of water. Kudo followed after. A ewer sat in a corner of the room, filled to the brim with fresh, clean water. Los poured it into the pot, which she then hoisted onto a trivet atop the stove.

"Young Kudo, a fire, if thou wilt. Canst cast such a spell, canst thee not?"

"Answer me, Professor."

"I am in the very midst of the attempt! Come, light the fire. Quickly, now!"

Kudo clicked his tongue, but obediently lit a fire in the stove. Flames rose through the opening to heat the bottom of the pot, accompanied by Los's happy cries of, "Oh, how convenient! Lovely!

"And I have already given thee my answer, young Kudo. Entertainment is the stuff of my life. I shall stop at nothing to eliminate those who would take this from me. And, at this moment," she paused, pointing at Kudo, "mine entertainment is you three."

"Huh?"

"You call me Professor, do you not? Titles mold the people who bear them. In merely a matter of days, I have completely given myself over to this role as your teacher. Though our time together has been brief, the fledglings I have protected and guided into the air are about to be brought cruelly crashing down to earth—an end I do not wish to see. I have no love for simplistic tragedies, nor shall I allow anyone to trample upon my beloved students' denouement."

"I have no idea what you're talkin' about... You tryin'a say we're just here to amuse you?"

"And I shall gladly risk my life for such amusement."

Having steeped the leaves until their color and fragrance permeated the water, Los now poured the boiling, pale green brew into two cups. One she brought to her lips, while the other she handed to Kudo. Without a word, the beastfallen accepted the cup, and, taking a sip, felt a refreshing tingle pass through his nostrils.

"I do not give up, nor do I compromise. After all, I live for pleasure. I obtain the outcome I desire, by whatever means necessary. And in the service of that," Los smiled, "I do not shrink from death."

Kudo opened his mouth to speak, then shut it again.

*You sound like Saybil. No point in saying so, 'course. But—*

"I'm afraid."

Repeating Hort's words, Kudo drained his cup and left the room.

Hort did not fear scorn. The solution for that was simple: win over those who disdained her. When she turned the full force of her beguiling smile on someone who didn't like her, Hort almost felt as if she were going into battle.

But indifference—that, more than anything, she couldn't stand. She could brush it off when people insulted her, called her "devil child," but seeing them awkwardly avert their eyes destroyed her. She would take a hateful fist over a cold shoulder any day.

That's why it had shaken her to the core when Saybil showed her such indifference. Sure, they hadn't known each other long, but in that time, they'd traveled together, faced a murderous Arbiter together, scraped by with their lives, and shared deep secrets they'd kept hidden up 'til then—for Saybil to outright deny any meaningful connection in the face of all that, well, it shocked her beyond belief.

Fleeing pell-mell from the vacant house, Hort eventually found herself outside the small chapel. She stepped in apprehensively, only to find it empty. Hort quietly prayed to the statue of the Goddess enshrined there, and almost immediately, her wild heart slowed its pounding. She let out a long sigh.

"Ah, dammit… Look at me. I seem more like a devoted believer than a mage…"

"…Is that bad?"

Hort flinched, not having expected a response to her soliloquy, and whipped around to see where the voice had originated. There she saw a small—as in no taller than Hort's waist—child standing at the entrance to the sanctuary. Cloaked from head to toe in a robe, hood pulled down low over her eyes, the child was somehow unsettling.

"Are you...with the Church?"

"Lily was cleaning nice and tidy," said the child—Lily—as she hugged the broom tight to her chest.

"Oh... Sorry, I didn't mean to get in the way," Hort replied. "Why are you dressed like that?"

"Um..." Lily looked around cautiously. "I-It'll be bad if they see Lily talking to you. But you were crying, so..."

Surprised, Hort hurriedly wiped away the tear stains that remained on her cheeks.

"Are you sad...?"

"Uh-uh. No, I just got into a fight with a friend...but it's okay, we'll make up."

"Oh, good," said Lily. Though she couldn't see her face, Hort could tell from her voice that the child was smiling. After looking around furtively again, Lily pitter-pattered closer to the mage. "You know, um, it's okay."

"Huh?"

"Mages can be believers, too. The Father always says so."

"...He does, huh."

*I know she's just a child, but hearing that does make me feel better. Does she live here in the chapel? Maybe if I talk to her, she can help me prove the priest isn't lying to us.*

"Hey, Lily. Do you like the Father?"

"What...! H-How? How did you know?" Still hugging the broom close, Lily squirmed bashfully. The cuteness of it all almost made Hort reach out and pat her head.

However—

"Lily."

—the priest's voice made them both jump.

"Eep!" The hooded Lily squeaked and scurried off in a flash. The priest listened as her footsteps retreated, then quietly sighed.

"Goddess help me... After all my warnings not to come out here..."

"Um, I'm sorry! She came out to comfort me because I was crying. So please, don't be mad at her!"

"Are you really in any position to be worrying about someone else?" the priest asked, exasperated. Puzzled, Hort cocked her head.

"Your chaperone has great misgivings about me."

"Oh, right. Umm... Guess not?"

"I see. So you're a naughty student." Amused, the priest grinned, which made Hort smile back. *Tnk, tnk*, his cane struck the stone floor, echoing through the nave. He walked over to the door Lily had left wide open as she fled, shut it, then leaned against it facing Hort. "So, you had a disagreement with your friend?"

"Y-You heard that?!"

"My hearing is one of my better qualities," he replied, tapping a finger beside his ear.

"Oh, right... It's, um, really not that big of a deal. I just, like, had kind of a shock, and I know my friend didn't mean to hurt me or anything, but I just kind of started crying and ran away..."

"I see... Sounds like a simple misunderstanding. In that case, I believe you two can still find ways to forgive each other."

*Forgive each other.* The reassurance lifted a weight off Hort's shoulders. *I know what Saybil's like. I know that he actually thinks really deeply about things under that unmoving mask. It's just that he doesn't know—how to express his emotions, how to relate to other people, what's normal, what constitutes a connection.*

Hort realized she shouldn't have simply run away crying. No matter what Saybil thought of her, she viewed him as a friend. She should have told him that.

*Right, it's not too late.*

She wanted to make up with him as soon as possible.

"I should get back. It's kind of like I ran away from home, so I'm sure my friends are worried about me."

"Indeed, it was most reckless of you," agreed the priest. "Running off on your own in a village controlled by a witch."

Again, the priest's staff clicked against the floor, and Hort's attention was drawn to it. It was no longer wrapped in cloth as it had been the first time they met, giving Hort a better view of its structure...and there was something odd about it.

*Is it, like, a folding cane? It looks like it could get longer if you stretched it out.*

As she studied the cane closely, Hort's eyes came to rest on a design engraved into it: the stake and flames of a witch-burning—the emblem of the Dea Ignis Arbiters.

*But how could a blind man ever be—*

"On the subject of misunderstandings and forgiveness—Hort," the priest said tenderly, calling the girl by name—a name she hadn't yet shared with him. "I hear you betrayed the Church?"

*Ahh, Professor.*

Los's instincts had been correct. Hort shouldn't have underestimated this man just because he "looked weak." The Tyrant had obviously reported Hort's treachery to the Church after escaping in the commotion caused by the Staff of Ludens's berserk rampage. And that message had been passed on to the blind priest standing before her now.

*But why would a Dea Ignis Arbiter be stationed in a witch's village? The residents seemed to trust him. Even that little girl, Lily, had so clearly been attached to him. Why would such a man—*

"Oh, no need to be afraid. I do not mean to blame you for it." He took a step closer. "After four years studying at the Academy of Magic, it was only natural your heart would waver. Not to mention, the Tyrant's comportment is a touch violent for my taste."

The next thing Hort knew, she was paralyzed. It felt like something had bound her, rendering her physically unable to move. The restraints cut lightly into her skin as she struggled, drawing blood that trickled—through the open air.

*They're strings!*

Threads too thin to see had bound Hort in place. The priest whipped his cane through the air. A razor-sharp blade slid out with the force of the motion, transforming the cane into a huge scythe.

"H-Help! Professor Los! Sayb! I'd even take Kudo right now! Is anybody out there looking for me?! Hello?!"

"Quiet." The priest pressed a finger against Hort's lips. The blade of his scythe was already at her throat. "Let's you and I have a little chat. Please, don't worry. As long as your heart proves righteous, no one has to get hurt."

**4**

There was something strange about this village. The beastfallen mercenary they had met first, the blind priest, even Laios, Uls, and the other villagers—all of them felt off in some way. The same went for this house, too, which was unusually well-stocked and tidy for a supposedly uninhabited home.

So when Saybil returned crestfallen from his fruitless search for Hort, Los felt a sense of validation.

*I knew it. Something is afoot.*

"Did the villagers witness anything?" she asked Saybil.

"Actually...nobody would come out of their houses to talk to me... Uls said he hadn't seen her, and there was no one at the chapel." After that he just sat there saying, "What are we gonna do?!" over and over.

Los lambasted the dithering youth, then pulled him to his feet and set out toward the forest, following Hort's trail. An exceptional witch could track the presence of another magic-user they had encountered even once, and Hort had cast spells in Los's presence. The bright, powerful trail her magic power left did not require much searching; it almost demanded attention.

"Gracious... 'Tis a more taxing business than I'd ever dreamed, chaperoning these students. Rescuing them from witch hunters, searching for them when they go missing after a lovers' quarrel... Even though we've finally arrived at our destination, I cannot even find time to properly investigate the situation!"

Half lecture and half petty grumbling, Los's muttered soliloquy went on endlessly as she traced Hort's mana trail, with Saybil and Kudo following close behind.

"But I cannot very well leave the other two behind, or they shall be whisked away the very instant I turn my back, taken hostage at the most inopportune moment. I am no fool. I adore theatrical dramas, and as any aficionado knows, one must keep one's weaknesses by one's side at all times."

"Aaargh, quit yer whinin' already! If you hate chaperoning us that much, why doncha just quit?!"

"Preposterous. When did I ever claim to dislike it? I merely called it a 'taxing business.'"

"But that's bad, right?"

"I resent no hardship I have chosen for myself. 'Tis far preferable to boredom."

"Then stop complaining!"

"Whether I complain or not is my prerogative. If thou dost wish to be free of my grumbling tongue, shouldst focus on becoming a mage proficient enough not to require a chaperone— Hmm?" Los stopped short.

"What's that? A cave?"

"So...it would appear."

"Is Hort in there...?"

"So...it would appear," Los said again, peering into the opening. "Halloo!" she called, her voice echoing into the depths. "'Tis a natural cave, and a rather deep one at that."

"But Professor, there's a torch here on the wall."

"Indeed. Caves remain cool within, which suits them perfectly to storing foodstuffs during the hot summer months. Most caves this close to a settlement will have been modified in some way by the nearby residents."

"I know she wanted to be alone, but hiding out in a cave? Who does that?" Kudo said. "What a weirdo."

"I knew it, she must've been kidnapped... And it's all my fault! If I hadn't been so awful to her, she wouldn't have needed to be alone...!"

"Good grief," Los sighed. "Thou art constantly assigning all guilt to thyself...be it now or when Kudo was attacked... Wouldst likely blame thyself if some geezer died after thou didst sneeze in his presence."

"I mean, obviously it'd bother me if an old man died because I sneezed."

"Then stop breathing, dumbass."

"C'mon, Kudo," Saybil protested. "Take it down a notch."

"Young Kudo, a light, if you please. There is some such suitable spell, is there not?"

"It's not meant to be used in place of a torch, ya know..."

"Yet that is how 'tis used."

Kudo silently activated Solm, conjuring up a ball of light that floated in mid-air.

"Whoa, amazing. I didn't know you could cast Solm without the incantation, too."

"'Course I can. Someday I'm gonna be able to cast every single spell there is without saying a word."

Los laughed. "The incantations do make thee blush, after all."

"Shut up! Got a problem with that?"

The three stepped into the cave. They were able to proceed without difficulty thanks to the illumination Solm provided, but Los quickly stopped in her tracks. Saybil and Kudo paused as well. They had no words.

The glow of Kudo's Solm reflected off dark red stains trickling along the ground.

"Blood."

Los stared into the depths of the cave. "And the mana I sense from deep within...belongs not to Hort alone."

Saybil knew instantly what that must mean.

"'Twould appear this is the notorious witch's den. Perhaps she dangled young Hort before us to lure us in like unsuspecting fools."

"Then we're screwed! Shit, this is no joke! Let's go back!"

"No, 'tis a development in our favor. The reigning witch is in essence expressing her wish to meet with us. She's saved us the effort of looking for her."

"How stupid are you?! It's a trap! She's gonna kill us all!" Kudo shrieked.

Los drew in a shallow breath. "A trap...you say?" she mused, a calm smile playing across her lips. No child of her apparent age would ever have adopted such an expression. It was very much the look of a witch, aloof and detached.

"A battle betwixt witches, young Kudo..." Los began.

"Yeah?"

"...is a battle of wits, pitting each against the many layers of traps laid by the other. Unlike the magic you lot study, sorcery can send forth clouds of poisonous gas to far-away lands. In ages past, the Knights of the Church would storm the witch's stronghold to dispel the pestilence, knowing full well all manner of traps awaited them."

Los took a step. Forward. A black mist flowed out of the Staff of Ludens, slithering into the far reaches of the cave. Saybil could tell it was observing what lay within. In a witches' battle, traps were a given. The true contest lay in seeing through them. Los proceeded further into the cave. Saybil followed after.

"I hear from Sayb thou wishest to join the Church and Mage Brigade, young Kudo. As the Church's sword and witches' shield, they do not fear battle with witches. Take that knight who soars through the skies on dragon-back, for one—he challenged a great dragon without a lick of magic at his disposal, and magnificently brought it down. I adore his tales, the deeds of the Dragon Conqueror King—king of a country laid waste by dragons, and symbol of the Church and Mage Brigade."

"Rgh...gh...!" Kudo growled.

Saybil had heard about the Dragon Conqueror King, too—from Kudo, no less. Although the beastfallen was hostile to anyone and everyone, he took on a childlike wonder when (and only when) he spoke of the famous knight.

"Wilt thou be a brave and dauntless warrior, or a terrified villager fleeing in confusion? The choice is thine."

Kudo lifted a foot, but could not seem to take that step forward. "Th-This is bullshit! I'm not stickin' around for this!"

When Saybil looked behind him, Kudo had already turned his back and begun trudging off towards the entrance.

"You're just headin' to your deaths! Runnin' straight to your own doom isn't courage! Go get yourselves killed if you want! I don't give a shit even if I do get expelled!"

"Kudo...!" Saybil started to call out to him, but gave it up. He had nothing he could say to stop him—because he knew he shouldn't.

Once Kudo had gone, Los paused and glanced over her shoulder. "A sound argument... 'Twould seem he needed one more push," she muttered to herself.

"Were you trying to light a fire under him?"

"And yet the tinder would not catch. A young man's heart is a fickle thing. Well, so be it. Come, Sayb, produce for us one of those balls of light. 'Tis unbearably dark without young Kudo."

"R-Right!" Saybil began the incantation. At which an abnormally brilliant flash of blinding light flared into existence.

"Egaaah!" Los screamed. "What was that?! An explosion?!"

"S-Sorry. I'm a little nervous... I'll get it this time. I'll do it right."

Saybil invoked the spell once more. This time a tiny ball of light no bigger than his pinky nail appeared. They looked at each other, stone-faced.

"...Didst not say thou hadst all thy currently known spells under control?"

"...Um... Should I go get Kudo...?"

"...No. We shall make do with this." The witch sighed.

"I'm sorry..."

"Good grief... If only I could use magic myself..." Suddenly, Los blinked and whipped around to look at Saybil. "I do believe I've had a marvelous idea," she announced, smirking. And what a sinister smirk it was.

"You leave 'em for dead?"

Kudo jumped at the voice that addressed him as he left the cave. A shadow pulled away from behind a tree—a *white* shadow.

"You—You're that—!"

"So? You leave 'em for dead or what? You done with them?" The beastfallen mercenary brought a hand to the hilt of his sword and stared Kudo down.

"What if I did? It's none a yer damn business."

"Oh, but it is. I like you, kid."

"Wha...What?"

"If you're finished with them, there's nothin' to stop you from joinin' up with me, is there? As you know, it's my job to watch over the village. That said, I'm basically a glorified shepherd. Thing is, my master's lookin' to add some sheep to the flock— So? How 'bout it? The villagers'll hate ya, but it ain't bad livin'. Better than bein' a bandit or a soldier, anyway."

"Shepherd." The beastfallen had tossed the word out as if he thought of the villagers as nothing more than livestock. But he had known Kudo and the others were part of the special field training program. In which case, he probably also knew they'd get expelled if they couldn't fulfill the requirements. Most failed beastfallen mages eventually wound up as either robbers or mercenaries—an eventuality the man standing before Kudo knew very well.

But—

"Why the hell would I wanna work for some witch?!" Kudo hissed. "If you're lookin' for friends, look somewhere else."

"You could learn more magic, *friend*."

Kudo froze in his tracks. "...What?"

"You were at the Academy, right? Then you should know that witches who've studied sorcery can create their own magic—magic that Wenias won't be able to interfere with. The way I hear it, the Academy wipes away all your memories of magic if you get kicked out. But you could start over from scratch."

"...Not interested. It's not that I wanna be a mage—I just wanted to get into the Church and Mage Brigade. Once you graduate, you can get a recommendation from the Academy."

"That right?"

"So it won't mean shit if I learn magic *after* I get expelled!"

"I can get you in. To the Brigade, I mean."

Kudo's eyes widened.

"Stay in the merc business long enough and you meet all sortsa people. So as long as you agree to work for me until I find another shepherd, I'll get ya in. I promise."

"Wha... Are you for real, old man?!"

"Who the hell you callin' 'old man'?!" the mercenary growled, then cocked his head. "Huh, maybe I am gettin' to be that age...? Well, whatever. Glad you finally turned around. If you're good with those terms, I'll even sign a witch's blood contract with you. Then if I go back on my word, the demonic power in the contract'll rub me out forever."

Kudo looked back toward the cave. In that instant, his wavering heart once again came to rest. He remembered why they'd come to this cave in the first place: that patronizing girl who was always shouting at him and telling him off. She wasn't the type to disappear without saying a word. And the blood in the cave—it had definitely smelled like her.

"...Hey, old man."

"You've really got a shitty personality, you know that...? Not that I mind."

"What happened to Hort?"

"Hort? ...Oh, the brat with the cap." The mercenary chuckled. "I snapped her neck and had me a snack. Tasty little thing, too. Young girls really do have the tenderest meat."

"Eh...?! Wh...huh?! Y-You...ate her...?! Huh?! You ate Hort?!"

"What? Never eaten a human before? Man, you must've had a pretty easy life. Whenever we start feelin' a real deep self-loathing on account o' these bodies of ours, beastfallen get hit with a craving for human flesh. Carnal rage, we call it."

Kudo put his hand over his heart. The impulse to kill and eat humans was one he had admittedly felt. But he'd never let it overwhelm him. And yet, this guy was talking about it like it was the most natural thing in the world.

"If you do come on board, I'm gonna need you to do a job for me first," the mercenary explained. "Go run after your little friends. The witch I work for is waiting deep inside the cave. They're heading down there to fight her, right? I want you to go along and pretend nothing's changed, then flip at an opportune moment and kill them."

"...You slimy piece of shit...!"

A current of rage shot through Kudo's body, setting all his scales standing on edge. He'd turned his back on Saybil and Los only moments earlier, telling them he didn't care if they threw away their lives. He'd thought they were being reckless. Unlike Saybil, the thought of death terrified Kudo. He always put on a tough act, but in truth, he was constantly trembling with fear. He'd thought studying magic had made him stronger, until the Arbiter had made mincemeat of him like that. What could a weakling like him ever do? At most he'd probably just lose his head and end up getting in Los's way.

That's why he'd turned back—no, run away. And yet here he stood, facing a battle-hardened mercenary who was overwhelmingly more powerful than he was, but Kudo didn't feel afraid. Another emotion had completely overridden any fear: rage.

"Whaddaya say? Up for it?"

"Not a fucking chance!" Kudo erupted. He had his incantation ready to go. His scales raced straight past the red of excitement and turned a slightly phosphorescent blue.

The mercenary's ears drooped in disappointment—or so it seemed, until he broke out into a toothy grin. "Now I like you even more. You pass—or at least I'd like to say so, but I think I'm gonna let you show me just how willin' you are to put your money where your mouth is!"

## 5

The path leading into the belly of the cave continued in a long, gentle decline. All Saybil and Los heard as they walked along were their own footsteps echoing around them. All conversation had dried up some time ago. This being a witch's den, they had almost certainly attracted her attention the moment they set foot inside. Los said there was no point in trying to conceal their presence, but at the same time, it made Saybil nervous just waltzing in like they owned the place.

"So tell me, young Sayb," Los began, as if it had just occurred to her. "Regarding Hort..." Saybil flinched, his whole body going stiff. "Though in fact...this regards young Kudo as well."

"...Huh?"

"In both cases, thou didst decide to go save them because didst blame thyself, correct? What if their plights could not be blamed on thee...? If thy friends' lives were in danger for reasons unrelated to thee, what wouldst thou have done?"

It was true that Saybil had felt obligated to take responsibility for both the attack on Kudo and Hort's kidnapping. Though he couldn't explain why, he always felt this need to punish himself. And the thought of anyone getting hurt because of him terrified Saybil—in fact, it scared him so much that he was willing to put his life on the line to prevent it from ever happening. But what if he wasn't to blame? He thought it over.

*Actually, not much to think about.*

"I'd try to rescue them, even then."

"Wherefore?"

"I mean..." Saybil cast his eyes downward and mumbled, but Los couldn't hear what he'd said.

"Come again? Thou shalt have to speak up. These old ears don't hear as well as they once did."

"But you look so young!"

"For my age, perhaps."

"I mean... Th-They're my...friends..." Saybil mumbled, feeling strangely awkward and shy.

"I see, I see." Los nodded. "A lovely thing, friendship. I, too, had friends once. I grew tired of losing them, however, and have avoided forming deep attachments ever since."

"Th...The same goes for you, Professor Los."

"Hm?"

"I would try to save you, too. But...I might wind up being more trouble than help. Again..."

Los gave Saybil a nice, crisp pat on the back. "Oh, how thou dost love to shower me with praise! To what end art thou so ardently seeking to raise my opinion of thee?"

"P-Please don't make fun of me...!"

*I shouldn't have said anything.*

He'd only spoken up because Los had looked somehow pained despite her smile as she spoke of the burden of losing friends, but he should've seen the ridicule coming.

"Never forget thine impulse to protect thy friends, Sayb. Always, always remember that there are those who care for thee, just as thou carest for others; remember the bonds that connect you, and that thou shalt just as surely continue to form new bonds."

"Wow... Why do you sound like a teacher all of a sudden?"

"Now that irks me! I've been comporting myself as a teacher this entire time!" Los swung her staff around and pointed down the passage. "Look." Amid the blackness of the cave stood a door illuminated by torchlight. "The witch lies within. She has patiently awaited our arrival, without activating a single trap. Dost thou grasp what that means?"

"Uh... Ummm...?"

"'Tis a ploy of placation. Young Sayb, thou must take careful stock of thine own value. If the Arbiter did in fact report our doings to the Church, then word of how thou didst take my staff in hand has almost certainly spread. Every witch in the land will seek thee out—the apprentice mage with a wellspring of never-ending mana."

*Badump.* Saybil put a hand on his chest to suppress the pounding of his heart. Suddenly, it felt hard to breathe.

"Sayb? Whatever is the matter?"

"I—I don't know... My heart just started racing..." Saybil took a few deep breaths to calm his palpitations. "I think I...almost remembered something..."

The next instant, the door flew open. Vines shot out of the gaping portal, barreling toward Saybil with tremendous speed and stifling his cry of surprise. They coiled around him and yanked him through to the room beyond.

"Sayb!"

Panicked, Los tried to run after him—but something jerked her small body backwards. Even as she grasped her predicament, her precious staff was torn from her hand. Almost as if it had been whisked away by some invisible string... The witch turned to snatch it back when a powerful blow took her in the stomach. It was only after she'd sailed through the doorway and crashed at Saybil's side that she realized she'd been kicked.

"Gah—ufh...!"

Distracted by Saybil's situation, she'd been unable to dampen the full force of the blow. Los knew without looking who she had to thank: the blind priest, who she'd suspected from the very start.

"I *did* warn you." On the other side of the door, she heard the priest suppress a chuckle. "You should have killed me when you had the chance." And with that, he slammed the door shut.

"Fiend! How darest thou fix thy greedy eyes upon my little Ludens...! Oi, Priest! That staff is more precious than thy life! Handle it accordingly! Thou *shalt* return it to me later!"

Los pounded on the door with her fists, but it wouldn't so much as budge. Clicking her tongue at her apparent confinement, she studied Saybil as he stood in a stupefied daze, and frowned.

*What is he staring at?*

"Young Sayb, what is the matter?"

Los followed the young man's gaze. Torchlight flickered around the dim cavern, but from the very center of the chamber came another source of luminescence: a faint glow emanating from a grandiose magic circle drawn on the stone floor. And in the heart of that circle stood a woman. She was devastatingly, breathtakingly beautiful, with long silver locks and bluish-purple eyes—eyes just like Saybil's.

"Professor Los, that's her. She's the..." *only memory I have. The only person I remember.* Saybil could not peel his gaze away from the woman's stunning visage for even a second. The instant he'd seen her, he knew.

*That's her.*

*—Hmm. You have my eyes, young man.*

That gentle voice.

That sweet scent.

The warmth of her body.

*—Come. I shall take you to a world which befits you.*

*I remember her. I can still feel the cold rain hitting my cheeks, the warmth inside her cloak as it enveloped me.*

"You have done well to reach this place, young man."

"Um..."

"Come. Long have I awaited you." The witch reached out a hand to Saybil.

"Me...? But, you—" *You never once visited me at the Academy these past three years.* Plus, this woman—this witch—had not only driven out her beloved predecessor, she was also extorting taxes from the villagers.

A smile graced the witch's lips. "I finally found you, only to have the Academy of Magic steal you from my bosom and keep you these past three years. I have leveraged every asset at my disposal to retrieve you, young man—including this village." She spread her arms wide. "I took it for your sake."

"For...my sake...?" he repeated, mentally turning it into *because of me—it's my fault.*

"But the headmaster told me to come here. If she took me from you, why would she go out of her way to...send me back?"

*I shall take you to a place which befits you,* the witch had told Saybil.

*Wasn't that the Academy?*

"The Mooncaller Witch—the headmaster of the Academy, as you know her—has a somewhat myopic view of the world. She did not realize it was I who had taken control of this village. In her ignorance, she attempted to exploit it for her own ends, a convenient pretext to compel students she deemed unworthy of graduation to seal their own expulsion."

"So...the priest..." *wasn't lying.*

Albus, fully aware of the village's precarious situation, had sent

her students there to force them out of the Academy. Even Saybil, with his extremely limited knowledge of the world, could imagine plenty of reasons why the headmaster might want to be rid of Kudo, a beastfallen; Hort, with her uncomfortably close ties to the Church; the two treacherous students who returned to the Academy from the inn; and Saybil, with his bottomless reserve of magic power.

Saybil began to quake. The emotions he always managed to keep bottled up began to slowly trickle over the brim. Los took his trembling hand in hers.

"Calm thyself, Saybil. Nothing she has said comes as a surprise."

"Anyway," continued the witch, at last turning her blue-purple eyes disinterestedly to the staff-less Los standing next to Saybil. "So this is the witch who delivered you unto me. And yet, she is powerless—an *imposter* with no mana of her own, able to use neither sorcery nor magic."

"How's that?? Heed my words, thou insolent witch. Hundreds of years have I lived as the ancient and—"

A sharp *snap!* cut through the cavern, and Los was hurled backwards.

"Professor Los!" Saybil screamed, running over to help her sit up. The witch's limp, unmoving body shook Saybil to his core.

"The incompetent master will corrupt her pupils merely to pass the time. I'll do away with this piece of obsolete rubbish."

"Wh-What are you...!"

"You belong to me, young man. *I* will guide you. *I* will love you, for you are worthy of such. Even if your memories of the Academy are sealed, what of it? I will give you everything—including the memories the Mooncaller Witch stole from you."

Saybil was thunderstruck. "Headmaster Albus...took my memories...?"

"Yes, she sealed them away. And yet still you held on to your memories of me... She is, as I've long suspected, a poor excuse for a witch indeed, one unworthy of your talents—much like that imposter."

The witch's icy glare fell upon Los as she lay motionless in Saybil's arms. Parted from her staff and without any magic power of her own, Los had no means to fight.

*I have to protect her.*

"Young man," the witch called out to him, her voice cold and unfeeling. "You must not underestimate your own worth. You are special—much more so than the one you hold in your arms. And—" She tossed something onto the floor. It was Hort's trusty cap. "—a god in comparison to the parasites that would cling to you for your power."

The cap was stained with blood. Saybil caught his breath. "What...did you do to Hort...?!"

"I gave her to my mercenary. The flesh of a young maiden makes for a delectable reward. And there was one other pest...the lizard that fled. I imagine my mercenary is having his way with it even as we speak."

Saybil felt no sadness. An emotion far more violent—and more intense than he'd ever felt before—swelled larger and larger inside him with every beat of his heart.

"Listen to me, young man. Once you learn to master your gift, far more beautiful and powerful creatures will kneel before you. All will desire you, as I will." She held out her hand, as if instructing him to take it. "I will love you. I will guide you. As long as you are by my side, none will ever harm you. Now, come."

Memory intersected with the present moment.

*—I shall take you to a world which befits you.*

Saybil tightened his embrace around Los. "...What does a 'world which befits me' look like?" he asked. "All I see is the sadness of the villagers...and death...! First Hort and Kudo...now Professor Los... And it's all my fault..."

"Insignificant pests will only stand in the way of your pursuit of greatness. You understand, don't you? I did this all for your sake."

"But Hort—!" Saybil clenched his fist. "Hort was kind to me, even when I was just a nobody, a washout... Over and over again she complimented me. And...she told me she was scared of me dying."

*She's my friend.*

*She* was *my friend.*

"She wasn't some bug... Even Kudo... He was honest to a fault and always angry, but he treated everybody exactly the same. He never tried to hide who he was, or change his terrible attitude for anyone... He was brave...!"

Saybil had loved the way Kudo swished his tail from side to side, the perpetually irritated look on his face shouting, *This is who I am!*

"And Professor Los is no different!"

An imposter, the witch had called her. The person who had protected and led them here all the way from Wenias—the same person who taught them how to hunt and camp outdoors just for fun, even though she had no obligation to do so.

"She brought us all the way here. She stood up to an Arbiter for Kudo, and even threw away her precious staff to protect us...! We were totally ignorant, and she taught us everything we needed to know. She's no imposter—she's my professor! And you—!" Saybil glowered at the witch before him. "You were my only memory. Not a single day went by that I didn't think of you. But I don't need you anymore. Out of all the memories I have now, you're the one I need the least!"

The witch's lips curved up into a smile that was at once so beautiful and so hideous as to remind any who saw it of the specter of death.

"You do not want me…? *Me?* You mean to deny my hand, when I would give you everything you could ever desire? Even if it means death?"

"You—" Saybil insisted, his anger forcing forward a body that wanted nothing more than to cower in fear, "—do not befit me."

The Staff of Ludens was nowhere to be seen. Los had lost consciousness. And Saybil couldn't use magic.

Except that he could.

Saybil's magic was an exercise in extremes. Either it failed to activate—or it ran wild. So, what would happen if he put all his magic into an enchantment? What if he poured every ounce of the limitless mana he possessed into the strongest spell he knew?

*I remember the incantation. I should be able to do it.*

If he was going to get killed anyway, he might as well strike one final blow in return. And if that would save Los—even if she were the only one to survive—Saybil would not regret giving up his own life.

He parted his lips—only for something soft to press against them. Moist and wet, something slipped into Saybil's mouth and twirled around his tongue.

"Ngh…gh…? Nngh…! Nmm?!"

Los had sat up in his arms and kissed him—a kiss that sent

Saybil into a fluster the moment he realized what was happening. But he felt power flowing out from him and into the lips pressed against his, into the tongue dancing with his own. At last Saybil fell backward, and found himself flat on the ground, looking up at the witch straddling him.

Los held his face with both hands and slowly, very slowly, pulled her lips away. She got to her feet unsteadily, a brilliant light flashing in her eyes. Her slightly parted lips and drowsy, half-closed eyes made her seem like an exquisitely crafted doll, an elaborate stage prop, the numerous glass marbles with which she adorned herself floating gently in the air around her.

"'Tis ages since I last felt this, these torrents of magical power surging through my body."

"Profes…sor…?"

"Didst mean to let thy spell run amok, didst thou not? And after all the times I warned thee that such self-destructive acts are naught but foolhardy recklessness!"

Saybil withered under her glare.

"Now then, youngling. Thou didst call me 'imposter,' yes? Me, the Dawn Witch, who has lived lo these three long centuries!"

Her opponent raised the corners of her mouth, her amused smile seeming strangely full of life in contrast to Los's doll-like visage.

"So you siphoned mana from the young man. Now what do you intend to do with it? I can cast a spell long before you finish an act of sorcery. Your age has long been in its twilight, impotent one, yet you claim to be the Dawn, ever in search of the new? How laughable."

"So thou thinkest."

An unnatural, high-pitched keening resounded through the cavern, setting the air atremble. The temperature around Los instantly skyrocketed. She cried out:

*"Bahg doh gü Laht!* Hellsfire, rally to me! Blast and burn!"

She flung her arms wide as if in the throes of a dance. Serpents of flame crawled out of the void and slithered up the length of her body. Upon her arms collected the flames—of Flagis.

"Professor Los...you're—!" *using magic?!* Saybil shouted, but the roaring flames devoured his exclamation.

"Young Hort cast this once in my presence. A spell of this caliber I can easily recreate after having seen it done. I am, after all, a genius!" Then, with a self-satisfied smirk, Los declared: "Chapter of Hunting, Final Verse! Flagis! Heed this call by the power of my name—Loux Krystas!"

Serpents of fire rushed at the stunned witch.

"Amazing," Saybil whispered. *That's the most advanced spell they teach at the Academy. It's hard to activate it at all, but Los did it after only seeing it once—and more powerfully and beautifully than any of the students could.*

"Behold, young Sayb! What thou seest is powerful magic under complete control! Never again art thou to attempt something so unlovely as a wild spell!"

"Flagis, eh? Interesting," remarked the mysterious witch, grinning with genuine amusement as she gracefully reached out a hand toward the oncoming serpents of fire. Then, she made her own declaration.

"Void the call. Heed me now, for I am Zero."

The raging flames Los had released instantly bounced back and fizzled to nothing.

"Huh?" Saybil blurted. *She negated the attack. Just like that.*

A low, guttural laugh—the triumphant chuckle of a victorious witch—echoed through the chamber.

"Do not underestimate me, Dawn Witch. That spell is mine. It is my wisdom incarnate, my power. You thought you could turn my own weapon against me? Don't make me laugh."

"Professor Los! What's going on—?!"

"This is what's going on, young man," said the witch—the Mud-Black Witch—as she took a step toward Saybil, her long silver hair flowing behind her. "The techniques you call 'magic' and study in place of sorcery were all begotten from the *Grimoire of Zero.* I am that Zero. The *Grimoire* is my creation."

Despair fell like a thick fog over the chamber. They had never stood a chance. No mage, no one wielding magic as a weapon, could ever hope to overpower this witch—Zero.

"It is past time you learned. It is I who draw meaning from the meaningless, and substance from nothing. I am the Mud-Black Witch!"

Saybil raced forward to protect Los, who stood paralyzed in her amazement. He jumped to his feet, ran to her, grabbed her arm and pulled her behind him. In that instant—

*Badaah.* A somehow farcical *pop* broke the silence.

Bits of confetti began fluttering down all around.

"Huh? What? Wh—What the? Confetti?!" Unable to process the situation, Saybil looked every which way until he realized that Zero now stood immediately before him. Terrified, he instinctively staggered a half-step back. Zero poked the end of his nose.

"And, as of today, I am the witch who will be supervising your field training program. As a side note, I also authored the textbook you use at the Academy, the *Magic Manual that Begins with Zero.*"

"Huh? What? Huhhh...?"

"Welcome, young mage. I receive you gladly."

"Wh...Wh...Whoooaaaaa!" yelled the dumb-struck Los as she snapped back to life, pumping a fist in the air. "D-Didst thou see, Sayb? A voided call! In the flesh! And the spell I poured all my magic into disappeared in a flash! My heart! Oh, what a happy thing to have lived all these three hundred years!"

Flailing her arms about with childish enthusiasm, Los reenacted the scene she'd just lived again and again. Saybil, meanwhile, remained frozen in a daze, unsure how he should react.

Los finally noticed his confusion and said, "Oh, come. Look alive, young Sayb. 'Twas a test, a test! And thou didst pass!" She gave him a loud, congratulatory smack on the back.

"Ouch!" he yelped, jumping with surprise, his eyes a-goggle. "A...A test...? Wh-Which part?"

"All of it, ever since you three saved the child Laios in the forest."

"You're kidding, right?!"

"Saaaaaayb! Congraaaats!" cried a voice so high-pitched that it seemed to be squeezed out the top of the speaker's head. He didn't even need to look—it was Hort. As he turned around, a girl-sized mass slammed into him and toppled him onto the ground.

"H-Hort? Hort! You're alive! Wait, you're alive?!" Saybil threw his arms around her without thinking. Her body felt warm in his embrace; he could even feel her heartbeat. "You're all right...! I'm so glad...! Oh, I'm so glad...!"

"Me too! I'm so glad you're okay, Sayb!" Hort smiled with all her might, tears welling in her eyes. "If you'd agreed to go along with Master Zero, you would've failed on the spot and been expelled. It's all part of the test, apparently. They said everyone in the town were proctors and were watching us to see what we'd do!"

It was all too much. Saybil had no words.

"The priest tested me, too! He said he'd save me if I promised to turn on you and keep leaking information to the anti-witch faction of the Church…but then I spat right in his face, and I passed! I think he's probably some kinda perv!"

"Who are you calling a perv…?!" demanded the priest, suddenly appearing out of nowhere to give Hort a crisp smack on the top of the head. He then produced the Staff of Ludens, which he'd wrapped just a little too thoroughly, and held it out to Los. "I believe this is yours."

"My dear Ludens!"

"Goddess help me… I wish someone had considered the precarious position I was put in, tasked with stealing an accursed staff that kills anyone who touches it from an ancient witch. Among all the proctors, I was the only one who had to risk his life."

"My, my, and steal it thou didst. I had expected some sort of machination, but never did I dream thou wouldst think to take by force a staff sure to kill any who touch it," Los said cheerfully, ripping off the wrapping before lovingly rubbing her cheek against the staff as always.

"And yet…you had already realized this was a test, hadn't you, Loux Krystas," the priest remarked.

"Why, certainly!" boasted the witch. "Not for naught have I deceived and been deceived lo these three hundred years. Your lies were far too tepid and naive to pass muster."

"Whaaat? I couldn't tell at all!"

"M-Me neither..." Saybil chimed in.

"For example," Los began, "the first inkling I had that something was afoot came with Laios, the only child to be born these past five years—or so his father Uls did claim. Would it not then stand to reason that the boy should be no more than five years of age?"

"Oh, uh huh."

"However, the last witch disappeared two years ago, according to the villagers. So, were we to believe all the stories Laios told us of her were drawn from his memories as a three-year-old? When he spoke as if he'd seen her only yesterday?"

"G-Good point..." Saybil mumbled.

Hort nodded, too. "If that were true, Laios would need to have, like, a crazy good memory...!"

"Furthermore, not only did the beastfallen who attacked us lack any hint of genuine hostility, but anybody who knows that blasted Albus at all would recognize she is not the type to allow a strange witch to take possession of her village. Given her character, I would imagine her stomping her feet in rage before storming over to wrestle back the reins."

The priest chuckled wryly. "That I cannot deny. Our plans originally depended on a witch who was not quite so familiar with Headmaster Albus escorting the students here..."

"Wait, that's right," Saybil recalled. Another witch, not Los, had originally been assigned to lead him and his friends to the village.

"The most outrageously obvious clue, however, came in the form of that vacant house."

Hort cocked her head. "Huh? I was only there for a second, so I didn't catch anything. Was there something weird about it?"

"Was there anything *not* weird about?! In what fantastical world does an abandoned house that has stood vacant for two years after the tragic deaths of its previous inhabitants come complete with tidied beds, cabinets stocked with clean dishes and fresh herbs, and jugs full of fresh water?! It was painfully obvious that the house had in fact been prepared in advance for guests. And as for those dreadful dolls so pointedly hung for us, they bore no sign of having weathered the last two years, during which they supposedly dangled as a warning for all to see. Farcical indeed!"

"Hmm… You are unsettlingly perceptive. Perhaps I should have expected as much from the Dawn Witch, the eternal traveler who seeks all that is new—Loux Krystas. I may have underestimated you slightly," conceded Zero with a serious expression.

"Bumbling fool! Anyone could have seen through this mockery!"

"This is exactly why I insisted we shouldn't clean and prepare the vacant house like that," said the priest.

Zero knit her brows. "Simple enough to say, Father. But I could not in good conscience have sent these children to sleep amid the dust and cobwebs after their long journey."

"There is a world of difference between that and hand-picking a careful selection of herbs for the kitchen."

"I simply couldn't wait to have the children try my original blend, perfectly formulated to provide the taste and fragrance one craves most after a tiring journey," a pouting Zero mumbled, continuing to make excuses for herself.

Saybil blinked his eyes a few times. The terrifying witch who had mere seconds ago directed such intense menace toward him now felt terribly familiar and relatable. Just then—

"Yooo!"

—a deep voice boomed through one of the chamber doors—the one which led to the exit—causing all heads in the room to turn toward it. Two large figures lumbered into the cavern.

"Don't mean to interrupt the festivities, but we've got another successful candidate over here."

It was the hulking beastfallen mercenary. Hort and Saybil jumped to their feet the minute they saw the figure walking a half step behind him.

"Kudo!"

The two raced over to his side. Kudo looked them over, then asked, "You guys, too?"

They nodded. Without another word, Kudo enveloped the other two apprentices in a tight embrace. "...I'm so glad." His voice was trembling. "I'm so glad...nobody died...! That bastard... He told me he ate Hort, and I...!"

Every eye in the room shot daggers at the mercenary, piercing through his white fur and plunging into his heart.

"Wh-What?! It's not my fault! I just went by the script! If you've got a problem, talk to the priest—he wrote it!" he insisted, pointing at the clergyman he'd just thrown under the wagon.

"After all, the test requires we rouse the students' fear and anger, and get at the very root of their sense of inferiority." The priest shrugged without a hint of guilt.

"Hmm... I suppose I can take this to mean all three students who arrived in the village have passed the test?" Zero said, once she saw the situation had settled down to some degree. "Hmmm," she murmured again, stroking her beautiful chin with long, slender fingers. "I must admit, even I am slightly taken aback that all three of you passed, when not a single student managed the feat last year."

"They had an excellent teacher, after all." Los, standing next to Zero, patted herself approvingly on the shoulder with her staff.

Zero gazed down at the diminutive witch and smiled warmly. "Loux Krystas, Dawn Witch. That spell you cast was impeccable. And though I only spoke them in the context of the test, I would like to apologize for the disparaging insults I directed at you."

"What dost thou mean?" A mischievous smile on her face, Los looked up at Zero. "Being an *imposter*, I have something of a terrible memory."

Zero blinked, taken aback, then frowned slightly. "Dawn Witch...you're in fact quite angry, aren't you? I sensed it, you know—the unbridled murderous intent with which you released that spell."

"Oh, yes, I was in deadly earnest. Wert thou not Zero, I might have fried thee to a crisp. Thank goodness I did not incinerate my students' proctor before their very eyes!"

Zero had not revealed her name before Los attacked, so the Dawn Witch would have had no way of knowing whether Zero could negate the spell—though she had known that her opponent was proctoring the test, at the very least. It all added up to a terrifying picture if one looked close enough—but Saybil and his friends remained blissfully ignorant of that fearsome truth.

# [ Interlude ]

"Egyaaaaah!"

Within seconds of hearing a freakish howl emanate from the headmaster's office, Holdem raced in. He nearly kicked down the door as he burst through to find Albus holding a letter in her tremulous hands.

"Did you just go into labor?! My lady, were you keeping a secret pregnancy from me?!"

"Don't be stupid, you third-rate manservant!" Albus snapped, swiftly chucking a thick book from her desk at the beastfallen's face. Then, "Th-They all passed..."

"Huh?"

"All the students we sent to Zero! Aside from the two traitors that came back, they all passed!" shouted the headmaster, waving the letter in the air.

It was no ordinary letter she held. This was a witch's letter, a form of correspondence that immediately replicated the contents of one paper onto the other, no matter the distance between them. It was an extremely valuable tool, and Zero and Albus each had one of this pair. As a result, Albus could stay up to date with all the goings-on in the village—as long as Zero didn't slack off in her duty, that is.

"They all passed...?" Holdem repeated, his face frozen in confusion. "Isn't that a good thing?"

"It's a wonderful thing! A brilliant achievement! Holdem! Prepare for a celebration immediately!"

Going back to the beginning—Albus had indeed sent all the students to Zero's village to get them expelled. Of this, there could be no question. Fortunately, they secured sufficient evidence to banish the two students selling Academy information. But the remaining three—the strikingly uncouth beastfallen, Kudo; the Church's spy, Hort; and Saybil, the boy with unlimited magical reserves—each had the potential to grow too powerful for anyone to stop them, should they veer down the path of evil after graduation. So Albus sent these potentially dangerous mages to face Zero, originator of all magic, to put them through a trying test with little chance of success, and expel them should they fail.

Passing the examination demonstrated that they were "both talented and virtuous," and that they posed only a vanishingly small risk of betraying their friends, attempting to subjugate the world, or engaging in other such nefarious deeds. Albus knew Zero and her compatriots would have tempted the students from every possible angle: mercilessly threatening them, shaking their convictions, and drawing out their basest desires. Despite all that, Zero had nevertheless judged them worthy. Albus knew all too well what a remarkable accomplishment that represented.

"I was a little worried after I heard that Arbiter had attacked them along the way, and I considered putting the test on hold...but I'm glad I trusted them to pull through..." Albus let out a contented sigh.

"That so?" asked Holdem. "If anything, I think they might have the attack to thank for their success."

"What do you mean?"

"Facing that life-or-death situation together must've given them a sense of solidarity."

"Ah, right. That may be so. Hmm... I've got mixed feelings

about this, but I guess that means we owe that Arbiter our thanks. Oh, all right, I'll throw him a bone."

Albus smiled. On her desk lay a wanted poster for the Tyrant.

*Wanted dead or alive.*

Albus quickly edited this to say:

*To be taken alive.*

"Who knows? He may be of use to us if we keep him alive, after all." She tucked a lock of blonde hair behind her ear and handed the poster to Holdem. "Send this to every mage, Church and Mage Brigade battalion, and bounty hunter in the kingdom," she ordered. "No one hurts one of my students without paying for it—no one."

# Chapter Six

## 1

"So, I think some proper introductions are in order. As you all now know, I am Zero, a witch of rare genius who runs a humble magic shop in this village."

"Wow, if you don't say so yourself..." Saybil blurted out, only for Hort and Kudo to give him a very physical chiding.

"Sayb! If you don't have anything nice to say, keep quiet!"

"Careful who you're talkin' to, you jackass! She literally *invented* magic!"

"S-Sorry..." Saybil apologized, clutching the spot on his head where he'd been whacked and his ribs where he'd been elbowed.

They had relocated to the small tavern in the middle of town, where almost literally every other villager in the settlement had joined them. Everyone welcomed the young mages, heartily toasting them and reveling in their accomplishment. It was a marked difference from the standoffish reception they'd gotten earlier in the day. Evidently, the villagers had holed up in their homes so as to not let on about the test if they spoke to the students.

"Well done making the long journey here. And congratulations on passing the examination. You have each proved yourselves virtuous through and through, fending off all manner of fearful and tempting trials. We all had our hearts set on your expulsion, but you betrayed our expectations."

*So wait, that means—*

"You...were the one who took me to the Academy, weren't you...?"

Zero nodded. "Yes, I was."

"Then you also know why I can't remember anything before that?"

"You do not remember?"

Saybil cocked his head.

"If not, then those memories are just as well forgotten."

"Y-You're not going to tell me?"

"If you need them, they will return to you," Zero replied, just as Headmaster Albus once had. After that, Saybil could say nothing more.

"Um, question! I have a question!" Hort's hand shot into the air. "Why did everybody want us to get expelled that badly?"

"Your talents are too great."

Hort blinked.

"You three are significantly more gifted than the ordinary mage. Should you continue to progress as you have thus far and then one day set out to conquer the world, for instance—it might be more than just the northern half of the continent that gets destroyed this time."

"Whaaat?! Aw, come on, you're just saying thaaat..."

"Listen to me, antlered one."

Hort flinched, subconsciously reaching for the horns hidden in her hair. She no longer wore her cap, which was now stained with blood.

"Your ability is comparable to that of the Mooncaller Witch—whom you know as the headmaster of the Academy of Magic."

"Whaaa?!"

"Her talents incline towards the Chapter of Protection, however, whereas your forte is the Chapter of Hunting. In ten years' time, I foresee you wielding the power to vanquish an army of thousands in a matter of seconds."

Hort's breath caught in her throat.

Zero shifted her gaze to Kudo. "Young lizard, your gifts are fearsome indeed, a powerful combination of regenerative ability and talent for spells from the Chapter of Protection. Should your mastery of both continue to evolve, you will learn to regrow your limbs before you even feel the pain of their loss. None will be able to harm you, and you will be known far and wide as the undying mage."

Finally, the witch turned to Saybil. "Limitless mana... Not even I can fully estimate the potential you hold. Over the next several hundred years, you may very well become the longest-lived mage in history—he who bestows magic upon those who have lost it, a savior to all witches. And a long lifespan means endless opportunities to sharpen your skills."

As she spoke, Zero conjured a ball of ice in her hand. "Young man, this represents you as you are today. However, with time—" The ice began to melt. Droplets trickled down and refroze, slowly sharpening the sphere into a jagged icicle. "—you will gain the power to penetrate anything and everything."

The three young mages fell silent. They found it hard to believe they possessed any such potential.

"Fearsome possibilities, no?" Zero grinned. "I, for one, fear them."

"Possibilities..." Saybil repeated. *In other words,* "What you just said...won't necessarily come true?"

"Exactly. Not even I can predict what sort of indolent mages you might degenerate into should you neglect your studies and waste your days lounging in bed. That eventuality would be terrifying in its own right."

The icicle in Zero's hand shattered into a fine dust, which then gathered together like snow to form an adorable rabbit. The snow rabbit hopped off her palm and melted away to nothing in mid-air.

"The scenarios I have just described are merely previews of the futures that await should you hone your talents to a keen edge. While they represent no more than possibilities, the risk is far too great to leave you unattended. That is why you're here."

"All right, all right, you can get down to the heavy business later. Right now, it's time to feast! Dig in!" announced the owner of the tavern—who happened to be the white carnivorous beastfallen, known to everyone simply as Mercenary—as he lined up dish after decadent dish before the mages.

*I was definitely surprised to hear he owned this place, but I still can't wrap my mind around the idea of a beastfallen cooking. Not to mention the fact that it's so freaking delicious!*

"How did a beastfallen mercenary come to own a bar?" Saybil asked.

"This is the house I grew up in," Mercenary replied as he ladled out soup from a huge tureen. "Went through some things and wound up runnin' out o' here, but eventually I came back and took over the place."

"Wowww! I'm amazed they let a beastfallen take over the business! They must've been really wonderful parents!" Hort marveled, her eyes sparkling.

"They sure were," the beastfallen agreed proudly.

"This meat is safe to eat, right…? It's not, like, human or anything...?" Still traumatized by Mercenary's assertion that he'd eaten Hort, Kudo refused at first to touch anything the beastfallen served them. But after nibbling at plates of fish and vegetables, he eventually began wolfing down the meat dishes, too. It was just that good.

"And I am the village priest, entrusted with leading its faithful. I may as well tell you, since Hort already knows and there's no point in hiding it, that despite appearances I am in fact an Arbiter of Dea Ignis."

"*Former* Arbiter. Former," Mercenary cut in.

Dea Ignis had been officially disbanded once the Church accepted peace with the witches. Given that many of their members had originally been condemned convicts, some were apparently executed as planned, while others were pardoned in light of their contributions. Theoretically, that meant the Arbiters who remained were relatively good people—but given their run-in with the vicious Arbiter who'd attacked Kudo, Saybil found it difficult to put much faith in that notion.

"What's an Arbiter who used to hunt witches for a living doing proctoring an exam for mages in a witch's village?" Hort inquired innocently.

"It's a long story," was the priest's brusque reply.

"And just so you know, he can see," added Mercenary.

"Wha?!" the three youngsters exclaimed in astonishment, looking over at the blindfold covering the clergyman's eyes.

"Then why do you wear that?" asked Saybil.

"Fashion? Are you trying to look cool?" Hort ventured.

"You gave up your eyesight just to look cool...? Damn, that's pretty badass... These Arbiters don't screw around..."

Mercenary roared with laughter at their various responses,

while the priest pressed an exasperated hand against his forehead.

"My eyes are sensitive to light, so I can only remove the blindfold at night."

"Ah, so then you really can't see in the daylight."

"Aw man, I thought for sure you were going for a look," Hort said, instantly losing interest in the priest and turning her attention instead to the steamed chicken and vegetable stew in front of her.

"So, um... What should we call you?" Saybil asked.

The priest just shrugged. "They called me 'the Mask' in the Church, but within the confines of the village, simply 'Father' will suffice."

Saybil had wanted to know the priest's real name, but that information was not forthcoming. Like Mercenary, he was apparently known by his trade.

A thought seemed to occur to Hort, who suddenly started scanning the room.

"Hort? What's up?"

"Hmm... Um, Father, did the little girl from the chapel not come today?"

"What sort of a nonsense question is that?" the priest asked dubiously. "There are no children in the chapel."

"But..."

"If you mean Lily," he continued with a sigh, "she's already over twenty years old."

"No waaaay!! But she's, like, sooo much tinier than me!"

"In any event...I will introduce you in time, but she has a rather timid personality and dislikes crowds. Perhaps I should have dragged her along regardless."

"No, no, no. Bad idea." Mercenary smiled wryly. "That pipsqueak's scary when you rile her up. If she wants to see ya, she'll take care of it herself."

"So, students," Zero began. "As I believe the Mooncaller has explained, you must each achieve something here in the village to prove your advancement as mages. It would be inefficient to expect you to do so while aimlessly spending your days here, so I would like you all to run your own individual enterprises."

"Enterprises...?"

"Yes. You are free to choose whatever appeals to you, so long as you can provide the villagers with some sort of service. Alternatively, you may also join an established business—coincidentally, I run a modest magic shop here in the village, though fundamentally I'm more of what you might call a handymage. If you three could take on some of those odd jobs yourselves, it would be a boon to me as well."

*I hadn't actually given any serious thought to what I'd do once I got here, but... A business, huh?*

"I hadn't thought about it... What about you, Sayb?"

"No, me neither..."

"Couldn't we just be, like, bodyguards or something?" Kudo suggested.

"Huh? But you don't have to be a mage to do that," pointed out Hort.

Zero smiled warmly at the three students *hmm*-ing to themselves, deep in thought. "I will give you three days to think about what kind of enterprise you would like to run. Our job is to support you in this process, after all."

Once he'd filled his stomach to the bursting point and all but drowned himself in drinks, Saybil tottered back to the vacant house. That's when he realized he hadn't seen Los in a while.

"Where's Professor Los?"

"I think she said she was going to Master Zero's shop," Hort answered as she plopped down on the bench by the window and kicked off her uncomfortable shoes. "She said she was dying to read all the books Master Zero has written."

"Oh, right. Zero did write the *Grimoire of Zero,* after all. I bet she's got tons of books."

*Plus, Los wants to read the* Grimoire *more than anything. I can see her champing at the bit to get her hands on everything Zero's ever written.*

Kudo apparently had something to discuss with Mercenary, and stayed behind after the tavern closed. In other words, Saybil and Hort now had the whole house to themselves. Suddenly, the silence between them felt heavy. At the same time, it also provided Saybil with what he considered the perfect opportunity.

"Hey, Hort?"

"Yeah?"

"I'm sorry about earlier... The thought that you'd be sad if I died had never even crossed my mind..."

"Huh?! Are you really bringing that up now?!"

"I mean, I won't stop worrying about it 'til I say something... I'm really sorry!"

"It's fiiine." Hort smiled. "I mean, what else could I expect? It's who you are, Sayb."

"So you've given up on me...?"

"No! I just realized I should've used my words. Like, I should've told you that you're my friend, that I have a lot of fun with you, that I'd be sad if you weren't around."

All of this probably should have gone without saying. Most people could surely recognize that others would mourn them if they died; they could call those people's faces to mind. But not Saybil. He didn't understand what most people could intuit without being explicitly told.

"...Sorry." He apologized again, feeling abashed.

"It's okay. Plus, you got mad on my behalf."

"Huh?"

"When Zero told you I'd died, you got *real* mad."

Just as he was about to ask what she was talking about, Saybil remembered exactly what she meant, and flushed bright red. "You heard that?!"

"I sure did. And I had a front-row seat to that sexy smooch with Professor Los."

"Wa-awa-wa-whaaaaa...! N-No, that's not—! She was—Professor Los was just taking mana from me, it wasn't a real k-kiss or anything...!" Saybil squirmed as he relived the memory of Los's lips and tongue.

"Ahhaha! That face! Sayb, your emotions are really starting to show!"

Just then—

"Y-You guys! Get out here! Come outside! Come look!"

—Kudo screamed as he burst into the house, his face agog with excitement, before racing right back out without another word. Saybil and Hort ran after him.

Kudo pointed up at the sky. "Look! It's a dragon—and it's coming this way!"

A silver dragon raced across the moon—the very same dragon they had seen when they were leaving the Kingdom of Wenias. It circled above them, then slowly began to descend, spiraling down to the village square. A large crowd had already formed by the time the three mages arrived. Nimbly, the silver dragon alit in the center of the throng.

Dragons were sacred creatures, said to slumber for a hundred years each time they slept. And as they lived in terrain unsuitable for human habitation, some even wondered whether they actually existed outside of tales and legends. But then, six years ago, after the Disasters of the North devastated half of the world, a battalion dedicated to destroying witches was established, and a dragon bearing a human rider appeared out of the chaos. King of a country laid waste by dragons, that man—the Dragon Conqueror King, as he was known—now belonged to the Church and Mage Brigade. And, as should go without saying, it was this man that Kudo admired more than anyone, the hero who'd inspired his dream of joining the Brigade.

That very same legendary hero now hopped lightly off the dragon's back. He had fiery red hair, and his expression was set in a perpetual frown. His black armor was a humble and unadorned black, and a sword hung at his waist.

The Dragon Conqueror King scanned the crowd. "Are the students from the Academy of Magic here?" he asked.

"Y-Yes!" the three stammered, weaving through the villagers to the front of the crowd. Kudo stood ramrod straight, his usual bad attitude nowhere in evidence.

One by one, the Dragon Conqueror King studied the mages. "Saybil, Hort, and Kudo...I presume?" he said brusquely. The three nodded in response, and he handed each a sealed letter. "I bring you word from Albus, Royal Mage of the Kingdom of Wenias," he announced. Then, grumbling to himself, he continued. "Unbelievable... Never expected when she insisted I leave at once on an urgent matter that I'd be asked to play errand boy, delivering mail of all things..."

The dragon rider gave a weary sigh. At that moment, two figures raced up.

"Well, if it isn't the Dragon Conqueror King! It has been too long!"

"Hey, Heath! Look at you—you're huge!"

It was Zero and Mercenary. The former trotted over to the rider, while the latter approached the dragon—Heath, as it was evidently named.

As soon as he spotted the two approaching visitors, the legendary hero snapped, "How many times have I told you not to call me that?!"

Saybil and Hort exchanged a glance. *Huh? What the...? Do they know each other? Are Zero and Mercenary friends with the Dragon Conqueror King?* They were dying to ask all this and more, while Zero and Mercenary joked and roughhoused with the two visitors like playful puppies. Unfortunately, neither Saybil nor Hort had the audacity it would take to cut in, to say nothing of Kudo, who'd been reduced to a bundle of nerves.

"No need to be so humble. The whole world knows your name by now. It's high time you accept the title and move on."

"It's overblown at best... Look at me, I'm nothing more than a glorified postman."

"They must be important letters indeed, if Mooncaller entrusted them to you," Zero said. "Students, go ahead and read them."

At her urging, Saybil and his friends opened their letters. They all let out a "Huh?" and looked to each other.

+++

*Apprentice Mage Saybil*
*Appointed to service in the Witch's Village.*
*All restrictions on magic are hereby lifted.*

+++

So went Saybil's letter.

"All restrictions on magic…are lifted…?"

"Yours says that, too?" Hort asked.

"Same here," added Kudo.

*All restrictions on magic are hereby lifted*—normally, that privilege was reserved for mages who had graduated from the Academy and been officially recognized by the Kingdom of Wenias. For these three whose graduation was still in doubt, the news brought more bewilderment than joy.

"Unrestricted use of all magic…? These children?" Not even the Dragon Conqueror King, who had himself delivered the messages, could hide his discomfiture.

"Oh, hush. Clearly, they are worthy of the distinction," Zero said, sounding for some reason proud. "Nevertheless, the anti-witch faction would have much to say about entrusting such power to apprentice mages who have not yet completed their schooling. In other words, this is a top-secret dispatch. So? Rightly befitting of a message sent by dragon, wouldn't you say?"

"Your cheap flattery won't work on me," said the Dragon Conqueror King, scowling even more than before.

"You never change, do you?" Zero teased with a grin.

All of a sudden, Kudo stepped forward. "Excuse me, I—!"

"Hm?"

The beastfallen mage's legs were quaking. "I— You...You saved me...once...years ago..."

"Right, I remember." The Dragon Conqueror King nodded, his expression unchanged.

"Huh?" spluttered Kudo nervously.

"You were the young beastfallen I found in the ruins of that freak show up north. You couldn't get out of your cage, so you staved off starvation with the dog carcasses that were lying within reach."

"You...remember...?"

"My heart is not so numb as to forget such a horrific tragedy. If I remember correctly, you said you wanted to fight by my side. I believe I told you only magic could make that happen, though I wasn't implying you should become a mage..."

"What?!"

"I meant to say it was impossible. But look at you. This *is* a surprise. At this point, you may be more formidable than I, since I have no skill with spellcraft."

"O-Of course not! I could never compare with you! But, um..." Haltingly, Kudo asked, "D-Do you think...I c-could make it...into the Ch-Church and Mage Brigade...?"

"Not my concern."

His dreams dashed with the brutal curtness of the reply, Kudo almost buckled at the knees.

"I have nothing to do with recruitment," the Dragon Conqueror King went on. "However, I believe you would be an asset to my battalion."

"—!"

The dragon-rider patted Kudo on the shoulder. "I have high

hopes for you."

"Th-Thank you, sir!"

Kudo's scales shivered through every color of the rainbow, making it impossible to pin down his exact emotion. Even so, Saybil got the impression he could've died happy in that moment.

"So, what now, Dragon Conqueror King? You're staying the night, right?" Mercenary asked as he offered Heath some water.

"That was my plan, if you don't mind the imposition."

"No trouble at all. Make sure to drop by the chapel later, though. The pipsqueak'll want to see Heath."

## 2

"What?! Wherefore did you not call for me?!"

Los rolled back and forth on the ground without a care for how it might dirty her dress, flailing her arms and legs about in a full-blown tantrum. "I would see the dragon up close, too! I would touch it! I would ride it, if it were permitted me!!"

Worried since Los had still not returned the following morning, Saybil, Hort, and Kudo went to Zero's shop to check in on her, and found her burrowed in a pile of books, completely engrossed in the one she held. When they called out to her, she'd looked up and asked, "What? Time for dinner?" She had clearly lost all sense of time, and after they told her it was already morning, she'd exclaimed, "What, already?!" They then explained that a dragon had arrived the previous night and left that morning, which brought them to the present moment.

"We speak of the *only dragon* whose flight has been confidently attested in all the world! How could you not immediately call for me, your dear professor, when presented with something so unquestionably interesting?! How could you?! Oh, the humanity!"

"I-It's okay..." Saybil said. "The Dragon Conqueror King seemed to be friendly with Master Zero and Mercenary, so he'll probably come around the village again soon..."

"*Soon*, thou sayest? How canst thou be sure I will yet remain in the village when this *soon* comes to pass?!" Los petulantly puffed out her cheeks and sat cross-legged on the floor.

"So...she is leaving, after all."

"See, I *told* you so. She just came here to drop us off, then split."

Los blinked in surprise as she listened to Hort and Kudo. "What's this? Of what do you speak?"

"We were all talking about what you were gonna do once your chaperoning duties were finished," Hort explained. "You said your goal was to meet the Mud-Black Witch, but you already have, so..."

"I will set out in search of frolic and revelry, naturally. That is how I live my life."

Dejected, the three mages' shoulders drooped. They'd hoped beyond hope that Los would stay in the village with them for a little longer—but also had a sinking premonition those hopes would go unfulfilled.

"Nevertheless, I *do* believe I will require more time to finish perusing all of these books, and I plan to remain in the village until such time. I furthermore have much yet to discuss with Zero. And, most importantly," she said, looking up at her students with her usual composure, "watching to see what progress this village achieves with the introduction of three new mages will, I imagine, provide thorough entertainment in and of itself. In fact, it is entirely possible it may prove a more titillating affair than any of the thousands of dramas I have delighted in thus far..."

"Professor Los!"

"Though I shall promptly depart at the first sign of boredom." Los pointed her staff threateningly at each young mage in turn. "Study for all you are worth. I have a great love of growth and change. As long as you three aim for greater heights and ardently pursue self-improvement, I shall assist you in whatever way I can. That, above all else, is what shall entertain me most.

"Now go! Delight me!" she commanded pompously. All three—though Kudo more or less got roped into the mix—flung their arms around her.

"Nghaaah! I am becrush'd...! Unhand me, you coddled whelps!"

Los pushed away her pupils, and they raced out of the shop.

*We've got to find something to do—and quick!* A welcome impatience now spurred the three young mages forward.

Zero entered the shop just after the students left.

"So, thou hast returned," Los said.

Zero furrowed her brows. "Quite a mess you've made here... I myself don't much care, but Mercenary will have some angry words for you."

"What's this? Does that beastfallen double as a housekeeper as well?"

"Yes—but only for me." Zero picked up the books Los had strewn about the floor and stacked them into a tall column, then sat down on it.

"'Tis more than a casual connection, then."

"Indeed. We love one another deeply."

"I should like very much to hear all about it."

"In time," Zero said, nipping that conversation in the bud. "So you will remain, Dawn Witch?"

"The prospect promises to be most interesting. And, O illustrious Mud-Black Witch," Los continued, "thou hast run dry of magical power, hast thou not?"

Zero lifted an eyebrow. "Oho... So you did catch on."

"Naturally. Hadst thou not voided my spell, I would not have believed thee the Mud-Black Witch. How did the renowned witch of rare genius fall to such a state? What couldst thou possibly have done to use up so much power?"

"Oh, I traded it to save the life of one I love."

"My, how dashing."

"Right?"

"Add that to the list of stories I should very much like to hear. However," Los said, changing gears, "Sayb's arrival must surely seem divine providence for a witch drained of all mana like thyself. That pupil is one of my darling little fledglings. I should not like to hear it on the wind that a certain witch had dug her poisonous fangs into him and brought him crashing down to earth."

"You think I would make the young man a tool to replenish my magic?"

"Without it, thou shalt grow old and die. I imagine such a prospect would terrify a witch of such beauty and limitless power, who hath lived already a hundred years and more."

"Do you know what lies in his forgotten memories?" Zero suddenly asked, referring to the past Saybil could not remember.

"Albus sealed them away, did she not? As to why, I cannot say."

"He killed someone."

Los sprang to her feet. "How dost thou know this?"

"I saw the witch's corpse myself. That young man has been as he is from birth. Hardly difficult to imagine that witches might seek him out, is it? This witch first murdered his mother before his very eyes. She then tried to wrest mana from him, but destroyed herself with an overdose."

"So," Los said, "Sayb did not in fact kill her. The greedy fool sealed her own fate."

"Not in his eyes. 'My mother was murdered because of me, and this strange witch died all of a sudden because she touched me. My very existence is a sin.' He was convinced of this. Unable to withstand the immense pressure of that guilt, he sealed the memories away himself. Bereft of his memory, the orphaned boy wandered aimlessly through the city slums, enduring every imaginable type of pain and suffering. Destitute, starving, and abused, he had lost all feeling by the time I found him. His heart was frozen over. The one and only emotion that remained within him..." She paused. "... was guilt. When I found him, he cowered from my touch. He was afraid of salvation. He didn't believe he deserved it. All that time, he had been putting himself in those wretched circumstances as a kind of punishment."

*I'm not afraid of dying,* he had said. And indeed, he had chosen to touch the Staff of Ludens at the cost of his own life.

*Did that reckless bravery arise from a sense of guilt? Or did it stem from the way he valued all other life above his own? If so—how terribly wretched. Far too pitiful an act of self-sacrifice to label either reckless or brave.*

"Mooncaller and I considered what to do. The psychological wounds he had endured were far too severe for him to handle. So we decided the best course of action would be to seal away *all* of his memories for the time being, and give him a chance to rebuild his life—an opportunity to create memories that would sustain him, and cancel out that anguish when the day came that he finally remembered his harrowing past. The Academy of Magic provided the perfect environment for him to build that foundation. Fortunately, the boy has an innate talent for magic. However, his unusual constitution affected even the other students at the Academy. There was also the risk that he would force immeasurable magical energy into difficult spells to compel them to activate, only for them to then run wild and cause great harm. Extraordinary abilities can at times invite great suffering. And so we decided—"

"To expel him?"

"We thought a life away from magic might bring him more happiness. Perhaps, with all his memories concerning the art sealed away, he could enjoy living in the village much like the other children here, for instance."

"Hmph," Los snorted. "How arrogant. Why go so far to meddle in one human's life? Sayb's gift poses some risk, that I understand. Nevertheless, that does not justify the illustrious Mud-Black Witch's meticulous involvement. Witches are fundamentally selfish creatures, after—"

"He is my elder brother's son."

Los's mouth snapped shut. "Thy brother's?"

"Do you understand what that means, Dawn Witch?"

"That would make Sayb's father—"

Zero and Los spoke in unison.

"Thirteen."

Los looked up at the ceiling. Every ancient witch knew the story by heart: the tale of Zero, the Mud-Black Witch and author of the *Grimoire of Zero*, and Thirteen, the sorcerer who stole the *Grimoire* and incited war in the Kingdom of Wenias. The sordid tale of a sister and brother, bound by blood.

"Your eyes... I see, a hereditary trait." Los had risen to her feet,

but now plopped back down into a sitting position. "I must admit, I had not heard Thirteen had a child."

"As far as I could gather from the available records, it was roughly sixteen years ago, shortly after he stole the *Grimoire*. In his effort to establish a foundation from which to spread magic throughout Wenias, he sought support from a famous witch, who asked him to sire a child for her in exchange. Evidently, he agreed."

"A loveless tale, indeed."

"Nevertheless, I have love for the boy."

"Hmph," Los snorted again. "Even though thou hast not once spoken his name?"

Zero cocked her head. "His name...? What's the problem with that? I do not even call Mercenary by his name."

"Dost thou not know? No, I suppose not." Los rose to her feet. "That is why I shall stay."

Zero did not press Los further. She simply nodded, with an expression that said, *I see.* Whether she accepted Los's reasoning or not, however, remained unclear.

"You are most welcome, Dawn. I take heart from your presence."

"And well thou shouldst, Mud-Black. Look to me for guidance as much as thou wilt. After all, I have lived a vastly longer life than thee."

## 3

Many of the houses in the village were uninhabited. The townspeople had repurposed an abandoned village to build their own, and as a result, many of the original older buildings still remained. The first thing a budding enterprise would require was a storefront. But—

"So, the clinic asked me to help out," Kudo had announced, officially becoming the first of the mages to land a job. The physician there had told Kudo his proficiency with the Chapter of Protection made him a goddessend for the clinic.

"Oh, that's a great idea! We can start by helping out other people at first! Actually, that's how it usually goes in business, right?! You work for someone else, then try to branch out on your own!"

Armed with that new outlook, Hort put up a poster on the bulletin board at the tavern that read "Accepting Job Requests," and began taking on work as a handymage. She'd apparently decided to use Mercenary's tavern as her headquarters, and helped him with the bar when she could.

As for Saybil—

"Well, there's not much I *can* do..." Not much at all. Saybil turned over the few options he had in his head, but it didn't take long.

Since the vacant house Uls had brought them to had one bedroom each for the three mages, they decided to use it as their dorm—and Saybil converted the first floor into his shop.

He didn't have many customers, but Saybil still felt his service filled an important niche. And he didn't need much in the way of furniture or equipment. A few comfortable chairs and some mugs for tea were plenty.

"Sayb, guess what! I got a job today! At the next village over! That lightning storm yesterday knocked over a tree and blocked one of their roads, right? So they asked me to do something about it with my magic! And let me tell you, I blew that thing to smithereens! Then the villagers started clapping and cheering, and they asked me to do all kinds of different things for them. So yeah, I'm like *totally* out of mana!" This all came out in a rush the moment Hort came flying into the shop.

"Wow… That's so cool you got work from another village."

"Apparently, they were gonna ask Master Zero or Mercenary for help, but then Mercenary told them there was a new handymage in town, and why not try her out!"

Beaming, Hort stretched out her hand to Saybil, who took it in his. He focused his mind, imagining a link between their blood vessels, then pictured the mana in his body flowing over to her through his bloodstream…

"Wh…Whoaaa! I feel it! I can feel it, Sayb! The mana's flowing into me!"

"Sh-Shh! Quiet! I need to concentrate or you're gonna burst at the seams!"

"Nooo! You better concentrate real hard! Actually, I think I'm good! Aah, i-it's too much! I'm gonna pop!"

A single drop of blood dribbled from Hort's nose. Saybil dropped her hand in a panic.

"S-Sorry, Hort!"

"Uh-uh, it's fine… Mmm, I'm full up! Your shop is the best, Sayb." Hort wiped away the blood and finally took a seat in the guest chair. "It was such a great idea to open a mana shop for other mages! Now Kudo and I—and even Master Zero!—can cast magic without having to worry, and it's all thanks to you."

"I mean, this is pretty much the only thing I *can* do right now, so..."

Sayb's Mana Shop—that was what Saybil named his business. Though it only catered to other mages, people had already come to see it as an important service in its own way.

Suddenly, there was a knock on the Mana Shop's door. Saybil and Hort turned to look.

"Oh!" they both exclaimed. There stood a witch with long, blonde hair, dressed in men's clothes.

"Headmaster Albus?!"

"Hello, you two. Feels like ages since I last saw you. I just ran into Kudo, too. He *really* let me have it... Something about 'too bad you didn't manage to expel us'... I just let him get it all out..."

A wry smile playing on her lips, Albus leaned against the doorframe and pulled out an envelope. "By the way, I was hoping I could put in an order..." Her smile left no room for protest. "I've looked all over the world, but yours is the only mana shop I've found. You'll help me out, won't you? Mister mana merchant."

# Afterword

I always have a hard time starting these afterwords. And when I'm writing one for a new publisher for the first time, it feels just as difficult as doing the one for my debut novel did.

It's totally different from doing the second volume in a series; it's the space where you get to introduce yourself to new readers, after all, so you get the urge to sex things up a little, add a dash of humor, that kind of thing. Then again, the fear of sounding corny makes you want to rein in that impulse, too.

Eventually, you end up pulling out all the books in your house and excavating their back matter for any useful tips or tricks. But at the end of the day, all that effort doesn't really yield much in the way of valuable lessons. Either the authors take far more liberties with their writing than you're comfortable emulating, or they play it too safe and it ends up totally boilerplate.

There's a huge gap dividing authors who enjoy writing afterwords and those who don't. As for me, I'm in the former group, and I like to make 'em nice and long.

Consequently, I decided to let it all hang out, like I always do. My editor S gave me the go-ahead to make it as long as I want, so I get to write to my little heart's content. Huzzah! What incredible relief!

And so, without adding to that already overlong preamble, hello everyone. This is Kakeru Kobashiri. As I imagine many of you have already realized, this story takes place in the same universe as my debut series, *Grimoire of Zero.* Let's be honest, it's basically a sequel. In terms of the timeline, the order goes: *Grimoire of Zero* → *The Witch and Beast's Extremely Normal Village-Building (online publication)* → *The Dawn of the Witch.* Though this series has all-new main characters, many of the people from *Grimoire* also appear, and even more of them are slated to show up down the line.

That said, I absolutely wrote this first installment as the beginning of an entirely new series, one that readers unfamiliar with the world could just jump right into. I'll have to leave it to you to decide whether I succeeded. Do let us know by writing to the editorial department—your letters may very well affect the fate of this series.

*Why?* is the question I imagine must be resting on many of your lips. *Why would you publish this series with a different publisher, when the universe and timeline are connected to the previous one?* Honestly, I would feel uneasy leaving the question totally unaddressed, so without getting into all the details, the real answer is: it just kinda happened?

All things being equal, this book would've been published four months after the end of the previous series, but due to the workings of some kind of mysterious force field, that couldn't happen. Kodansha's light novel imprint picked up the series instead, which led to the book you now hold in your hands. To be totally frank, even I still can't shake off the *What happened here?* of it all. I'm pretty sure I'm not alone in this, and there are plenty of others who feel like some wily fox has been messing with their heads.

After many discussions amidst the chaos, I received my previous editor's blessing and was encouraged to continue unfolding this universe with Kodansha. And despite the unexpected turn of events, we still managed to publish this book in 2018 thanks to incredible fate, luck, miracles, and good will. This work avoided a cold death on the cutting room floor thanks to the efforts of so many wonderful people. I thank you all so, so much.

And now, I'd like to turn to the content of the book itself. I think it should go without saying that the guiding force in this story is none other than Loux Krystas. She is, in a few words, a *thou-dost loli*, the quintessential loli hag. Yes, dear readers, we're dealing with a loli hag.

Some characters the author carefully crafts into existence, while others are born all on their own. Los is unquestionably the latter. I decided I wanted something to happen before Saybil got to the headmaster's office, and there was Los, standing right in front of the door. The rest basically happened on auto-pilot. Los took her students, and me, by the hand and tugged us along, leading us through the story.

Her appearance, however, took a while to cement. "Zero's got silver hair and Albus is a blonde, so I guess Los should have black hair? Oh, but Sayb's already got black hair. Well, let's just go with this for now. I'll make her clothes frilly, diametrically opposed to Zero's..." This was my thought process as I put together the story and the characters, my head permanently cocked in uncertainty.

However, as anyone who's read the book—in fact, anyone who's seen the cover—can tell you, Los is very much a blonde. Doesn't that just feel right? Trust me, it does. The illustrator Takashi Iwasaki played a great role in this. At my wits' end as to how the characters should look, I went to Iwasaki-san and my editor for advice. We changed Los's appearance at the very last minute, which meant rewriting all the relevant parts of the book. Iwasaki-san also proposed a few options for little Ludens's design, which I then filled out with even more detail. As a result, I think you would be hard-pressed to find another character whose external appearance better complements the contents of the novel than Los. And her SD character is unbelievably adorable.

I'd like to take a moment here to thank Iwasaki-san from the bottom of my heart for readily agreeing to my unreasonable and sudden request to draw the illustrations for the sequel. So many of the characters from the last series pop up in this one, and I needed an illustrator who could stay true to the image readers already had of these characters while also designing amazing new ones. The only person I could even imagine being up to the task was Iwasaki-san. This series is truly fortunate that he was willing to take it on.

I also owe the great Yoshinori Shizuma a debt of gratitude for allowing us to keep the characters he designed consistent in this series. Thank you so very much. The generosity of your heart knows no bounds. Seriously, I've got half a mind to start worshiping the Sacred Shizuma.

I've already gotten approval to publish a second volume in this series, so it looks like this story will continue for at least a little while. I also have a completely unrelated SF (somewhat fantastical) story in the offing, and hope to announce the details of that soon.

I look forward to seeing you in the next volume, or the next series!

# Afterword

# あとがき

Hello!!
This is Takashi Iwasaki, the illustrator who took over for Mr. Shizuma!

I feel truly honored to get to draw Zero and Mercenary again! I really tried to keep their height difference in mind when designing Los and her students.

Hope you like them!

**Kakeru Kobashiri**

An eternal newbie writer who loves fantasy and beauty-and-the-beast stories above all else. I always insist I'm not a furry because I love robots and monsters, too. Really I just love all relationships that involve some kind of difference.

Illustrator

**Takashi Iwasaki**

I'm so glad to have the opportunity to draw Zero and the others again. I sure hope I do justice to this series, since I'm a faithful reader too! Plus it was my first time ever drawing a lizard.